Raphael Remeris is a Chicago policeman with a dark secret of childhood abuse. This abuse led him to choose a vocation where the paramount duty is to protect the innocent. But has he lived up to his ideals?

Angela Reed is a freelance writer from a nearby Chicago suburb. When her brother is arrested and found involved in gang activity, then locked away in Statesville Penitentiary, Angela goes on a crusade to prove his innocence and to find the dirty cops her brother swears framed him. Raphael Remeris may be one of them. With time running out, Angela increases her efforts to free her brother and moves into a rough area of Chicago in order to find the evidence she needs. Angela runs into officer Remeris and her hatred of him fuels a battle for dominance. But she soon finds that Raphael stokes up more than her anger. He may have started a fire in her heart.

Indigo Love Spectrum

An imprint of Genesis Press, Inc.
Publishing Company

Genesis Press, Inc.
P.O. Box 101
Columbus, MS 39703

Copyright © 2007 by Dyanne Davis

ISBN-13: 978-1-58571-248-9
ISBN-10: 1-58571-248-5
Manufactured in the United States of America

First Edition

Visit us at www.genesis-press.com
or call at 1-888-Indigo-1

TWO SIDES TO EVERY STORY

DYANNE DAVIS

Genesis Press, Inc.

DEDICATION

This book is dedicated with all my love to the men in my life:
William Davis Sr. and William Davis Jr.
You're both heroes.

To Cassandra Boozer, with much love.
May your every dream be fulfilled.

ACKNOWLEDGMENTS

As always my acknowledgments begin with God. I give my thanks to my Creator who has given me everything that I possess, for reminding me every step of this journey that You are indeed in control. I thank You for each breath.

I want to acknowledge the readers. No writer is complete without readers, so thank you very much. Your loyal support is priceless.

To all the different people who checked my Spanish, I thank you all for your different wordings and different meanings (smile): Fatima and Iris Gomez and Wendy Byrne.

Jackqueline Jackson, my sister and friend, thank you for your continued support and love.

As always I have to thank Sidney Rickman, the world's best editor. What can I say to you that I have not said a hundred times in the past? You make the editing process a thing of magic. I know that you go above the call of duty in your editing. I want you to know that I know it, and I appreciate it, and you, from the bottom of my heart.

To loyal friends, none of this journey would be so joyous if you were not cheering me on.

To all the ladies at Windy City Romance Writers of America. I am proud to have been voted in for a second term as your president. I hope each and every one of you realizes your dreams. You're an extremely talented group of women.

To Jackie Wallis, Adrienne Maynard and Theresa Steven, you are the most exceptional board in all of RWA, I'm sure, and I'm proud to have served with all of you. Thank you.

To the Genesis Press family, thank you for giving all of my characters a home. To Deborah Schumaker, thank you for all that you've done and for your understanding during difficult times.

CHAPTER 1

"You will meet a woman of fire and ice, a woman you will love always, one you cannot live without. You will perish without having her love."

Raphael laughed at the prediction but he remained seated out of courtesy. The old woman was a friend of his family and his godmother, his *madrina*, but Raphael didn't believe in fairy tales, nor did he believe in *el decir de fortunas*—the telling of fortunes.

"I know you don't believe me," the old woman smiled. "It's there in your eyes."

Raphael attempted to protest but she stopped him. "Is not necessary for you to believe. It will happen."

Raphael continued smiling, feigning interest. He wasn't looking for a woman. In fact, a woman was the very last thing he either needed or wanted in his life. He was a Chicago cop; loving a woman could get him killed. It was better for him to not have that burden. In fact, he thought the department should make a rule: Cops are forbidden to ever fall in love. He thought the reasons were obvious. Cops endangered the public and themselves when they did, not to mention the person unfortunate enough to receive their love.

"Raphael, listen to me. Your mother has told me of your foolish wish to never fall in love. Love is about to find you. Soon, Raphael, very soon."

"Don't I have any say in the matter?" he joked.

"No."

"No. Why not?"

"Because this woman is the other half of your soul."

"How do you know I have a soul?" he asked quietly. He'd had one when he first joined the police department, but he didn't know if he still possessed it.

"It's in you, Raphael. And you will have to fight to get it back where it belongs, in the light, just as you will have to fight for this woman's love."

"If she's my soul mate why will I have to beg her to love me?" He felt his jaw tightening. "Beside, *Titi*, I don't beg, and especially not for a woman to love me."

"Don't *auntie* me. You will beg this woman."

"I will not."

"You will."

Raphael was tiring of the game and of the old woman. "Tell me, why will I beg her?"

"Because she will hate you. She will hate you with a hate so fierce it will stop your heart."

'Then why the hell would I want her? Excuse me, *Titi*. I didn't mean to swear, but why would I want a woman that hates me?"

"Because when she learns to love you, she will love you with a fire more powerful than the ice with which she hates you. Her love will stop your heart but it will also restart it again. She will be true to you till death." The old woman smiled. "That is, if she discovers that she loves you. If she doesn't she will be the one to seek your death."

"Thanks, *Titi*," Raphael said, rising from his seat. "I think I'll pass. The one thing I know for sure is that I don't need is a woman who wants to kill me."

"She's beautiful, Raphael, and she's your soul mate."

"I don't care. A beautiful Puerto Rican woman who will love me if she doesn't kill me? No thanks," he laughed and walked away.

The old woman watched him leave, a knowing smile on her face and a twinkle in her eyes. "I never said she would be Hispanic, Raphael," she half-whispered under her breath, deciding not to tell him. He didn't believe her anyway. He needed to learn a lesson the hard way.

"License and insurance, ma'am."

"What did I do?" Angela asked, her eyes blazing. She refused to adjust her defiant stare, not caring that her manner alone might annoy the man. After all, it didn't take much to antagonize the Chicago cops.

"Sixty in a thirty-mile-per-hour zone."

"God, I hate this!"

"Then I would suggest that you don't speed."

For a long moment Angela looked at the officer, her dislike of cops coalescing in this one man. She closed her eyes briefly, feeling the trembling begin to wrack her body, knowing she was about to do something stupid.

"My insurance card is in my dash and my license is in my purse. If I move to retrieve them, are you going to shoot me?"

She saw the officer blink. A look of surprise came into his eyes and then a mask fell over his face.

"Why would I shoot you?"

"Why are citizens shot every day in Chicago for no reason?" She glared at the officer, challenging him, her gaze unwavering. When his demeanor remained unchanged, she frowned in surprise.

"License and insurance, ma'am."

Angela reached for her purse and held it toward the officer. "I'm going to open it," she said. "I don't have a gun."

She knew her unspoken accusation was angering the man. She'd seen the way he'd visibly stiffened. *So what?* If it wasn't for the Chicago Police Department, her brother wouldn't be sitting in Statesville Penitentiary on trumped-up charges.

Angela retrieved the wallet and slipped the plastic-coated license out and handed it over. She fished her cell phone from her purse and punched in a number, her eyes never leaving the man's face.

"Simone, I'm on Damen and Cermak. I'll be a little late; I was stopped for allegedly speeding." She glanced once more in the officer's direction, this time a little more intently.

"I'm calling so you can listen; I want a witness in case I end up on the evening news. I'm cooperating and being extremely pleasant."

TWO SIDES TO EVERY STORY

She knew what was coming before it did. She heard the sigh and for just a nanosecond she thought she saw hurt in the cop's eyes. So what? Her gaze swung to his name tag. Rafe Remeris. What the heck was an Hispanic man doing with green eyes?

"Your insurance, please."

His tone indicated he was losing patience. She could continue and cause a scene, get arrested, thrown in jail, but at this point that wouldn't help her brother. She had to find the woman who could help him. With any luck she'd also find the cops responsible and make them pay.

"I'm reaching into the dash for the insurance card," she said into the phone. "I don't have any weapons. I'm cooperating."

She fished the card out, handed it over and snatched her hand back when his fingertips touched hers. "What did you do to me?" she screamed. "You shocked me."

She searched his hands for the cause. She'd seen nothing in them before and didn't now. "He shocked me," she said into the phone.

"Lady, calm down. I didn't do anything to you. Give me a minute to check your plate. Stay in the car," he said firmly, and walked away.

"Angie, are you there?"

Mesmerized by movements of the cop, she was slow to respond. "I'm here."

"What did he do to you?"

"He touched me."

"Touched you? Where? Did he try and feel you up, what? Come on, tell me what's going on."

"He touched me. He touched my fingers and it shocked. Now my skin is burning where he touched me."

Angela kept her eyes on the cop as he walked to the patrol car, got in for a minute, then came back to her. She swallowed when she noticed the officer's hand resting on his gun and fear swept over her. In a flash her mind flew to the latest reports of police shootings of civilians, then to her brother, and she wondered if this was how he'd felt. She moved several inches away from the open window and readied herself. The phone that was at her ear slipped.

4

"Here's your ticket. You can pay it or you can go to court. The date's on the ticket."

Angela's heart caught in her throat. She could almost breathe again. He wasn't going to shoot her. "I'm going to court. I'm going to fight it."

"That's your right. You have a great day now and take it easy."

For one long lingering moment Angela remained still. There was something about that cop that had taken her aback and stirred a feeling of unease.

Raphael Remeris was shaken. He got back in his cruiser and kept his eyes on the woman as he started backing away. The woman's words, 'you shocked me,' still rang in his ears. The tips of his fingers also tingled from touching her. He rubbed his hand over the leg of his trouser. The tingle had turned to a mild burning sensation.

A fist twisted in his gut as he remembered what his *madrina* had said to him. If he ever met a Puerto Rican woman who so obviously hated him as much as this Black woman did, he would run as fast as he could to get away from her.

Of course he'd known what game the woman was playing. The department had been taking a beating for quite awhile now. Sure, there were lots of cops in the department that used deadly force but he wasn't going to second-guess them. No one knew until their own life was on the line how they would react.

Raphael had felt compelled to escape the fury in the woman's eyes by returning to the squad car and had written the speeding ticket there, finding the need to close his hand into a fist and shake it out before being able to complete the task. His skin still tingled from the contact with the woman.

A sense of danger had overwhelmed him as he walked back toward the woman's car. He'd actually switched the ticket to his left hand and positioned his right hand on the butt of his stun gun, just in case.

TWO SIDES TO EVERY STORY

He didn't spook easily but he had been spooked by that woman. Her extreme dislike of him seemed so personal and so intense that it had permeated the very air that he breathed. Her hatred had nearly stopped his heart. He wondered how many people out there loathed him so much that it could affect him as intensely as this encounter had.

This surely was not what he'd expected when he'd made his decision to join the force. He'd done it to gain respect, to help, to not be a bum. But respect was the last thing he'd gotten on the job. He'd been spit on, kicked, hit, cursed, called every name in the book, just because he wore a badge. But never in the eight years that he'd been on the force had he ever felt the revulsion as much as he had today. Raphael hoped he never would again.

Once again the old woman's prediction came to him. Maybe this woman was the precursor. He imagined all of the fire of a Latin woman combined with the ice of the woman to whom he'd just issued a ticket, and he shivered. *Fire and ice. What a hell of a way to start the day. Only blocks from the station,* he thought, as he continued his patrol.

Angela sat in her car until the officer drove away, then let out the breath she'd been holding. She wondered what had made him put his hand on his gun and what had kept him from pulling it. She could even now smell her own fear surrounding her. But it wasn't the very real fear that he would shoot her. It was more personal, as if he would destroy her life in some other way.

"Angie?"

She'd almost forgotten she still had Simone on the line. "I'm okay. I was just harassing the cop."

"But you were screaming. Did he use a stun gun on you? Did he really shock you?"

Angela realized how silly that sounded. The man had had no weapon, just his hand. She rubbed her fingers together. The slight burn was fading. She wondered if her own prejudice had created the electrical energy." *Stun gun?* She'd never thought of that.

"I don't know," she answered. "It's just . . . I just got back from the prison and I wasn't in a mood to be stopped by the cops."

"Were you speeding?"

"I don't know. I wasn't looking down but I'm going to fight it anyway. I don't like being harassed." She ignored the fact that she'd just confessed that she was needling the cop. He deserved it, she didn't.

"Are you still moving on Saturday?"

"Yeah, I need to live in the neighborhood to find out what happened. Eventually someone will talk."

"You don't have to live there to find out what you want to know. Besides, your parents hired an investigator. He's trained. Why don't you allow him to do his job?"

"It's not his brother in jail. He doesn't care about Adrian, I do. I'm going to do everything in my power to get him out of there."

"It's too late."

"It's not too late," Angela screamed at her cousin. How would you feel if it were Trae instead of Adrian? Maybe you can not care since it's your cousin and not your brother."

"You know better than that. I love Adrian. But maybe I can see things a little more clearly. He's not an angel, and neither is Trae."

Angela winced. She knew her brother wasn't an angel. She'd long feared he was involved with things he shouldn't be. But she'd let it go when he would smile at her and tell her not to worry, that he could take care of himself. But now he wasn't saying that. He was begging her for her help. Her tough-as-nails big brother had had tears in his eyes when she left him. And he'd begged her to hurry and get him out. She had no choice but to follow through with her plan.

"You're playing a very dangerous game. You could get hurt. You don't know anyone and you're deliberately putting yourself in a known Hispanic gang territory. You're Black, Angela, not Hispanic, and you don't even speak Spanish. How do you hope to do anything but get yourself killed?"

Angela wanted to tell her cousin that if she was so worried about her safety maybe she should join her, be her roommate. But what her cousin said made sense and she didn't really want to endanger anyone else with her plan. She didn't even want to endanger herself. But if she lived in the neighborhood where Adrian had been accused of the crime and where he'd been beaten, maybe she'd find some answers. She knew for sure the Chicago police didn't care about finding out the truth.

"Everyone does what they have to do," Angela said. "He's innocent."

"How do you know he's telling the truth?"

"He's my brother."

"That doesn't mean he can't lie. I hate what happened to him also, but I know there's more to what happened than what he's admitted to. There's always another side."

"Not in this case. In this case there is only one side I'm worried about and that one is Adrian's. He wouldn't lie to me, not about anything this important. I believe him. He just happened to be in the wrong place at the wrong time. He has a right to be wherever he chooses and so do I. I want to know what happened."

"And if the same thing happens to you?"

"At least maybe then you won't think I'm crazy for trusting Adrian."

"You're hoping for more confrontation with the police?"

Angela shuddered, remembering the fear she'd felt only moments before, remembering the Hispanic cop with the green eyes, his hand on the butt of his gun. She wasn't looking to die. She was looking for answers. Her death would not help her brother.

"Thanks for talking to me," she said abruptly. "I'll call you after I move in."

Angela crumpled the ticket she was still holding and threw it on the floor of her car. There was a time when her heart had not been filled with such anger, such rage. All that had ended two years ago when her brother had been beaten by police only a couple of blocks from the Damen police station. They'd accused him of gang activity, attempting to deliver drugs, and resisting arrest.

Angela didn't believe it. No one would be stupid enough to do that right in their faces, not so close to the police station. Any Black person with a lick of sense knew the reputation of the police department for profiling. And considering the increasing number of shootings of Blacks on a weekly if not daily basis, one would have to be a stone fool to try some mess like that. Besides, she'd looked in her brother's eyes and seen no deception. He'd told her it had to be a case of mistaken identity or profiling. She didn't know which but she was going to find out.

CHAPTER 2

Angela sat in her new apartment. She had nothing to do now but wait. Hopefully she could return to her home in a few months but for now this was home. She looked at the rented furniture, cringing at the cost. She'd had no choice in that either. She couldn't bring her own furniture. Her parents had to believe she was out of town. It was good to know that they would be taking care of her home while she was gone. Only her brother and her cousin would know where she really was. If she encountered the private investigator they'd hired, he wouldn't know her. All he'd ever seen of her was her checks.

Lucky for Angela, her parents always used the cell to reach her. Her job as a technical writer with Kline, Inc., which she could do at home, provided her with the means and the time to look for the mysterious woman who could alibi for her brother.

She had a reason for undertaking the investigation herself. She didn't believe the investigator was doing all that he could. Even as she thought it, Angela knew the man didn't have the one piece of information that she possessed: a name. Even so, she still thought he could do more. And when she found the person she was after, she was personally going to fire the investigator. Until then he could keep looking. Besides, they were working different angles.

Angela felt chilled and wrapped her arms around her body to stop a sudden tremor. She hoped that what she was doing would help her brother. Her plans did not include getting arrested by the cops before she even moved into the neighborhood. The possibility of her parents having grief over another child was definitely not on her agenda.

She smoothed out the ticket she'd retrieved from her car. At least that gave her a chance to focus on something other than her extreme loneliness. She didn't like lying to her parents about what she was doing, but she couldn't tell them. They would be worried, and in the last two years they'd had enough of that to last them the rest of their lives.

Angela thought about the cop who'd given the ticket to her. Something about the man niggled at her way down deep. She told herself it had nothing to do with his green eyes but she could see herself getting lost in them. She shuddered and shook that thought away. She wasn't there to drown in a man's eyes. She was there to find Teresa Cortez, the woman her brother said knew the truth.

Still, thoughts of the green-eyed Hispanic pushed their way into her mind. She wondered how he'd shocked her and made her burn with just his touch.

Raphael did his job the same as he did every day, only now there was something just a little bit off-kilter. He found that he was on the alert for a speeder, and not just any speeder. He was looking for the woman who'd had such ice in her eyes when she'd glared at him that it had seemed to stop his heart.

In the few minutes it had taken to issue her a citation he'd seen a lot that she'd more than likely wish he hadn't, like the visitor pass on the passenger side of her car that told him she'd recently been to Statesville. Maybe that was the reason for her hostility, but he doubted it.

Despite her anger he'd noticed her big beautiful brown eyes. *Iced topaz*, he thought. And the sound of her voice had been pleasant in spite of the sarcastic bite. Raphael bit his lip. His thoughts should not be going in this direction but he couldn't help it. The woman had intrigued him; he wouldn't deny it.

For days all that he'd thought about was the way his skin had first tingled and then burned on touching her, and his godmother's prediction. *I shouldn't be listening to Titi Nellie*, Raphael thought. *She's just a foolish old woman. There is no way that a person's hatred could stop your heart.*

Yet his had stopped for a moment.

And it made him wonder.

Raphael laughed at his foolishness. There was definitely no way that love could restart it. But for the first time in his life Raphael was wondering if he'd been right to shun the thought of loving someone.

Why was he thinking of these things? He didn't want a woman in his life; his job was too dangerous. Still, he wondered how it would feel to have someone love him as much as the Black woman had hated him. He had to admit that would be some powerful loving, because the woman's loathing was definitely strong.

Angela came from the store loaded with bags and rushing to avoid getting a parking ticket. She groaned and walked faster when she saw she was too late. "I was only in the store for a second." she said to the police officer.

He glanced at her and she immediately recognized the crystal green eyes of the cop who'd given her the ticket days earlier.

"Are you handicapped?" he asked her.

Smart ass, she thought and opened her trunk, forcing his foot from the bumper. "Look, I couldn't find a parking spot."

"You mean one that was close to the door?" His eyebrow shot up. "Handicapped parking, in case you weren't aware, is meant for those with disabilities." He smiled. "Physical disabilities, I mean."

Angela glared. "Just give me the ticket. In case you haven't met your ticket quota for today, I just saw two squad cars parked in the handicapped spot at the donut shop down the street."

When she snatched at the ticket, his fingers accidentally brushed the back of her hand and she stared at him. This was not her imagination.

Angela sucked in a breath and eyed him curiously, wanting to ask if he'd felt it, knowing that because of their little war she couldn't.

The officer walked away, but not before Angela saw him glance over his shoulder toward her. His expression was one of bewilderment. She got in her car knowing he'd answered her question. He'd felt it too.

As Angela waited inside the courtroom, she looked around, then smiled. The dark-haired, green-eyed cop wasn't around. In the past weeks she'd seen him several times but had managed to avoid direct contact with him. Twice he'd been poised to write her a ticket, but on spotting her had turned in the opposite direction and closed the flap on his book of tickets. It had been evident to her that he no more wanted to see her again than she wanted to see him. That thought gave her confidence that he wouldn't be in the courtroom. She settled back in her seat, more determined than ever to plead innocent. Who could dispute it?

"Angela Reed."

Angela blinked. The rough gravely voice that called her name sounded impatient, and the judge looked it. She gathered her belongings; it was time for justice. She walked to the podium as the judge spoke to the person standing alongside him. A second later she heard a voice and turned. The green-eyed cop was walking in the door heading toward the podium, smirking in her direction as he made his way to the front. She glared at him. Nothing had changed. She was still determined to declare her innocence.

"Fifty dollars' fine and traffic school. It looks like you may not be familiar with the rules of safety, or why they're in place."

"But . . . ," Angela protested, wondering what had happened to her plea. It was as if the judge had not heard her. She shouldn't have to go to traffic school. "I pleaded innocent. You're not listening to me."

"Be thankful that this won't be on your license. Three moving violations and your license would be suspended. So I suggest you slow down."

The same gravelly voice called out, "William Davis," indicating that Angela had been summarily dismissed. She glared again at the cop who was staring back at her, a curious expression that she took as a sneer on his face.

Raphael felt the same sense of danger emanating from the woman that he had the day he'd stopped her. He immediately scanned her body for bulges and saw none that shouldn't be there. What he saw was a slender, rather short, beautiful Black woman with shoulder length black hair that she wore in a ponytail. The only bulges he saw were in the right places. A nicely rounded rear and ample bosom, he thought as his eyes met hers. Not too much, and not too little.

She'd caught him staring at her and was again glaring at him. He could swear he could see a wavy line coming from the woman toward him, and the word *energy* flashed into his mind.

The woman wasn't carrying a weapon; she was the weapon. She was a danger to him, and he should do everything in his power to stay away, yet he found himself searching his mind for ways to see her again. He had to find out more about her, about her reaction to him, his reaction to her. She continued glaring and again he froze, his heart seizing until she looked away and released him from her arctic hold.

Angela entered the building and looked for directions to the room where traffic school was being held. Finding the room, she sat down to wait for someone to come and tell her what she knew already. She was not to speed, it was against the law, it could get someone killed. Well, so could beating them almost to death. Her eyes lifted and widened. There was no way the green-eyed cop should be here. Angela marched to the front of the room. "Why are you teaching this class?"

"For money," he replied. She closed her eyes and counted to ten.

"Are you doing this to annoy me?" She watched while he looked around the room.

"There are at least fifty people in this room that have disobeyed the law. Do you think you're so special that I've singled you out? Listen, if you don't want to be here you're free to leave. Reschedule. It's your choice." He turned away from her and she stood for a moment, unsure. She didn't have time for this. She was not spending another Saturday in a musty room being told what she already knew. "I'm staying," she announced through clenched teeth. He held a paper toward her and didn't speak. Her eyes remained on him. She wasn't sure if she'd intended to touch him, but the tips of their fingers met, and for the third time she felt a definite electrical shock followed by the same burning sensation. Angela snatched the paper away angrily, wondering what the heck was happening.

Raphael pretended not to notice her reaction to him, or his to her. But he was intrigued. The entire eight hours the woman glared at him, not smiling, not speaking. Wanting to make sure that he knew she hated him.

He knew. And Raphael was beginning to have a funny feeling. He no longer thought the woman his godmother had been talking about was Puerto Rican. He didn't understand how anyone anywhere could have as much hatred for him as this woman seemed to have. All of this couldn't be over a couple of tickets. Her hatred of him seemed personal, and he wondered why.

Raphael approached the car that had flown by him as though he wasn't there. "Damn I don't believe it. The woman's crazy," he muttered as he walked to her car. He'd followed her for nearly two blocks with the lights and siren on before she finally stopped.

"License and insurance."

"You're beginning to make this a habit. It's becoming irritating."

"You're speeding. Look, I'll make it easy for you. Don't speed on my beat and you won't get a ticket."

"Are you from the Damen station?"

"Yes, why?"

"I'm going to report you."

"For what?"

"For harassment."

"And just what have I done to harass you?"

Angela looked into the emerald green eyes and spoke softly. "Because you're a cop, and just because you breathe." She scanned the front of his shirt. "You, Officer Rafe Remeris, are a symbol of everything that I hate. I would suggest that you find something to do with your time other than stopping me."

Raphael backed a bit away from the car, from the intoxicating presence of the woman sitting inside. He mentally shook himself, releasing the strange hold that had suddenly come over him.

He looked at the woman's driver's license. "You live in Naperville. Why are you always speeding here? Are the traffic laws different in the suburbs?"

Sudden laughter bubbled up into her throat, but Angela quickly tamped it down. She'd not expected humor. She had been going for anger. She ignored him, preferring not to speak. The man caused too many extraordinary things to happen when she was in his presence. Her entire body was on fire. She could feel the heat rising to her face. All she wanted was for him to write the ticket and leave her alone.

"So that's it," Raphael said smiling. "In Naperville you're allowed to fly down the streets doing sixty in a thirty-mile-per-hour zone. I thought we covered all of this in traffic school. This doesn't speak well of my abilities as a teacher if my students can't remember not to speed. How long has it been, Ms. Reed?"

She didn't answer, so Raphael did. "A week? Maybe it's not me; maybe you're slow." He cocked his head and looked into the window, directly into her icy stare.

"I'm letting you off with a warning today, ma'am. Please have yourself a good day." He flipped her license over to the empty passenger seat, noting again that a fresh visitor pass was sitting there.

Angela sat for a moment holding her breath, sucking her belly inward toward her spine. She didn't want the cop touching her again. But when he flipped her license past her, it angered her to know that he also didn't want to touch her. Her eyes slid over to the license and landed on the Statesville visiting pass, and she cringed.

The knowledge that the cop now possessed personal information about her angered her further, and fueled her decision. She was a few blocks away from the station, and turned at the next light and headed back toward Twenty-third and Damen.

CHAPTER 3

Angela picked up the phone at the counter, hating that she was in the building. "I want to file a complaint," she said to the blonde woman who was staring out at her through the bulletproof glass with a bored expression on her face.

As the woman's face suddenly became animated, Angela dropped the phone from her ear, remembered what she was supposed to do, and picked it up again.

"Someone will be with you in a moment," the woman finally said.

Angela looked around, leveling her gaze on the white bench across the room. She paced around the perimeter, waiting for someone to come through the door. Her eyes landed on two display cases.

She didn't want to see anything proclaiming the good work the police had done, but she paused in front of a display case and began perusing the contents. A pamphlet on Alzheimer's was the last thing she expected to find in a police station. She lifted it from the bin and began reading. Finding herself reading the same line over and over, she began to wonder if at twenty-eight she wasn't showing signs of Alzheimer's herself.

When she looked again toward the bulletproof glass and saw several officers inside talking together, she became annoyed. They were deliberately making her wait. Maybe she'd complain about the entire department.

Now she knew why they kept the public so far away from the cops. She was feeling pretty darn hostile just sitting there waiting for someone to come and take her report.

At last the door opened and someone came toward her. She looked down at her watch. Forty-five minutes had passed. She frowned at the man approaching her and looked again at her watch for emphasis.

"I'm sorry it took so long, Ms. Reed. I understand that you want to file a complaint against one of our officers. Is that right?"

"Yes."

"Then would you come with me?"

Angela had a moment of panic. She'd seen her share of police shows; she knew what she was doing could cause problems for Officer Rafe Remeris.

She stiffened her spine. She didn't care, she asserted to herself as she began to follow the officer across the room to another closed door. She didn't care that the man had beautiful green eyes or deep dimples when he smiled. She didn't care that he had a sense of humor. And most of all, she didn't care that his touch sent a zillion volts of electricity cascading through her. If for nothing more than that reason alone, she wanted him out of her hair.

He was a cop and she had moved into the Pilsen neighborhood to destroy cops. She couldn't begin to think of even one of them as a funny, strikingly handsome man with marble green eyes and fingers that ignited her soul. Angela shuddered and took the seat she'd been offered.

"What did Officer Remeris do?"

"He stopped me for speeding."

"You're angry that he gave you a ticket?"

"He didn't give me a ticket; he gave me a warning."

"And you're here to file a complaint against him?"

Angela frowned at the man behind his desk. "I'm here to complain about the manner in which he treated me. He called me stupid and he threw my license back at me. He didn't hand it to me. He threw it into the car. I don't know about you but I find that disrespectful."

"I agree, and I'm sorry that you had to be treated in that manner. But I'm wondering if you may have misunderstood what happened. Officer Remeris is a good officer, very respectful. It seems highly unlikely that he would do the things that you said. Do you want to reconsider filing this?"

"Please don't patronize me. Am I to understand that you also think I'm stupid?" She lowered her eyes and allowed her gaze to rest on his name plate. "What was your name again?" she asked pointedly.

The officer cleared his throat. "I'm sorry, here's the form. Just write what you want to say in the comment area, sign it and I'll put it through."

He pushed the form across the desk toward Angela. When she tilted her head slightly, he lifted the paper and held it out.

Angela wrote on the form, pushing the face of Officer Remeris from her mind. Nothing would happen to him, she assured herself. Nothing ever happened to the Chicago cops. She just wanted him to leave her alone. She signed her name, thinking that should at least take care of that. No more heat from unwanted sources.

—ɷ—

Raphael couldn't believe it. The woman had actually carried through with her threat. He'd known from the moment he looked at her in the courtroom that she was a danger to him. Now she was trying to ruin his career. He'd given her a pass when she didn't deserve one.

"Did you throw the woman's license back into her car instead of handing it to her?"

"Yes, sir." Raphael squirmed.

"Did you call her stupid?"

"Not exactly."

The commander glowered. "Look, the department is taking enough of a beating as it is. The mayor doesn't want any undue attention on us, got it? Now what did you say exactly?"

"I've stopped her before for speeding. She was even in the class I conducted at traffic school a couple of weeks ago. So I told her it had to be either her fault or mine if she hadn't learned that she wasn't allowed to speed."

"Did you call the woman stupid?"

"No."

"What did you call her?"

"I called her slow," Raphael admitted.

"Is there something personal going on with you and that woman? I've got eyes, she's beautiful. What? She makes you hard and you think this is the way to go after her, by harassing her? Do your screwing around on your own time. That squad car is not your own little personal pickupmobile."

Raphael was getting angry. He was being reprimanded for things he hadn't done. "Look, sir," he tried again. "I didn't harass the woman. I gave her a break."

"And you're telling me you weren't thinking with your di—" The commander stopped short, glanced over at Wendy, the new recruit, and glared at Rafe.

"You should have given her another damn ticket, not a warning. She was doing fifty-nine in a thirty-mile zone. She deserved a damn ticket. Get some stones. You want to get laid, go get laid! But don't use the department as your pimp. Now get the hell out of my office."

Raphael walked out of the office averting his eyes as he walked away, wondering how much ribbing he was going to have to take for what had just happened. There was no such thing as a secret reaming in the department. Before the end of the day the story would have circulated across the city and into the suburban departments. He hated to think what he would be accused of when it made the rounds.

He took the steps two at a time, wishing he'd at least handed the woman her license. But he'd seen the fear in her eyes, had seen her holding her breath and he'd shared her fear. There was some phenomenon at work when they touched. And he had no more of a desire to repeat it than she did. He'd thrown her license in the car thinking he'd relieved her mind and his. Now look what it had gotten him— written up.

TWO SIDES TO EVERY STORY

For the next six weeks Raphael was engaged in his own private war. He was pissed and being pissed he'd chosen to ignore his commander's orders to leave Angela Reed the hell alone.

At least twice a week he would spot her car illegally parked and would ticket it. And at least twice a week she would go into the station and file a complaint against him. The entire thing came to a head when one Thursday she blew a stop sign and he followed her onto private property to give her a ticket.

The thing was, he wasn't allowed to enter private property unless the police department had a deal with the owner. In this particular case they didn't. It was also too bad for him that Angela Reed knew this also.

"You can't give me a ticket," she said, a smirk on her face.

"Why not?" he asked.

"This is private property."

"We give tickets all the time on private property."

"Yeah, but you have to have consent, and the owner won't give it, so you have to leave."

Raphael went inside, talked with the owner and came back out to hear the woman laughing at him. "I'll give you the ticket when you leave."

"I'm not leaving," she declared. And they'd begun their wait. Actually, he'd been the one waiting as she got out of her car, marched down the street, and did some shopping. Then he'd sat there watching as she pulled out a disposable camera and began taking pictures of him. He knew where that was going. Another complaint.

Raphael had wanted badly to leave his spot and go buy his own camera, but if he did she'd leave. He was aware that he was behaving like a fool. Besides, he'd already lost that battle. She was going about her business while he in the meantime had made himself a prisoner in his squad car to watch her car that she wasn't even in.

He had no idea how long he would have stayed watching her car if a call hadn't finally forced him from his position. He'd never gotten a chance to write her a ticket that day. But still she'd filed a complaint.

He'd noticed that a pattern was beginning to emerge. When he worked Tuesday or Thursday, she was much more hostile on those encounters. And always he noticed on those days there was a pass from the prison sitting in her car. He was getting some of the fallout from her visits to the prison. That much had become obvious to him.

After awhile Raphael had invested a small fortune in disposable cameras and flashed his own proof to counteract hers. It hadn't worked. He'd still been ordered to back off, and that time the commander had been livid.

"Leave that damn woman alone," the commander had screamed, his face red as anger filled him. "IAD is already on your ass over this. What are you bucking for, a suspension or what? Have you suddenly gone loco? This is an order: Leave the woman alone!"

"So what am I supposed to do, let her break the law?"

"Yes," the commander screamed.

"Can I have that in writing?" Raphael countered. When he saw he'd crossed the line, he quickly changed his tactic.

"Look, sir, do you think I picked up her car and put it into those no parking spots? They're always empty because people know they'll get tickets if they park there. She seems to be drawn to these spots. If you don't want me to ticket her, maybe you should take down the signs, or say no parking except for Angela Reed."

Raphael watched while the commander sighed and rubbed his face roughly with his hands. He was pissed. That much was obvious.

"The woman hates you. Why?"

"I don't know."

"You sure she's not some woman you nailed?"

Something bristled inside of Raphael. He didn't like talking about the woman in this manner, regardless of what she was doing to screw him over.

"I haven't touched her."

"See to it that you don't. She wants your badge. You make a mistake and forget that for a moment and she'll have it. Don't let those big brown eyes of hers fool you. The woman's cold as ice."

That had been Raphael's reaction to her in the beginning but he now knew better. There was something about the woman that produced a heat in him that he was afraid would consume him. The slightest touch of her fingers on his skin and he burned.

He'd admit to himself that he looked for her car when he was on patrol. She intrigued him and he wanted to know why. He wanted to know if she knew why her touch had ignited a fire in him that he'd never known existed, a fire that was dangerous and that he didn't want. At least he was still telling himself he didn't want it.

For over a week Raphael ignored Angela's car illegally parked in the neighborhood. He was following orders. He wasn't the only cop on the street; let someone else have a few of her complaints for a change.

He did as he'd been ordered, until the day came when he couldn't ignore her. He was sitting at a red light when a car pulled up on his right side, took a quick look in his car and ran the light, right with him sitting there. The driver on the left of him looked over at him as if to say, "Well, aren't you going after her?"

He almost didn't. He really didn't want to, not today, not when he'd just been thinking of her. Still, he had to do his duty, or more than likely the person sitting there witnessing it all would report him.

Raphael turned on the lights and siren and went after her, wishing she'd waited the three seconds it had taken for the light to turn green. Now he had to give her another ticket.

"What are you trying to do?" he asked angrily as he stalked up to her car.

"Oh, it's you. I was beginning to wonder what had happened to my shadow."

"Are you getting pleasure out of busting my balls?"

She smiled at him. "If you're asking if I'm enjoying this . . ." She stopped and stared. "Are you recording me?"

"No."

"Then yes, I'm enjoying it. How does it feel to be the person on the receiving end of harassment?"

"Look, lady, I haven't harassed anyone."

"You're a cop."

"And that makes me a bad person?"

"Yes."

Raphael rolled his eyes. There was no reasoning with the woman. He glanced at her passenger seat and her gaze snagged his as he brought his eyes back to her. She knew what he was doing. Today there was no pass.

"Why me?" he asked.

"Why not you?" she answered.

"You're going to lose your license if you keep this up."

"Maybe I don't care."

"If you lose it, how are you going to be a nuisance to me?"

He saw her blink. This time he wrote out the ticket. "I'm just trying to do my job." He held the paper out to her and waited. He saw fear enter her eyes and for a moment he thought she wasn't going to take the paper. Her fingers gripped the end and he held on tighter. Her eyes found his and for a long moment they stared at each other.

Both of their hands moved on the paper until there was only an infinitesimal amount of space between them and still they stared. Then they touched and the electrical charge traveled from the tips of his fingers throughout his body and Raphael didn't let go. His mouth opened but no words came out. An electric current filled the air, circling around them, shooting through them, binding them in a strange awareness.

He wondered how long he would have stayed there like that if his radio hadn't crackled and interrupted the spell. The ticket was in her hand and she was looking at him strangely.

"Let's call a truce," he said as he walked away, not waiting for an answer.

CHAPTER 4

Angela sat at her computer, her mind not on her work, but on her latest run-in with her nemesis. He'd asked her if they could call a truce, and she wanted to. It would be the wisest move. She was literally playing with fire and like a stubborn child she was craving more.

She kept thinking back over the allegations she'd made against Officer Remeris. She'd attempted to harden her heart against remorse, but somehow he kept poking through her reserve. A little voice in her subconscious whispered that he didn't deserve what she'd done. Well, neither did her brother deserve what they'd done to him.

Unfortunately, Angela had not been able to uncover one single thing that would help to prove her brother's innocence. It didn't help that the majority of the Spanish she knew was swear words. And it definitely didn't help that for over a week she'd holed up in her apartment not going out, even to the store. The only place she'd ventured was the prison and only once. She hadn't wanted to run into Officer Remeris again.

In some strange way she'd found herself looking for him, enjoying their fights. With the realization of that came the knowledge that her heart was beginning to skip a beat when he stopped her. So she'd gone into hiding, determined not to venture out until she could properly sort out her rampant feelings, and make sense of them.

Angela sighed loudly. Being alone in Pilsen was getting to her, making her have crazy thoughts and even crazier dreams. Unable to sit still, she got up and scrounged her empty pantry for food. Finding none, she checked the refrigerator, which was nearly as empty. She had no choice but to venture out and buy groceries. Her only hesitation was where, to a big chain or to a neighborhood store where most of the customers spoke in Spanish and looked oddly at her.

Yeah, this entire plan needed some work. How the heck had she thought she could help her brother when she didn't even speak the language?

Angela reached for her purse. She'd try again. What did she have to lose? She'd do the same thing she'd done for the past two months since she'd moved into the neighborhood. She'd try to strike up a conversation with someone and hope that would help.

At this rate the search would take the rest of her life and she couldn't afford it. Not that she wouldn't devote the rest of her life to helping free her brother, but financially she could swing six months tops of paying for two places to live. If she didn't find Teresa in the next four months she would have to move back home and continue with an Internet search.

With that knowledge came renewed energy. Forget about groceries; she could pick something up from a local taco stand. She needed to walk the neighborhood, go into the shops, make her mission known.

She walked for several blocks down Damen, even stopping to go inside two of the ornately decorated churches, the first time to pray for her brother, the second time out of guilt, to pray for forgiveness for what she'd done to Officer Remeris.

When she came out of the church, she turned right and walked down Blue Island. Only a block into the street, a bad vibe hit her. She could swear she felt eyes watching her. She checked her watch, surprised that she'd been walking so long. Five hours. The fast approaching dusk should have been a warning.

She was aware of footsteps behind her and stifled a scream. She even resisted an urge to turn around to see who it was. The imminent sense of danger continued to mount and she couldn't shake it.

Angela prayed quickly, silently, and felt her prayers were answered when she spotted a store several doors ahead. She ducked in and stood for a moment as a wave of hostility hit her in the face. Seven or eight men lounged around and all halted their conversation as she made her way farther into the interior of the store.

Instead of lessening, her feeling of doom increased. She smiled, hoping to dispel the feeling. She walked down first one aisle, then another, hoping to buy herself time before venturing out again, knowing that as she was doing so it was growing darker outside. And she still had to retrace her steps to return home.

Every single item in the store had Spanish labels and she had no idea what most were. She walked toward a cooler and picked up a clear bottle. At least she knew it was water. When she attempted to turn around, she felt the heat from bodies pressing in on her. "Excuse me," she said and attempted to move.

"*Cuál uno de nosotros hacerle prefiere tu?*"

"*Tu tiene un hombre o es usted que mira?*"

"*Eres casada?*"

"*Tu eres tan hermosa.*"

"Excuse me," Angela said again, trying to move the men aside. When a third joined them, the tension mounted and so did her fear. She wanted to scream out for the owner. She searched her brain for Spanish but nothing came to mind. Well, nothing but swear words, and now with a fourth man surrounding her, she didn't think it was the wisest thing to tell the men to go to hell.

"Move," she said, and pushed at the man closest to her. "Move," she said again, louder this time, determined not to be pushed around by a bunch of macho bullies.

She gripped the bottle of water tighter in her hand. If she had to, she would clunk them all over the head. She wasn't going down easy. She wasn't going to be a victim. Just as she raised her arm to make her first swing, green eyes caught hers.

Officer Remeris was staring at her and he continued staring for a long moment before he spoke in rapid Spanish to the men surrounding her and they moved, making a path for him.

She trembled as he came nearer, her fear of him a thousand times more potent that the fear of the four men who'd surrounded her. Them she could fight; this man standing in front of her . . . She didn't know if she possessed the weapons necessary to win.

He leaned into her and whispered in her ear, "You'd better go along with me; they want to slit your throat."

She looked at the leering men. "Are you sure?" she questioned. That was not the feeling she'd gotten from the men. From the looks on their faces and the kissing noises one made, she'd thought they were more interested in sex.

"I'm sure. Just play along. I told them you're my woman, you're off limits. I'd advise you to go with it."

"You're the cop," she said quietly. "Do something."

"I'm trying," Raphael answered. "I'm trying to save both of our lives. I can't fight all of them. This is the best way to handle this, trust me," he said and lowered his head toward her, his breath searing her neck, his lips so close. He kissed the crevice of her neck, then lowered his hand to her waist, took the bottle of water from her hand and threw a dollar on the counter.

He allowed his hand to slide even lower and he patted her rear, pulling her closer as she attempted to pull away. The men laughed at them as they walked out of the store.

Raphael smiled inwardly, knowing he was taking the joke a little too far. He didn't care. Angela Reed deserved it. Why should he tell her what he knew to be true, that the men had no intentions of hurting her? They'd only made a stupid macho bet with each other as to who could woo her. The only scary thing had been that they'd all barged in around her at the same time, and they'd frightened her.

Raphael turned deliberately to look over his shoulder and turned back quickly. "Don't look," he ordered Angela. He should have felt bad for scaring her, but he didn't. After everything she'd done to him, she deserved some payback. No, he wouldn't tell her that the men had only complimented her, saying she was beautiful and asking if she was married. Besides, his cousin Carlos owned the store. He would never stand by and let anything happen to a woman in his presence, regardless of the odds.

"You can remove your hand from my butt now," Angela said.

"Not yet, they're still behind us."

Angela heard nothing, but wondered if the nearness of Rafe Remeris, his hand sending heat spiraling through her, might have something to do with her inability to adequately sense what was happening.

If only she'd sensed the danger of whoever was following her before she'd walked down Blue Island, before she'd entered the store. She wished now she'd turned and confronted the person.

She cringed, wishing she'd done things differently. She didn't like being afraid and she certainly didn't like feeling safe because the cop with the green eyes had his arm around her.

"Why were you in the store?" Suddenly something about the timing made her ask the question. "Were you following me?"

Yes, he had been following her, but not intentionally. He'd noticed her as he was out walking. And it was only when he saw she was aware of him and had become frightened that he'd decided to scare her. *She deserved it*, he'd thought, *the arrogant little witch*. She deserved it for messing up his life.

"Were you following me?" she asked again.

"I live in the neighborhood," Raphael answered honestly, avoiding her other question. "You should be grateful that I came along, or you'd be just another statistic on the morning news."

"Pilsen is mostly a Mexican neighborhood. Why do you live here?"

"One, because I want to. And two, because I work the area. I like it." He smiled slightly. "Besides, Pilsen is changing. You'll find a few of all races living here, even Puerto Ricans. Look at you. You're Black and you live in the area. Right? I mean, since you're out walking and not speeding, I'm assuming you live nearby." He dropped his hand a tiny bit lower, resisting the urge to caress her behind.

"Where are you walking me?" she asked at last.

"Home."

"How do you know where I live?"

"I don't. But I did assume if we were going in the wrong direction you would tell me."

Angela twisted her mouth to the side as she tried to determine if he was telling her the truth.

"Where do you live?" he asked. "I assume for whatever reason it's not in Naperville, not now anyway."

"No, it's not," she answered, wanting to remove his hand, yet at the same time wanting to press in closer to his heat. Wanting him gone, yet wanting him.

Her increasing awareness of him strengthened her resolve and she muttered, "You don't have to walk me home."

"I do," he answered. "It's my job to serve and protect."

"Is that why you still have your hand on my behind?"

"That's the only reason," he answered. "As soon as it's safe to do so I'll remove it," he promised.

He wouldn't admit to her that the feel of her body moving beneath his palm was doing things to him, robbing him of his good sense. He'd been ordered to stay away from her, to leave her alone and now—now he was walking down the street with his arm around her. And he had his palm firmly glued to her rear.

She had only to look down and she would know he was not keeping his hand on her out of a sense of duty. He was harder than he'd ever been in his life and he was burning from the contact.

His *madrina* should have warned him of his body's reaction to the woman who would stop his heart. Then maybe he would've been better prepared. Now he was helpless against what was happening. He thought of what the commander had said. It wasn't about getting laid, though making love to the woman walking alongside him would be a very pleasant diversion. It was about finding answers. It was hard to just put out of his mind the possibility that the woman might truly be his soul mate, that his *madrina* might have been right.

They came to Damen and Twenty-fourth. Raphael stopped and looked down the street toward the police station. "Do you need to stop in there to file any paperwork?"

Angela looked toward the police station. "I don't have any reason to file any complaints tonight."

"You didn't have any reasons before, but that didn't stop you." he murmured low, knowing that she'd heard him, knowing that he was baiting her.

"Just move your hand before I actually have a reason," Angela said, trying not to smile at him. "I don't think anyone is following us, at least not anymore."

She didn't bother adding, "if ever," but she was beginning to smell a rat. In fact, she knew she smelled a rat. It was just a little too convenient that he'd happened to be there to rush to her rescue.

And even though she didn't speak Spanish, she doubted that the men had meant to kill her; rape her maybe, but not kill her. But admitting that meant she had to admit that she had not made him move his hand from her rear because she liked the feel of his hand on her, of him being close to her. She didn't want to begin to contemplate what that would mean.

"I'm sorry, I forgot it was there."

For the next few minutes they walked in silence that was broken only when they reached Angela's apartment. Officer Remeris had done his duty. He'd walked her home.

"No need to go inside," she said, turning to him.

"I wouldn't be doing my job if I didn't check your apartment. To serve and protect," he repeated.

Raphael knew he was crossing the line. Damn it, he should turn and walk away, forget about the crazy way this woman made him feel.

She'd written a ton of complaints already and he knew he was going to give her reason to write more. He was going to give her the proof. And when she complained he would admit to it.

She was leaning against the frame of the door, watching him, her eyes blazing with heat. For a long moment they stared intently at each other. He licked his lips as the words *sexual assault* thundered through his head. He'd take his chances. He had to see if her lips affected him also.

Raphael lowered his lips to hers. From just a scant millimeter away, he could feel her heat. Their lips touched and he could feel the electrical surge. He lowered his eyes. If she wasn't giving permission he didn't want to know it. He had to taste her. So he did.

—⟋⟋⟍—

Angela sucked in her breath, feeling the tremble of awareness claim her body. She'd known from the moment he stopped talking that he was going to kiss her. In actuality she'd somehow known it when he'd taken it upon himself to be her hero and step between her and the men surrounding her.

She'd definitely known it when he'd firmly clasped his hand about her waist and walked her home. Neither of them had talked much, not after he'd asked for her address and she'd given it. And now as she stood there waiting, she knew she wanted it.

Angela felt the heat of Rafe's lips before they even claimed hers. She was shivering as his breath caressed her face. She wanted to move away from him, from what he represented, but she couldn't. He was the enemy, yet she supposed she'd always known this moment would come.

His lips closed over hers at last, and she moaned at the touch. The same heat that had filled her from the touch of his hands filled her now from his lips. She felt his tongue jabbing at her closed mouth and her lips parted to allow him entrance. Angela moaned at the sweetness. She tasted no mint, no gum, just him. His arms went around her and pulled her closer, taking her deeper into the kiss, and her own arms went around his neck.

She felt his erection pressing into her hips and moved so that it could press against the spot she wanted it most, the juncture of her thighs.

When he released her, she was breathless. His eyes were asking a question and hers were answering yes. They went inside and she only prayed he would keep his mouth closed and not spoil the dream. What was happening was magical. She watched as he locked the door, then slid the dead bolt in place. Only then did she remember that she didn't have any condoms. Her eyes snapped to his face.

"Don't worry, I have something," he said as his arms slid around her. She felt him loosening the rubber band from her ponytail and running his fingers through her hair. He lifted her in his arms as though she were a feather.

"Where is it?"

She pointed the way to her bedroom, afraid to speak, afraid of wanting him. This was crazy. She hated the man, had done nothing for the past two months but make his life miserable as she tried to get him into trouble.

"Why?" she asked as he entered her bedroom with her in his arms.

"The same reason that you're not screaming your head off. I want to find out why I feel this electrical charge when we touch. I want to know why it leaves me with a burning sensation."

At least he was honest. Neither had spoken of an attraction, just a curiosity and a need to know. One time and that would be the end of it. One by one he slowly undid the buttons of her blouse, looking at her in a way that affected her almost as much as his touch. It was as though he was dragging liquid fire across her flesh. He left a path of heat and she knew he felt it too in the way that he touched her.

She was trembling, partly out of fear that she was about to start something that wouldn't be as easy to stop as she wanted to believe. Surely this could be nothing more than lust. But Angela had known lust in her life and it had never felt like this. Not for one moment had her skin ever sizzled.

She was lying on her bed topless and he was staring down at her. She tilted her head and reached for his shirt and unbuttoned it as slowly as he'd unbuttoned her blouse. Then she allowed her fingers to connect with his flesh, running her hand down the plane of his abdomen, feeling his muscles tighten and bunch, feeling him jerk as she touched him. The heat from his body was scorching her skin.

Somewhere in the back of her mind Angela realized she was looking for answers. She'd hoped when he kissed her the feelings she was beginning to have for him would cool, that she could logically know what was happening, be able to put a word to it. But she couldn't.

She tossed his shirt into the same corner where hers had landed and lay back and waited, wishing she had on a bra that closed in the front.

It would be so much more romantic. Not only didn't she have that but she had on a plain white bra and to her chagrin, blue panties.

Who'd known when she'd entered the market that she'd care she had on underwear that didn't match, wasn't sexy, and wasn't her best by far. Now when it was too late, she remembered her mother always saying, "You never know if you'll be in an accident. Always wear your best underwear."

Angela was sure her mother hadn't meant the kind of accident she was about to find herself in. And surely it had to be some kind of mysterious accident that found her in bed with this man that she hated.

She looked into his green eyes and waited as he deftly undid the clasp from the back with a bit more expertise than she liked. She frowned slightly before remembering this for what it was. This was sex, nothing more.

"Tell me again, why are we doing this?" she asked, breaking the silence.

"To keep from killing each other."

That was as good a reason as any. At least Angela knew he was under no illusion that this was the beginning of a relationship. She wouldn't have to do a big song and dance about how she would never sleep with a Chicago cop. Scratch that, how she would never become emotionally involved with one. Because she knew within the next few moments there was nothing short of an earthquake that would stop her from making love with the man staring at her. And even an earthquake might not be enough.

His heated gaze swept over her, then landed on her waist and stayed for a moment before reconnecting with her eyes. She kicked her shoes off, not breaking contact, and lifted her hips, allowing him to pull away first her jeans, then her horrible panties.

He paused and she wished he'd hurry that part. Her panties were the worst thing for a seduction, not even silk, but cotton, courtesy of her mother of course.

Angela's eyes closed and she felt the cotton sliding from her hips, felt his fingers brushing her skin and heating the parts that he touched. She didn't think she could get any hotter, but she did.

She felt his lips kiss her belly. The coarse fabric of his jeans scratched her and she opened her eyes again. Their gazes locked as she sat up and unfastened his jeans and slid them down his hips, stopping every inch of so to caress his perfection.

Never in her life had she known a man who possessed a body that one could only dream of. He lay for a moment beside her and allowed her to pull the pants, then his briefs, from his muscular frame.

She sucked in her breath, felt a moment's hesitation and again looked at him, at his beautiful eyes, and she saw his own uncertainty. Suddenly his indecision dispelled hers.

She touched her finger lightly to his abdomen, ran it down his middle and found his center and circled him, his flesh in her hand hot and quivering. She looked once more into his eyes. All signs of hesitation had vanished.

For one moment Raphael wavered. He'd seen the hesitation in her eyes, and he'd halted in his exploration of her body while some semblance of common sense returned.

He wondered what the hell would be the price for making love to her. Would she scream rape? Then she touched him and he no longer cared. The only thought he had was to bury himself deep inside her. At the moment it didn't matter that she hated him.

Raphael's gaze was snagged by the iced topaz turning to fire. He plumbed their depths and saw the source of the heat. He shivered inwardly, thinking he'd taken a tiny peek into her soul. Her soul was pure fire, not ice. He wasted no time with amenities. He needed her now and as he slid the condom over his hardened flesh, his eyes remained glued on her face for any sign that she was changing her mind. He prayed to God that she wouldn't.

Raphael entered her. A supreme feeling of belonging overcame every objection about the right or wrong of his actions. Before he could stop himself, he fell onto her, crushing her to him. Hearing her gasp of pleasure, his moan combined with hers and they shook simultaneously. She might lie later, but for now he knew their joining was as spiritual for her as it was for him.

With a certainty he knew Angela Reed was the one his godmother, his *madrina* had spoken of. His flesh melded into hers and they became one. He heard the sounds she made in her throat, and saw the look of surprise before she closed her eyes. Her legs came around his waist and he knew what she wanted, to bring him closer. He was feeling the same. As close as they were he wanted more.

Raphael wanted all of her. His arms went around her back and he lifted her from the pillows. Her eyes opened and the look she gave him freed his heart. One by one the barriers that had protected him came tumbling down and in their place a tremendous fear was born.

He smelled and sensed danger for the third time now while in this woman's presence. And now it had a name. This woman had laid claim to his very soul. The truth of that was frightening. A woman who hated him was taking something from him that he'd never meant to give, his soul. And Raphael was unable to pull away.

He wondered briefly if she'd hexed him. When he heard her moan and saw the fear in her eyes, he knew she was wondering the same thing about him. He kissed her then, deep and hard, loving the feel of her, her nails digging into his flesh. He loved the sounds she made, the smell of her and for the moment he enjoyed knowing he'd found the other half of his soul.

He thrust into her hard and fast, feeling the slickness, feeling the heat, feeling hard. He grew even more as he rode her, his flesh harder than he could ever remember. As he filled her, the sheer tightness of her body inflamed him, and he growled loudly.

The sound was primal, as much so as that of a male bear finally finding his mate. He knew, his body, soul and heart knew. He couldn't get enough of her. Half of him never wanted the moment to end. The other half wanted it to end so he could begin again at the beginning.

When they came it was amidst a thunderous roar of sounds and lights. They were clinging to each other forever, it seemed. He never wanted it to end, never wanted to let go of her, to look into her eyes and see the fire replaced by the ice.

TWO SIDES TO EVERY STORY

He held her tightly, murmuring to her, "*Usted es el.*" He repeated "you're the one" in Spanish again, not wanting to feel vulnerable, not wanting her to know what he'd said without meaning to.

For the remainder of the night they made love in every conceivable fashion and when they were at last spent and sated, they slept in each other's arms. The words they'd uttered had been murmured in the throes of passions, words that could be forgiven, forgotten.

Raphael fell asleep knowing that the woman in his arms had to know that to destroy him she'd not needed the department, just the possibility that Raphael would find love. He didn't need that. He needed to remain apart. Damn. This woman had forever ended that. She had completed him and made him whole. Without a doubt he knew she was indeed his soul mate. There was only one problem with that: He wasn't in love with her and she sure as hell wasn't in love with him.

CHAPTER 5

Golden sunshine poured through the slates of the blinds and was barely filtered by the curtains that covered them. Raphael blinked in confusion, his senses alert, his body deliciously achy. He felt silk brush his arm and slid his glance over to the right.

Angela was cradled there, her hair caressing him. He looked down on her face in disbelief. Never in his life had he expected or even dared hope for the pleasure he'd received last night. He'd made love to an angel and he'd found the other half of his soul.

His mind screamed out, "This is just sex, just sex." But the pads of his fingers trailed the outline of her body, imprinting it for a lifetime. And he knew the words his mind yelled out were a lie.

He looked around the room trying his best to move as little as possible. He didn't want to wake her up. He glanced at the clock, grateful that this was his day off, or he'd have missed roll call. It was after eight.

He took in the contents of her bedroom, all feminine articles, nothing masculine. He smiled, then curved his body around hers and breathed in her scent. The smell of their loving clung to her but still he smelled her uniqueness. The scent teased him. He wanted to make love to her again but was unsure what her reaction would be when she awoke.

Raphael thought of a strong cup of coffee. That was what he needed, that and a shower. He moved away from the warmth of her body and eased from the bed. Leaning down, he kissed her eyelids. Again he smiled as he made his way to the shower.

Angela held her breath, not knowing how she had not moved. She'd felt his heat moving away from her body and had awakened instantly. She'd felt the butterfly kisses and held her breath, listening to the sounds he was making.

Only when she heard the noise of running water did she dare turn around. She held the pillow with the indention of his head to her chest. What had she done? A cop. A Chicago cop. And not just any Chicago cop, but one that worked at the very station she hated most. God, what a mess.

He'd made her feel things that she never had and still she was no closer to having an answer than she was before she slept with him. Yes, he had the power to make her burn, but why? She wanted to know. She also wanted to know why it was that she now felt a bond with Rafe Remeris like none she ever felt with another person in her entire life. Not her parents and not her brother. What did it mean that she felt this connection to a man she hated?

Angela trembled at the unwanted answer. This had been about sex, nothing more. The sounds of the water stopped, and she heard him at the sink and wondered if he was thinking of using her toothbrush. She'd kill him. Should she offer him one of the new brushes inside her bathroom drawer? She shook herself. Why was she worrying about his comfort?

Actually, it wasn't Rafe that worried her. It was the fact that she was worrying about him that worried her. As the door to the bathroom opened, she turned slightly away. Pretending to still be asleep she watched as he put on his briefs, then slid the jeans over his hips. She moaned inwardly at his masculine beauty.

She wondered if he would now leave without saying a word to her and how she would feel if he did. Still, she did not budge, just remained quiet, waiting to hear the sound of her front door closing before getting out of the bed.

The sound of the front door closing didn't come. Instead she heard Raphael moving around in her kitchen, opening things, and after awhile, she smelled the pungent aroma of strong coffee.

That smell alone pulled her from the bed and into the shower, where she made quick work of washing his scent from her body. She wasn't going to go all mushy over what had happened.

As she came into the kitchen, the sight of Raphael cooking was too comfortable, something she'd neither asked for nor wanted. She stood silently in the doorway, watching. He turned and smiled at her and her heart lurched in her chest.

No, she screamed inwardly. *This is only sex, nothing more.*

"Hi." Raphael held out a cup. "I'm making you breakfast."

"You've taken more than I offered and made yourself at home. This is not a relationship," Angela said, not reaching for the cup.

Raphael's eyes narrowed and for one moment she saw hurt before it was quickly replaced by anger. He walked toward her, his green gaze holding hers, and she watched as he silently fished his wallet from his pocket and withdrew a twenty.

"Will this cover it?" Raphael asked.

"Exactly what are you attempting to pay for?"

"The things you didn't offer freely . . ." He paused. "Your food. Will this cover the eggs and coffee?"

Angela took the twenty from his outstretched palm, looked at it for a second, folded it and looked back up at him.

"As long as you clean up your mess."

She watched as he shook his head and again extended the cup he'd offered her before. This time she accepted it.

"What do you think happened last night?" she asked as she looked away.

She had to know and was hoping he'd have the answer because she sure didn't. She took a sip of the coffee, glad that he'd moved away. Last night had been crazy. She could forgive herself for her error in judgment. But she couldn't explain what was going on now. Why her heart was beating so fast. Why the mere presence of Rafe in her kitchen seemed so right. Like he belonged there. She took another sip of the coffee.

"I think we may have called a truce," Raphael answered, fingering his mug.

She looked at him, seeing much more in his eyes than what his words were saying. "What are you expecting from me?" she asked.

Raphael tilted his head back, knowing there was no way in hell he was going to tell her what he expected or what he wanted. He watched as the ice returned to her eyes. What he really wanted was to have her cold hatred vanish forever. If he never saw iced topaz again in life it would be too soon.

What he wanted was the eyes that blazed with warmth, with desire, with lust. He took another sip of coffee, not surprised to find it now cold. The ice that flowed in the woman's veins had chilled his once hot coffee. He'd made love to an angel and now she had morphed into a hellion.

"Are you trying to tell me that you didn't feel the things I felt?" Raphael inquired, hurt, trying to keep his longing from his voice.

"I wouldn't know what you felt. I'm not a mind reader."

He swallowed. He'd hoped in vain, he now realized. She wouldn't admit that something had changed in the hours they had made love.

"You're right; you're not a mind reader, but I thought for sure we had at least ended the war. Like I said, I think we have found a way to not kill each other." He saw her trying not to smile and pushed on. "Would that be a fair statement?"

"I'll agree to that," she answered.

He noticed her embarrassment. "I don't know about you," Raphael smiled, "but I would rather we kept it like this than fight."

"Just sex?"

"Not exactly what I was saying. That's kind of crude and disrespectful to both of us, don't you think? Besides, I think it was more than just sex."

"Look, you're a cop. I might as well be up front. I hate cops. That's not going to change. Last night more than likely was a fluke. Probably because we hate each other, it made it more, more . . ."

"I'd agree if it had been once or twice, but it happened more than a dozen times. Even when I was a horny teenager that never happened."

He wanted to add he'd never before been to heaven with an angel, that his soul had never joined in the act of making love, but he didn't. He knew she would lie about her own feeling.

"Why do you hate cops?"

"I have my reasons."

"People change."

"I won't, not about this."

"I'm more than a cop."

"That doesn't matter. You're a cop and that's always what I'm going to see."

"Even when I'm making love to you?"

"You talk as if this is going to become a habit."

"Isn't it?"

"I'm not looking for a relationship."

"Neither am I."

Angela stared at Rafe, forcing him to return her gaze. "Let's make sure we both understand what we're saying so later there will be no misunderstanding. We're in this only for fun. When it stops being fun, we end it, no hard feelings."

Raphael lowered his eyes and deliberately let them wander over her body. He was being offered every man's dream—a fantastic physical relationship with no strings attached. "Can we at least be friends?" he asked.

"I'm not looking for any friends," she replied.

He couldn't help staring. "Well, can we stop snipping at each other?"

Angela stared hard into the marble green eyes. "The sex was good. I wouldn't mind . . ." She didn't know what to say. "We're not going to consider this dating or anything crazy like that. No going out to dinner, no movies, nothing."

"I got it," Raphael answered. "We're not a couple. No going out in public."

He saw the quick change that came over her. She could give it but taking it appeared to be a bit harder. It seemed his tough-as-nails angel wasn't as tough as she pretended to be.

"It's not a very good idea for me to be seen in public in the neighborhood with you anyway. I'm still under investigation. Besides that, I've been ordered to stay the hell away from you."

"So why haven't you?"

He grinned widely. "Do you really need me to answer that question?"

"Yes."

"The electrical charge," he answered. "I had to know why it happened."

"And do you know why?" Angela asked.

"No," Raphael nearly whispered. "I have no idea," he lied. What good would it do to tell her the truth? They were soul mates, two people destined to be together. Only he bet fate hadn't counted on the fact that neither of them would even like the other.

"I've never had a sexual . . . a . . . a . . . I've never made arrangements like this with anyone," Angela said looking away from Rafe.

He sensed her embarrassment. "I have," he answered, and waited until she turned to face him. "But I always paid for it." He watched while the iced topaz froze more solidly. "You're jumping to conclusions. That wasn't what I was saying about you. I was just trying to make you feel better about this."

"You didn't do a very good job."

"Then let me try again. This is a first for me also. I don't believe in becoming emotionally involved with people. In my line of work it's much too dangerous. Relationships can be a distraction."

"And I won't be a distraction?"

Raphael smiled. "You said it yourself. This isn't a relationship. It should work well for us both. I only ask one thing."

"What's that?"

"You didn't answer about the snapping at each other. Can we stop it?"

"We can try."

He grinned again. "Now that that's settled, want to tell me why you hate cops so much?"

"No."

"Want to tell me who you're visiting in the prison?" He watched the change come over her face, felt the chill in the room and wished he'd kept his mouth closed.

"Look, if this is going to work, there will have to be rules. No asking me personal questions. I don't like you, let's get that clear. What I do is my business. You're not privy to that information. You're not a part of my life; you're not a part of my heart. We've made a bargain for sex, no matter what you want to call it. What we do and say will be done in the bed. When we're not in bed, we're not anything."

She slammed the mug down on the table. "You are nothing to me. I don't care about you. Get that clear. You have no right to ask me questions." She stormed out of the room.

Raphael watched as she left the room. There was a lot more to this fiery woman than he'd thought. Not only wasn't she as tough as she pretended to be, she was hurting. He should have been angry with her but instead he felt compassion. He had his own share of loved ones in prisons throughout the country. He knew she thought of him as the enemy, only he wasn't.

He thought of leaving but didn't. Instead, he returned to fixing her breakfast, and when it was done, he made a plate for her and took it to the bedroom where she was holed up. Then he sat at the kitchen table and ate his own. He might not like her, but he did understand.

CHAPTER 6

In ways she had never imagined, Angela's life changed completely. She was doing the last thing she would have ever expected, and even if she never admitted it to Rafe, she was enjoying it. At least at night, in the darkness, in his arms she enjoyed it.

When daylight came, so did her doubts and the staggering guilt. She'd missed a couple of visits with her brother because she was unable to look into his eyes, knowing she was sleeping with her family's enemy.

As wrong as she felt it was when Rafe was not around, she felt a rightness when they made love. That was another thing about their agreement; she denied vehemently that they were making love, claiming it was only sex. It was getting harder and harder to protest when her soul and her body recognized the truth.

She shivered as she looked out the window, needing a diversion for her rampant thoughts. Who was she kidding? Rafe Remeris had invaded more than her nights. He was taking over a big chunk of her day and she was spending way too much time thinking about him.

With a sigh, Angela called her parents to get their schedule for the week. It was time for her to descend from the clouds. She couldn't avoid her brother forever. She'd have to eventually return to the prison and she needed to make sure she didn't run into her parents. She knew they mostly devoted their weekends to visit the prison. Anything else was secondary, even church.

"Daddy, how's everything going? I just wanted to check in on you."

"We're okay, baby. Your mother is getting ready to go see Adrian this afternoon for awhile."

"You're not going, Daddy?"

"Nah, baby. I have to talk to a real estate agent. Your mama and I talked and we're thinking of either selling the house or getting a second mortgage."

"Why?"

"We're running out of money to pay the investigator."

A lump formed in Angela's throat. If she weren't trying to help Adrian by living in the Pilsen area she could give her parents more money to help. She bit her lips and cringed. "Can you put that off for a little while?"

"We need the money to pay him."

"How much money do you need?"

"Honey, I wasn't telling you this to make you feel guilty or to have you come up with money. That's not what we want; we'll take care of this."

"But he's my brother. I want to help."

"You don't have that kind of money."

"How do you know? You haven't told me how much money you need."

"It varies but it usually runs about two thousand dollars a month."

"Daddy, hold off on doing anything with the house. I can handle at least one month."

"Will it hurt you, baby?"

"No, I was just saving it for a trip. I won't be taking any trips until Adrian comes home."

"Your mother and I don't want you giving up your life. You have a right to go on vacation. You work hard."

"Well, I'd rather give you the money," Angela insisted.

"Then what? You can't afford to pay it and neither can we. Why delay the inevitable? You help for a month, the month after we'll still have to do what I'm going to do today."

"But you may not have to. Maybe by then there'll be a break. Maybe the investigator will come up with something. Who knows? Just take the money and promise me you'll not do anything about the house."

"But your mother and I talked already. We made plans."

"Promise me, Daddy."

"Honey?"

"Promise?" she pleaded.

"I promise."

"Good," Angela answered. "Give me the detective's address and I'll send him a check."

For a long moment her father was quiet. She knew he didn't like taking her money and she knew that more than likely he knew it wasn't for any trip. "Don't worry," she assured her father, "this nightmare will be over soon."

"I don't know," he answered. "Even if it's over for Adrian it won't be over. Every day the Chicago cops are in the news. Every day they're beating somebody, shooting someone in the back. God, I'm glad they didn't kill my son."

"Me too," Angela whispered, feeling like a traitor. She'd slept with the enemy and it had felt so right. He'd felt so right. "I have to go now, Daddy. I have to work."

Angela hung up the phone, sickened by her own actions. She was sleeping with a Chicago cop. What in the world was the matter with her?

Two days later she was having the same feelings, only intensified. She was sitting across from her brother at the prison, wishing she had better news to tell him.

"Adrian, why won't you tell the detective about Teresa? Maybe with both of us looking for her we could find her. Do you have any idea the kind of money Daddy's paying him? It's almost two thousand dollars a month. They can't afford that for long, we both know it."

"What do you want them to do, let me rot in here?"

"You know I don't want that. But what's going to happen if they sell the house and have nowhere to live? Daddy can't work forever. They're going to lose everything."

"They haven't lost their freedom. They still have that. I don't."

Angela wanted to tell her brother how selfish he was being but didn't. She had never been in prison. She could only imagine how horrible it was for him. And she didn't blame him, he was probably going a little crazy being locked up.

"Did you deposit money in my account?"

"Yes. Why did you need so much?" She blinked at the hard look that came into her brother's eyes; it was such complete anger. "I'm sorry," she answered, imagining the worst. "I'm sorry," she said again.

"Look, just do what you went into Pilsen for. Find Teresa and get me the hell out of here."

"I'm trying."

"You're not trying hard enough. She's one woman, she shouldn't be that hard to find."

"I've asked people if they know her, and they look at me like they think I'm crazy and say, '*No habla ingles*' and I know that they're lying. I hear them speaking in English. They just don't want to talk to me."

"Did you tell them you're a reporter?"

"Of course I did," Angela said between clenched teeth, annoyed that her brother was treating her as if she were an incompetent moron. "That was the plan, remember?"

"Then take a camera, start taking pictures. No one can resist getting their picture in the paper. Look, I don't care what you have to do, but you need to do it quickly. I'm sick and tired of waiting." He got up from the table and walked away.

For ten minutes Angela sat there waiting for him to return. He was lonely and angry, but surely he'd come back. He'd not even said goodbye.

After ten minutes she gave up hoping he'd return and got up from the table. Her thoughts about her brother being lonely were quickly pushed to the back of her mind when she remembered all the people visiting him. Sure, that didn't make up for him being locked away, but no one had forgotten him. He could at least acknowledge that they were all doing their best. Right now Rafe Remeris was treating her with a lot more respect than her brother. The line between friend and foe was beginning to get a bit blurred.

TWO SIDES TO EVERY STORY

For three weeks Raphael had been spending most of his nights in bed with the woman who'd set out on a mission to destroy him. In that time he'd learned more about her. For one thing, he could tell when she'd been to the prison. She generally didn't want to see him, or if she did, she'd turn her back on him the moment they were done and order him to leave.

But a few days before, something strange had happened. She'd ordered him to leave and he'd been about to. Her eyes had blazed with hatred and self-loathing. He knew she hated being in bed with him. And he was getting tired of the look in her eyes. She'd started to cry.

"Do you really hate me that much?" he'd asked.

"It's not you that I hate," she'd answered.

"Can't I help you? I'm a good listener. You sound as if you could use a friend."

"We're not friends," Angela whispered. "Look at what I've done to you. I've tried to destroy your life. You're in trouble because of me. You don't owe me anything. Why would you want to help me?"

He shrugged his shoulder. "To serve and protect." He smiled at her.

"Why don't you hate me?"

"Hate takes up too much energy."

"I'm always so mean to you."

"I know."

"What we're doing is wrong on so many levels. I'll admit the sex is good between us, but I can't allow myself to have feelings for you. I don't want you thinking I'm someone that I'm not."

Raphael sighed. "All of this because I offered to be your friend?"

"No, all of this is because I think you might really be a nice guy and I'm not such a nice girl."

"Why do you say that?" he asked, stroking her face, caressing her neck, blowing her hair.

"I have too much going on," she whispered, not wanting to tell him of the anger and hatred she'd lived with for so long. Instead, she'd looked at him and simply stated, "It's consuming me. I don't know what to do any longer and I don't have much time to figure it all out."

A tear had slid down her cheek and he licked it away. "For one night let me be your friend, let me take your pain away."

Angela shook in his arms as a torrent of tears rocked her body. "I'm wasting time," she moaned. "And I don't have the luxury of failing."

He'd cradled her against his chest, crooning to her, touching her gently. And then he'd made love to her. Not sex. He'd made love to her and she'd clung to him and that damnable ever-present heat seared his soul. He'd wanted to stop her from hurting and had ended knowing it wasn't possible.

He hadn't wanted to admit it, but he was falling for her. As ironic as it seemed, Raphael's soul had been claimed by his soul mate.

Since that night, things had changed with them. She still held to the same rules but he could see a difference in the way she touched him in bed. She made love to him also and she no longer ordered him from her bed. Instead, she cuddled with him and fell asleep. And he fell asleep holding her near his heart, knowing she'd laid claim on it. Knowing she didn't want him. Knowing that because of her, he could possibly lose his job, his lifelong dream. And he wondered what would happen to them if that happened.

It was time. She glanced at the clock, knowing that within seconds Rafe would be knocking on her door. Her heart skipped a beat and she shivered, praying he didn't know how much he affected her life even when he wasn't around.

Angela opened the door, her heart pounding in her chest. She wished she could make her body behave, but it had a mind of its own. And when he was in the vicinity it went amok. She couldn't believe it. An entire month had passed and she was spending more and more time with him.

They didn't talk about their feelings but she was mellowing toward him. He was funny and sweet. When he was in her apartment, she could pretend that he wasn't a cop. He was teaching her Spanish and she was teaching him . . . She laughed as she opened the door. She was teaching him nothing at all. He already knew all that he needed to know.

—◆—

Angela pushed her hips backwards into Rafe. His arms were wrapped around her and it felt so right. He was nuzzling her neck and whispering to her in Spanish. She had no idea what he was saying but the sound of his voice filled her with an inner peace and lulled her to sleep.

When she woke she studied him as he slept. Even in sleep he held her tight . . . as if . . . as if he didn't want to let her go, she suddenly realized. The thought sank into her and a flame of awareness pierced her. She liked him and she didn't want to.

She'd wanted this to be only sex but he'd changed that. If she were honest, she'd admit he'd changed it from the first moment they'd been together. But none of his kindness had gotten to her.

Angela knew the exact moment when she'd felt the change. Only a few days ago he'd comforted her when she'd needed it most and he'd asked no questions, just held her and made her feel safe and wanted.

That knowledge alone had angered her at first and had almost given her the strength to send him from her bed. Almost. Then he'd begun making love to her and it had all been for her, not for him. It had been so different. He'd kissed her with such reverence, such, she hated to think it, but such love that she believed him. She'd looked into his eyes and she'd known. They were no longer enemies. She didn't know what they were, but she sure knew it wasn't enemies.

"Do you believe in fortune tellers?" he'd asked.

"Not really."

"Well then, do you believe in soul mates?"

"No." she'd replied.

"What do you believe in?"

"I believe in myself and in my family."

"That's enough for you?" Rafe had asked.

"It's my constant. My family will always be there for me, no fortune teller can tell me differently."

Her heart was pounding with awareness. She'd be a fool not to know what he was asking, but she couldn't accept it, not now. She didn't have time for soul mates in her plans, especially one who worked for the enemy.

"Do you believe in all of this, Rafe, fortune telling, soul mates and magic fairy dust?"

"Yes, I believe," he answered her, smiling. "But it scares the hell out of me. I don't really want to believe, but yes, Angel, I believe."

CHAPTER 7

Angela had mailed the check off to the detective just as she'd promised her father. She'd also increased her time on the streets, trying to strike up conversations, carrying a huge camera, doing fake interviews. Yet she'd gotten nothing.

Well, nothing wasn't quite true. She'd gotten Rafe. A big beautiful man that believed in magic and fairy dust and he was sleeping in her bed.

As they lay in bed, she glanced at his olive complexion and black curly hair and she couldn't resist. She blew and watched as the curl waved at her. He woke, looked at her, smiled and she melted. Then came the guilt.

The night before she'd heard on the news about another shooting involving the Chicago police. She knew both of her parents would call her later to talk about it and her brother. She hated thinking about Adrian when Rafe was looking at her with lust in his eyes and his emerging feelings so plainly there for her to see. The guilt increased.

She knew Rafe wasn't responsible for the shooting the night before. He'd been in the bed with her, making love to her. The knowledge both filled her with pleasure and with angst. The last man she should be liking was a Chicago cop. She wasn't in love with him, but she also didn't hate him anymore. And that was going to be a problem.

"Hi," he said softly, kissing her eyelids.

"Hi yourself," she answered back.

"You're beautiful."

"Am I?"

"You know you are." He nuzzled her neck. "And you smell good."

"You're aware you're breaking the rules."

"I don't think so," Raphael replied. "We're still in bed."

"Yes, but it's morning and . . ."

His lips came down over her and kissed her into submission. "Let's start again," he whispered into her ear, his hot breath doing things to her that made her moan aloud. "Don't you have to work?" she asked.

"Not today," he answered.

Angela knew where this was heading. They had never spent time together when he was off, no more than a couple of hours. He'd always insisted on making her breakfast before he left.

Raphael waited, wondering if she would let him stay, knowing it was Thursday, the day she usually went to the prison. The day she usually didn't want him around. He waited.

"What did you have in mind?" Angela asked, aware that it was Thursday, aware that if she played hooky and spent the day with Rafe she wouldn't get any work done. She wouldn't be able to patrol the neighborhood looking for leads. She thought of what her father had told her, that she deserved a life. *One day,* she thought. *What can one day hurt?*

"Are you saying that you want to spend the day with me?" Raphael asked, insisting on a direct answer.

"Yeah, I want to spend the day with you. Now get over it and tell me what plans you have."

He grinned. "I didn't make any. I didn't expect you to agree."

"Want to take it back?"

He kissed her deeply, came up for air and murmured, "What do you think?"

"So what are we going to do?"

He grinned.

"All day?" she asked.

"I'm up for it." he answered. "Well, maybe not right this second but I will be. We could go out to a movie, or to a museum or even to Navy Pier." He looked at her hopefully, knowing she'd say no.

"Not today." she answered.

"Maybe we could spend the day talking, get to know each other."

Angela pulled back from the heat of his body. "This isn't going to change anything."

"I didn't think it would."

"I'm not answering any personal questions, I'm warning you right now."

"Not even like why you're living here in Pilsen?"

She shook her head.

"Or where you went to school?"

"That I'll answer."

"And what church you go to?"

"You're trying to find out my religion?" She grinned.

"I'm just trying to figure out what will be a safe topic."

"I think you know what isn't. Just stay away from those and let's see what happens."

"What are we going to do for food?" he asked.

"We'll eat."

"You don't have any food in your kitchen."

"I do."

"You call those diet dinners in your freezer food? There's no ice cream or cookies and there's no meat. I want some food." Raphael pounded his fists on his chest playfully. "I need to eat."

She grinned at him. "I have some protein bars."

"Yuck."

"You like eating, don't you? How do you manage to stay so," she licked her lips, "so fit?"

"I exercise," he replied, grinning. "I'm a cop. I keep busy." He caught a flash of her biting her lips.

"Sorry, Angel, I know you don't want to hear about my job but can you tell me about yours? What are you, a reporter, freelance writer, what?"

"What made you think writer?"

"You're always at your computer writing and I don't see you rushing off to work in the mornings. So I know you work from home."

"Brilliant deduction."

"No deduction—" He caught her gaze and stopped. She didn't want to hear anything dealing with him being a police office. But surely she had to know as a cop he would notice these things.

"Mostly I'm a technical writer."

"What exactly do you do?"

"Anything that pays the bills."

"Anything?"

"Anything that has to do with writing," she amended.

"So go ahead and tell me exactly what a technical writer does."

"It's pretty boring stuff really. I can guarantee you won't find it interesting."

"Try me. I find . . ." He stopped himself from saying that he was beginning to find everything about her interesting. "I find writers very interesting."

"I write the words that describe the food in the restaurant menus. I write the copy for lots of ad agencies." She stopped, looked at him and grinned. "I even do a horoscope and advice column."

"I thought you didn't believe in fortune telling."

"I don't. I just told you I write that stuff; it's malarkey. How am I supposed to believe something that someone just like me made up while sitting in their kitchen chair in their bathrobe munching on toast and drinking coffee?"

"Do you make it all up?"

"Yes."

"You never consult a book or anything?"

"Maybe sometimes, but it doesn't mean anything. It's all for fun."

"Tell me about your advice column. Are you famous?"

"I wish."

"Seriously, Angel, would I have heard of it?"

"I don't think so. It's one of those free papers, a giveaway. I write an advice column for them and I get a steady paycheck. No big deal."

"Was that your goal, to write an advice column, tell people how to run their lives?"

Angela stopped and thought over what he was asking her. It had been a long time since she'd thought what her goal really was. For the past two years it had only been about freeing her brother, finding a way to make the cops pay.

Sure, maybe one day she would think seriously about some kind of career in writing that was more uncertain, but right now she needed money. She didn't have time to write for years and sit out the wave of inevitable rejections, hoping and praying to make a sale, then hoping and praying to get paid. No, what she did paid nicely, and she got to do it on her own terms. Her job was stable and for now she cherished the stability.

"I make good money doing what I do," she said to Rafe through clenched teeth.

"I wasn't criticizing you. I think it's very cool that you get to stay at home and work, yet make money. I wouldn't mind if I could do that."

"Are you saying you would give up being a cop?"

Raphael grinned. "No, I guess not. I've always wanted to be a policeman." He tilted his head and gazed at Angela. "Actually the word *cop* denotes something else. I dreamed of being a policeman and now I am."

"And you can't very well arrest the bad guy from your bed."

"So you admit there are some bad guys?" he asked, his breath moving over her cheek, his flesh lengthening. God how he wanted her. Just being near her made him throb with desire.

Angela was watching him. She saw the instant desire claim him. He couldn't hide it if he tried. Her eyes dropped down and she eyed his crotch, smiling at the quivering flesh. She enjoyed that she did that to him, that he was as weak for her as she was for him. She didn't want to be the only one caught in a trap of lust and desire. This had never happened to Angela before.

There was also something else that Rafe gave her and that was a sense of being young. She'd lost that and hadn't even known it. Now she felt playful teasing him and enjoying being teased in return. She pointed at his burgeoning erection. "Being a cop does that to you?"

She laughed as he looked down, grinning wickedly at her. "What do you think?"

"I think talking about it . . . well, they do say that men dream of using a gun to substitute for . . ." She laughed.

"Do you think I need help in that department?" he asked, placing his hands over his heart in a hurt fashion.

"Not in the least," Angela answered, deciding not to tease him anymore. "In that department you know exactly what you're doing."

"You know, this is the longest conversation we've had without one of us getting angry. It feels different, nice," Raphael stated.

Angela lay back on the bed, her fingers entwined with his, and smiled. She'd enjoyed it too.

"Would you like me to make you breakfast?"

"I thought you said I didn't have any food." She looked at him, bemused.

"You don't. But I come from a large family. You have to have something in there I can make into a meal. But you didn't answer. Do you like it when I cook for you?"

Raphael watched her closely, his eyes glued to the slow smile that curved her lips, the way she finally said yes as though she was giving away something precious. And he knew that, for her, she was. She was admitting to herself and to him that there were things she liked about being with him, cop or not.

"Do you want me to make breakfast for you, Angel?" he asked again, pushing a little.

"How did you learn to cook?" she countered.

"I told you I come from a large family. There are lots of things I know how to do, and do well." He leered. "You're stalling for time. Is it really that hard for you to say you want me to do something for you?"

Angela looked at his smiling face and his eyes that held a more serious question than the one he was asking. "I take care of myself, Rafe. I try not to live with illusions."

"Illusions about us?"

"About anything, it's too easy to get hurt that way."

"I've learned that you only fear the things that you long for, the things you wish in your secret heart of hearts to have, but you're afraid you can't have, so you push the hope away, have no illusions about it.

Why don't you try asking if you can have me? Is that what you want, Angel," Raphael teased. "Do you want me?"

"Give me breakfast." Angela smiled. "You're right, I secretly want to know what you can make from what I have in my kitchen." She hopped from the bed. "I'm going to take a shower."

"I could take one with you. What do you think?"

"I think I have a small shower and I'd better take it alone."

"Coward," he said and stared after her. Five minutes later he was still staring until he shook his head, realizing what he was doing. The secret heart of hearts he'd told her about was his own. He wanted her in his life, and not just occasionally.

CHAPTER 8

Angela leaned against the wall of the shower letting the hot water run over her body. What the heck was she doing? This was supposed to be about sex only, but it felt like so much more. It felt like friendship and comfort.

Everything about Rafe felt so right. She'd known the danger when she'd agreed to an entire day. She'd known her feelings for him were changing and she suspected that he knew it too. Scrubbing away at her body, she tried to ignore the fact that she wasn't visiting her brother today because she'd chosen to spend the day with Rafe.

"It doesn't mean a thing," she said in a whisper. "I'll go tomorrow. It doesn't mean a thing," she whispered again.

And later, when she was seated at her table across from him eating the fluffiest eggs she'd ever tasted, with a creamy cheese sauce, she felt the heat. And it scared her. His green gaze was hypnotic. He sat smiling at her, watching her eat, and with each forkful she saw things in his eyes she couldn't have, not with him. Not with a Chicago cop.

When she was done eating, he grinned at her and took the plates away to the sink and ran water. And for some crazy reason, that did her in. She walked slowly to the phone and turned the ringer off. Then she found her cell and put it on vibrate. Maybe she couldn't have Rafe Remeris forever, but for this one day she could pretend. Tomorrow she would return to her real life.

"Hey," Angela said, kissing her brother's cheek. He hugged her tight, then tighter, and for some strange reason she got a bad vibe.

"You stink," he said, pushing her from him.

Because her brother's voice was so vicious, Angela was stunned for a moment. She didn't stink, she knew that. But still he had her sniffing her armpits, blowing her breath into her hand, and all the time her face flamed with embarrassment.

Her brother's voice had been loud and she felt eyes on her. Everyone in the prison seemed to be looking at her, believing that she did stink.

But she waited until they were seated before turning to her brother. "What was that crack about? I don't stink."

"You do. I can smell him all over your body."

She went from being embarrassed to being completely mortified. Her mind flashed on Rafe and she cringed, wondering for only a moment if her brother could possibly tell that they'd made love only a few hours before.

But she'd showered after.

And made love again, she remembered.

Angela blinked rapidly, trying to ignore the anger in her brother's eyes. She was confused and was trying desperately to recap the entire morning. She focused on kissing Rafe at the door. She'd been in her robe. He'd left and she'd showered. She smiled triumphantly.

She'd showered.

"You don't smell anything on me."

"I smell sex. I didn't know you had a boyfriend."

"I don't."

"So what are you doing, banging some Pilsen Romeo?"

"Why don't you knock it off? I didn't come here for you to grill me about my private business."

"So you're admitting I'm right? Don't be stupid, Angie. Do you think I could bang a Hispanic chick without the entire neighborhood wanting to cut my throat?"

"That's stereotyping."

"Stereotyping exists because of some truths."

"And all the stereotyping about Blacks, is that true too?"

"Look, if you want to screw some illegal, I want you to know it's not okay. And if I wasn't in here, you wouldn't be doing it."

"What is this? Why the third degree? What are you doing?" Angela demanded. "I didn't come here for this."

"You sound like you're doing me a favor by coming. You don't want to come," Adrian glared at her, "don't come. You didn't come yesterday, so why did you come today?"

"I had things to do yesterday."

"I'll bet."

"What are you getting at? Because there is no way in the world you smell anything on me besides soap."

Angela glared at her brother. She was annoyed with him and was getting tired of making excuses for his rotten attitude for the past two years.

Yes, he might be the one sitting in a cell, but their entire family was doing time. They'd all become prisoners by proxy. When something befell one of them, it happened to the rest of them.

Now the very notion that he would begrudge her a boyfriend, even if she had one, angered her. She hadn't had a boyfriend since he'd been locked up. She hadn't had the time.

Brother and sister glared at each other for a few minutes until Adrian decided to end it by asking, "Have you found her?"

"No luck."

Then he glared again. "If you're not going to try you may as well leave the neighborhood."

"Adrian, I'm out there almost every day talking to people, asking questions. We knew this wasn't going to be easy going in, but I'm doing my best."

"Did you go out yesterday?"

"No, I didn't go out yesterday." she almost screamed. "I didn't feel like it. I took the day for myself. Do you mind?"

"No, I don't mind," he answered in a quiet voice. "But then again, if you're not going out every day you really can't say you're doing your best, now can you?"

It went like that for most of the visit and by the time Angela was on the expressway heading back toward her new home, she was exhausted. This was hard on all of them. She wanted her brother out more than ever. He was changing, becoming hard and mean. And she wanted him out before he changed any more. He was right; she'd have to work that much harder. Rafe's smiling face came into her mind and she pushed it away. She couldn't think about him now; he was distracting her.

"Hi," Angela said later that night as she opened the door to Rafe. She glanced at the shopping bags in his arms. "What's all of this?"

"Can I come in?" he asked, surprised that she was blocking his entry. He shifted the bags around to keep them from falling.

"What's in them?" she asked, moving aside to let him in.

"Food."

"Food?"

"Yes, food," he answered, puzzled.

She pulled back. He'd just ruined another moment. "Why are you bringing me food? I didn't ask you to. I have money; I can buy my own groceries."

"Calm down, Angel, this isn't a form of payment or a bribe. I know it's not a relationship with us." He carried the bags into the kitchen, set them down and turned back to face her. "But if you don't mind, when we're done making love, I'm done, poof, nothing left. I need food, not protein bars, so I brought some. Don't worry. The food even knows it's not permanent. When the carton of eggs is finished it knows it will be tossed in the trash and replaced. Everything in the bags will remain here for only a short time. Is that good enough?"

He glared at her before he turned and began unloading the bags. He would rather have told her the truth, that he was going to make dinner for her, but he knew she would not like it. He was falling for her hard, and wished like hell that he knew a way to stop it.

Falling in love was supposed to be fun, but this, it was brutal torture. She fought him over everything. The only leeway she allowed was when he made love to her. Then he could whisper words of endearments, but only in Spanish. He knew she could figure out what he meant but at least she didn't call him on it.

His *madrina* was right. He was definitely having to fight with her, and damn if he wasn't losing.

"I haven't had anything to eat in twelve hours," Raphael continued. "I'm hungry. Do you mind if I cook? As usual, I'll clean up my mess," he said between gritted teeth, hating that this woman was turning him into an *aseminado*. He had better hurry and decide what he was going to do before he completely lost his stones.

Angela didn't answer him. She bit her lip, wishing she could accept the little things he attempted to do for her without making such a big deal of it. She knew why she was being such a witch to him. She was becoming too involved, happy when he came, sad when he left, and that wasn't their deal.

"You want some help?" she offered by way of apology.

"Can you cook?"

"When I want to."

He stopped what he was doing and glanced in her direction. "Have you ever wanted to?"

Angela wasn't falling for that. She knew what he wanted was for her to cook for him, or to at least want to cook for him. Big macho Rafe was so transparent. He couldn't help it. He wore his feelings on his sleeve.

In the beginning he'd said he didn't think cops should become involved with anyone, that it made it too dangerous. Yet from the first night they'd made love he'd cared. Angela didn't believe he could make love to a woman without caring.

She shivered just thinking about his lovemaking. He put such passion into it, making her feel beautiful and worthy. She glanced upward and blushed, catching him staring at her.

"What are you looking at?" she joked.

"*Te ves buena para comar.*"

She blinked. His heated gaze washed over her, making her hot, making her want him. Making her want *them*. "What did you say?" she asked.

"I've taught you enough Spanish that you should be able to figure that out."

He was right, she could. But for once she wanted to hear him say the words to her that he whispered in her ear in bed. "Tell me."

"I said you look good enough to eat."

Her breathing slowed and she waited for him to touch her, to return normal function to her organs. "Rafe," she whispered as his hand touched her face and his lips caressed her hair. "What about dinner?"

"Later," he murmured. "I'm hungry for you now."

Her arms slid around his neck and she moaned as his tongue did an up and down dance over her carotid artery. She could swear his kisses were making her blood pump faster. "Rafe," she moaned again. "Do you have a sister?"

He halted in his caresses. "Yes."

"How would you feel if your sister were sleeping with a Black man?"

Angela forced her body away from his to peer into his eyes, trying to detect the slightest hint of a lie.

"Why are you asking me that?"

"Because I want to know. We both know there is as much hatred between Blacks and Latinos as there is between with Blacks and whites."

"When did this become about race?"

From the moment we began to care, she wanted to answer. "Everything boils down to it sooner or later. I didn't want to make it an issue. But then again, you seem to be having a problem answering the question."

"I'm not having a problem answering it. I was just wondering why now. I have four sisters. I've never asked them who they sleep with. I've never thought much about it."

"Think about it."

"Right now?" He leered. "I have other things on my mind."

"Right now," she answered, not letting it go. "Tell me the truth. When you see a Latino woman with a Black man, does it make you angry? Do you curse at them or stare at them? Do you call the woman dirty names?" She glanced away. "Or have you never seen a Black man with a Latino woman?"

Raphael shook his head and smiled sadly. "I never saw this coming. Angel, you've blindsided me here. Now I know why you don't want to go out in public with me."

"This isn't about us. Can't you just answer the question?"

Raphael moved his hands away and pulled out his wallet. "This is my family." He began flipping through the pictures, stopping at a picture of two beautiful women with long dark hair and brown eyes, both with husbands that looked to be Black. But Angela was aware that as with African Americans, Latinos also sported many hues and variations. "Are they Hispanic?" she asked, pointing to the men in the pictures.

"No, they're not."

"Do you like them?"

"Yes. Does that answer your question?"

"Did your parents object?"

"What does that matter? My sisters married the men that they loved and they're happy. Their husbands are a part of the family now."

Angela closed her eyes, thinking of the visit with her brother. She'd just spoiled a very nice moment and for what? "I had to know," she said.

"What about you, Angel, and your family? Are you worried about sleeping with a . . . what names do you call me, Angel?"

"I call you Rafe."

"You don't have any dirty little names that you whisper in the dark when you think no one is looking? I've heard the racial slurs people have not even bothered to whisper. It's always 'the Mexicans this,' or 'the Mexicans that.' Never mind that I'm not Mexican. And even if I were, why would that be someone's reason to sum up my worth? Since you're asking me about my feelings, Angel, tell me yours. Are you like that? What words did you use for me when we were fighting? Was I '*the dirty Mexican?*"

"You're not Mexican."

"So what?"

"If you're asking me if I've ever used racial slurs, I guess I would have to say yes, that I have. Haven't you?"

"Yes."

"Did you mean them?"

"At the time. Did you?"

"At the time."

"Where the hell did all of this come from?" Raphael asked, obviously puzzled.

"Someone pointed out to me that while Latino men have a problem with their women sleeping with men from other races, they will screw anything, anywhere, anytime."

Rafe's face scrunched up into a frown. "Is that what you've been wondering about me?"

"I hadn't."

"And now?"

"Now I wish I'd never asked you the question. There was no need. I never wanted this to be about race, Rafe. I was hoping that until it's over . . . I mean, when we're done we could just be us, no one having to make a statement, no declarations."

"What are you going to do with me when you're done, *mi amor?* Are you going to just toss me out in the trash with the egg cartons?"

She wanted to tell him never, to reassure him, but he was kissing her lips, cutting off her words. Then the time for words ceased as he began to make love to her while she stood in the middle of the room. His hunger was intense and the green of his eyes smoky and dangerous. Angela watched as they turned from jade to crystal and back again.

"Do you have any idea what I feel when I touch you, when I kiss you?" he asked. "Do you think it makes a damn bit of difference to me what race you are?"

His hands stroked her skin and she became molten lava. If only they could remain like this, the two of them, no worries, no differences between them. But it wasn't the way real life worked; this wasn't a fantasy. No one would come in to rescue her and give her her dream of a socially accepting world where race didn't matter, and it was not even worth the mention in a book. That day wasn't here.

People would always notice when they went to the movies and saw actors of difference races kissing. It would still be the main focus, no matter what the subject matter was. And an interracial love story would not be read by the masses because they would feel uncomfortable. Just as she knew seeing her with Rafe would make many Blacks and Latinos uncomfortable, and who the heck knew how many others?

Angela had done her best to not let the color of a person's skin influence her but she had her own prejudices. She blindly hated an entire police department. And now that her brother had voiced his objections, she saw more than Rafe's green eyes and she didn't like it. She didn't like knowing that either of them had those feelings.

"Are you going to throw me in the trash?" Raphael asked her again as his tongue flicked over her neck.

"No."

"Are you sure?"

"I'm sure."

"Why?"

Angela was shivering. She was falling for him and now was not the time. It felt as if the bones in her body had dissolved.

"Why won't you throw me in the trash, Angel?"

"Because you're much too good to ever throw in the trash." She watched the cocky smile that appeared on his face. "Don't smirk," she said.

"I'm thinking that you're liking me, Angel."

"I'm thinking that you're right," she admitted. "I do have a question, though, if you don't mind answering."

"Ask away," he said as his tongue again swiped the side of her neck over and over, sending delicious sensations flooding her body.

"Since we're on the subject, why do so many Spanish people that can speak English choose to speak Spanish when they're in the company of people that don't understand?"

"Because sometimes there are no words to explain what you want to say in English."

"I don't believe you."

"It's true."

"I still don't believe it."

"Does it bother you?"

"Of course it bothers me. It's rude! How would you like it if I spoke in a language in front of you that you don't understand?"

"That will never happen." He peered at her. "We never go out in public."

"But if we did?"

"If we ever do I'll make sure to not offend you. I'll speak in English."

"And if your friends are speaking in Spanish?"

"I'll tell them to speak in English." He smiled. "Does this mean you don't want me murmuring in Spanish to you when we make love?"

Angela couldn't help smiling in return. She rather liked it when he did that. "No, you can still do that. But I want you to teach me more Spanish, more than the words you say to me in bed." She blushed. "Things I can use in a normal conversation."

"Okay, deal. Anything else, any more questions?"

"Just one: why do so many Spanish women call their children and their husbands *poppi*?"

"It means father, but it's used also for a sign of affection. You could say it's used when there is the purest form of love."

"Oh, I didn't know that. I think I like it."

"Anything else?"

"No, nothing."

"Then can I make love to you?"

Before she could answer he was doing just that and she didn't have the slightest objection.

His hand slid up her leg so slowly that, knowing his goal, she wanted to urge him to hurry. Finally his hand was there and she squeezed her thighs together and allowed the moan to escape.

"Are you wishing that I were Black, Angel? Would this feel better if I were?"

"Shut up, Rafe."

She heard his deep laugh a second before her own hands began their explorations. She found him heavy with need, his erection full and throbbing, his excitement wetting the tip. She gave a little squeeze, felt him jump from the contact, and she laughed.

"Make love to me, Rafe, and let me make love to you," she said as she began to caress him in earnest.

His fingers plunged deeper into her and rubbed roughly across her essence. She was going to come and she wanted to prolong it, wanted to feel his hardness inside of her. "No, Rafe," she moaned.

"Yes," he answered, "come for me, Angel."

He gave another squeeze, his other hand cupping her buttocks, pressing her in closer to his heat. "Come for me, Angel." He groaned and shuddered.

With him touching her like that, Angela wouldn't have been able to hold back even if she'd had a mind to. And she didn't have a mind to.

"Rafe," she moaned over and over, letting the wave of desire fill her, the release surprising in its intensity. Then again, it always was. She wondered if it could always be like that.

Before her orgasm had subsided he was entering her, his muscular, hard body covering her own. His eyes burned with green fire. "Angel, *mi amor*," he groaned and each time he said it he pierced a little more of her reserve.

She wished there was a way to have this last forever. She felt his shudder and gave up thinking, seduced by Rafe and the massive trembling he was producing in her body. She groaned in surrender, knowing that she was producing the same immense effect on him as he was having on her.

TWO SIDES TO EVERY STORY

She loved it, loved the two of them together. They were a fit. She knew it and he knew it. *If only,* Angela thought, and that was her last thought before her release claimed her and she gripped Rafe's hair in her hand.

CHAPTER 9

Raphael was peeping in Angela's freezer, as usual. She now believed him when he said he needed nourishment after making love. Of course she couldn't blame him; they'd made love until neither of them had the strength to do anything but lie still, holding each other and nibbling at the other's lips. Angela rather thought it was Rafe's nibbling at her lips that had brought him from the bed to scrimmage for food.

"You have any ice cream or cookies?" he asked hopefully. He sounded so much like a little boy that she laughed in spite of herself. He was sucking her in big time, winning her over with his charm.

"I could make you a pancake."

He stared in surprise at her. "That's not ice cream and cookies," he said softly.

Since they'd begun whatever it was they had over two months ago, it was the first time she'd ever let down her guard outside of bed. To have her offer to cook for him was a first.

"I know," Angela answered, "but at least it's sweet with syrup." She cocked her head a tiny bit to the left. "Want some?"

"Lots of syrup?"

"Yes, lots of syrup."

He smiled. "Thanks."

At the grocery, Angela picked up the chocolate chip ice cream, envisioning the look on Rafe's face. She laid it in her cart next to the three bags of cookies and felt a ping in her chest. He was getting to her. He was doing what she had sworn would never happen. He was worming his way into her heart, making her think about him and what would make him happy. *It's only food,* she tried to console her subconscious, *no big deal.*

But it was a big deal and she knew it, just as her making him pancakes had been a big deal to both of them.

She thought of the way he'd looked at her as he sat at her table eating, his eyes never leaving her face. She doubted that he'd even tasted the food, yet he'd eaten every bite and held his plate out for more. When he was done, she'd refilled it and again he'd eaten while those darn green eyes of his continued telling her how he felt about her.

When he'd kissed her after he was finally done, she'd tasted the maple syrup that clung to his tongue and coated his lips. Thinking about it, Angela shivered as she emptied her groceries on the conveyer belt. A Chicago cop. What had she done?

Raphael walked hurriedly from one register to the next. He wished now he'd insisted on fast food from one of the millions of places around but Mike Tomas, his partner for today, had moaned that he wanted a sandwich from the grocery deli and he'd been relegated to go for them.

Every aisle had a half dozen customers loaded down with groceries, and not a one of them offered to let him pay for his sandwiches ahead of them.

So much for the respect he'd thought he'd get as a member of the Chicago police force. Finally he stood in what he hoped was the fastest moving line. At least there were only two people ahead of him, not counting the third whose groceries were laid out on the conveyer belt. The next person was beginning to unload when he heard a voice.

"I changed my mind."

Raphael peered around the mound of groceries and the two people in front of him and smiled. It was Angela. He stopped himself from calling out to her. Instead, he listened to what she was saying to the clerk.

"Take the cookies and ice cream out of the bag. I changed my mind."

Cookies and ice cream, his heart thumped in his chest. She was buying it for him, or more accurately, she wasn't buying it for him. He was hoping she'd change her mind again, but she was sounding more frantic by the second as she attempted to explain to the harried cashier that she no longer wanted the items.

He sighed as the bagger fished the items out of the packed bags, and his hope died in his chest. She still didn't want to care about him.

Raphael watched her leave the store. He saw a slight hesitation as she pushed her cart. Once again he hoped she'd come back and buy the treats but she didn't.

He sucked in the sudden hurt he felt, barely noticing that the cashier had finished with the other customers and was waiting for him to place his sandwiches to be scanned.

"I'll take that ice cream and the cookies off your hands," he informed the clerk, surprised at the words that came out of his mouth.

"Excuse me?"

"The ones the customer left. You have them off to the side. I'll take them." He ignored the woman looking at him as if he had two heads. He paid for the food and left the store.

"We have to stop by my house," he informed Mike as he climbed into the squad car with the bag. "I bought ice cream and I need to get it in the freezer."

"Did you see that nut job in the store?" Mike asked as he pulled away from the curb.

Of course Raphael knew who Mike was talking about. Maybe at one time he wouldn't have minded the comment. But that was before he'd found himself falling for the nut job in question. She was now his angel. Now he wanted to rip Mike's head off. "I don't know who you're talking about," he said instead.

"The Black woman who's been trying for months to get you fired. You know, the one that wrote out a dozen complaints against you."

"It wasn't that many," Raphael corrected.

"Yeah, right. I've never seen one person so determined. It was like she had a personal vendetta against you."

"Or against the department," Raphael offered.

"Could be. Why not? Everybody wants us to keep the city safe but they hate us for doing it. Anyway, when that woman came out the store, she stopped and looked directly at me."

Did she stop your heart with her eyes? Raphael wanted to ask as a wave of jealousy clutched at him. "Did you feel anything when she looked at you?" he asked instead, wishing that the words hadn't popped out before he could stop them.

"Feel anything? What are you talking about? No, I didn't feel anything. She stared at me as though she was expecting to see someone else, then turned and looked back at the store before walking to the lot."

"Did you see her drive away?"

"Nah, she must have gone out the other exit. Why? You think she's trying to find something else to harass you about? Did she see you in the store?" Mike frowned. "Did you see her?"

"Yeah, I saw her, and no, she didn't see me."

"You still being investigated?"

"Who knows?" Raphael turned the computer monitor screen toward him, wanting to stop talking about Angela. He had an appointment with IAD in a few days, but he didn't want that on his mind at the moment. All he wanted was a few minutes to think in peace and quiet about why Angela had picked up the ice cream to start with. Did it mean what he thought or was it only more wishful dreaming?

It seemed to Raphael that it was now becoming a habit for him to be standing on one side of the door and his angel on the other. He'd barely slept in his own bed in weeks. He didn't miss it one little bit. He knocked on the door and waited. "*Hola,* Angel," he said when Angela opened the door.

"Hola," she answered.

"Have you finished your work?" Raphael asked as he came in, closing the door with the heel of his shoe. "I find myself envying you more and more, being able to work from home, make your own hours, not having to go out, not even to the store if you don't want. Those protein bars of yours last forever."

"You think my job is easy?" she asked.

"Not easy," he answered slowly, sensing a change in her. She was in a foul mood and he suspected it had more to do with her increasing awareness of her changing feelings than it did with him.

"What's in the bag?"

Raphael glanced down, having forgotten the package for a moment and realizing that he'd picked the wrong night to get cute. "Just something I picked up. Nothing much."

He headed for her kitchen, opened the freezer and inserted the ice cream, knowing that from where she stood she'd seen the container. He had no choice but to take the cookies from the bag and put them in the cabinet. Folding the bag he put it under the sink into the container Angel kept them in. Then he waited.

She came over to the cabinet, opened it, and looked at the cookies. Then she opened the freezer and stared. He waited for her to speak, but she didn't. Instead, she turned toward the bedroom and he followed, removing his clothes and tossing them on the chair in her room. Without talking, they climbed into the bed. Without talking, they made love. And without talking, they went to sleep.

—⟋⟋⟋—

The feel of Angela's eyes on him pulled Rafe from his sleep. He blinked and rubbed his eyes before looking up at her.

"I'm going to be busy for the next few days," Angela announced. "I won't have any time to see you." She made an odd movement of her head. "I've gotten behind on my work and it's due."

"I thought you were caught up?" Raphael countered.

"Well, I'm not. I don't have to explain. I have a job, everyone seems to keep forgetting that."

"Suit yourself," Raphael said climbing from the bed and heading for the shower. He wasn't going to beg Angela and he sure as hell wasn't going to fight with her about that damn ice cream. He'd thought she'd find it amusing. She hadn't. *She's right*, he thought. They did need a few days apart.

For the past two months he'd almost forgotten that he was sleeping with the enemy. But he remembered now. Raphael showered and left Angela's apartment without another word to her. She was perched in front of her computer, behaving as though she didn't know he was there. *To hell with her*, he thought as he slammed the door. If she didn't want him, he didn't want her.

But he did.

Angela turned around at the sound of her door slamming. There was a lump in her throat. But she'd done the right thing. She was getting too close to Raphael Remeris. He was exerting too much of a hold on her. She knew it and he knew it.

She walked to her cabinet and took out a bag of cookies that he'd bought. She should have trusted her instincts. No wonder she'd been thinking so much about him in the store; he'd been there. And when she'd seen the squad car outside the store, she'd gotten chills.

He'd been there when she put the ice cream and cookies back and then he'd bought them. And he'd brought them to her home to let her know that he knew. She closed her eyes. She had to go and see her brother. She had to get Rafe off her mind.

Four days had passed and Raphael had gotten little sleep. He tried telling himself he was coming down with something, but he knew very well what that something was. He'd gotten too used to sleeping in the bed next to his angel.

Tossing and turning, he punched the pillows, willing himself to forget her, to pretend she didn't exist. A moment later he reached for the phone. Pretending she didn't exist wasn't working.

"Can I come over?" he asked as soon as she answered.

"I'm tired."

"Just for a little while."

"I don't feel like making love."

"Angela."

"What?"

Raphael sucked in his breath. "We don't have to make love."

"Then why would you come over?" she asked him, her voice filled with enough ice to chill the entire state of Illinois.

He sighed. "I have no idea. Who knows what I was thinking?" he said and hung up. But he did know what he was thinking. He was thinking he wanted her in his arms, wanted to feel her soft skin against his own, smell the scent of jasmine and vanilla on her, taste the sweetness of her when she wasn't growling at him. He wanted to fall asleep with her in his arms. That was what he was thinking. But there was no way he would admit that to her.

Angela turned in her bed; it felt empty. And she now hated that feeling. Always she'd wanted every inch of space she could get, but the last few nights without Raphael's body in her bed had changed her.

She hadn't lied. She was much too tired to make love. She'd been tired since returning from her visit to the prison and experiencing again her brother's coldness. He'd accused her of wasting time, of not trying hard enough, and she felt guilty.

Adrian was right. She'd spent time in the past two months doing something her brother would hate, and something that her entire family would condemn her for if they knew. And now she couldn't sleep because not having the one thing that she shouldn't have was eating away at her. She wished she hadn't snapped at Rafe. He didn't deserve that.

She picked up the phone before she could stop herself, wondering if he'd slam the phone down in her ear. Would he react the same way to her as she had done to him?

"Rafe," she said. "Are you asleep?"

"No."

"Neither am I."

"That's obvious."

"I guess it is," she answered. "Maybe you can come over and we can not sleep together."

He wanted to give her back the same words she'd given him but he didn't. "Are you still tired?"

"Yeah, I am."

"I'll be right over."

CHAPTER 10

Rafe curled his muscular body around hers and pulled her into his arms. His right arm was flung across her torso and his lips nuzzled her neck. Within minutes Angela heard soft snoring sounds and her heart shattered with swift understanding.

He hadn't been able to sleep in his own bed because he wanted to be near her, just as it was with her. They were breaking all their own rules and she didn't know what to do about it. She attempted to move away from the cradle of Rafe's arms but even in his sleep he pulled her back and held her tighter. She moaned.

"Rafe, what have we done?" she said into the darkness, then fell asleep.

In the morning she looked into his eyes and knew it was time to share the reason with him for her anger.

"My brother is in Statesville," she began without preamble, watching for his reaction. "I go to visit him a twice a week, usually Tuesday and Thursday. We're very close." Still he waited silently.

"About two years ago," she shrugged her shoulder, "actually, almost two and a half, he was in this neighborhood just minding his own business. Long story short, there was a big gang fight with the cops. My brother tried to tell them he wasn't involved but they wouldn't listen. He was beaten by the cops." She paused and waited for some reaction. "My brother went to jail."

"And you moved here from Naperville. Why?"

"I moved here to clear my brother," Angela continued.

"How?"

"To try and find the cops, the ones who beat my brother. I have to prove my brother's innocence. That has to be my primary function."

"That's your reason for hating cops?"

"That's not enough?"

"I'm just asking."

"It's been my reason for hating them for the last two and a half years. They give me new reasons to hate them every day."

"So why did you pick me for your poster child of hate?"

"I didn't pick you; you stopped me, remember?"

"I remember you were speeding."

"Maybe."

"Maybe?" Raphael attempted to laugh but his heart was pounding too rapidly in his chest. He was extremely familiar with the case Angela was talking about. He'd been one of the officers involved in the gang fight. The thought of the hatred in her eyes when she found out he was involved stopped him from telling her. He couldn't, not now, not when she was finally tearing down some of the barriers between them.

"Why are you telling me this?" he asked.

"I want you to know why we can't take this any further."

He eyed her sharply. She was contradicting herself. She was taking it further by merely telling him. In the entire two months they'd slept together, she'd never once told him who she was seeing in prison. He'd wondered if it was a boyfriend.

"All of this because of my job?" Raphael asked.

"It's not just any job, we both know that. Look, we knew going into this what we were doing. Remember, we both agreed it was just for fun?"

"I thought it was just sex?" Raphael said over the lump in his throat.

"Yeah, just sex," Angela amended, "until it stopped being fun."

"Has it stopped being fun for you?"

"No." Angela stared at him, wanting to tell him that the opposite had happened, what they'd vowed wouldn't. She was starting to care for him and she could tell from the look in his eyes he was feeling the same things.

"So why are you telling me this?" Raphael asked again.

"My brother has to be my main priority. That's why I'm here, to find evidence of his innocence."

"Don't you think that an investigation was done? If he were innocent he wouldn't be in prison."

Angela laughed, then, "Get real. Do you have any idea how many
men have died in prison that were innocent? Don't you keep up with
what's happening? Innocent men go to prison."

"And so do guilty ones."

"My brother's not guilty."

"What if he is?"

"My brother's not guilty."

Raphael closed his eyes, then reopened them. "How do you expect
to find the ones you think are dirty cops?"

"I have my ways."

Raphael knew what her ways were. He'd known from almost the
moment she'd moved into the neighborhood and begun asking questions. Only then he'd not known why, only that she was . . . he'd
thought she was a reporter doing an undercover expose on the
department. And there had been enough dirt in the past two years to
give her more than enough information to do her article. Now he
knew that the entire time it had been as he'd thought in the beginning. It was personal.

"Angel, you're playing a very dangerous game. Harassing the police
department is not the way to go about trying to clear your brother. And
you have no idea who you're talking to on the street. You can get yourself into trouble if you're not careful."

"I know what I'm doing."

"Do you?"

"Yes."

"If you find these dirty cops, what are you going to do to them?"

Angela wished for a millisecond that she could tell him, but she
couldn't. She also couldn't tell him that she was trying hard to find the
one witness her brother had said could definitely prove his innocence.
Teresa Cortez.

"Rafe, I think it's best if you stay out of what I'm doing. You won't
want to be in the middle of this when it all goes down. And it won't

matter to me if the cop is a friend of yours or your relative. I'm going to take them down."

"And if it's me?"

"It won't make a difference."

"Are you really sure of that, Angel?" he asked.

"Don't call me that," Angela reprimanded, though there was no fire in her words.

The need for more words was delayed when a ringing phone interrupted them. Both of their heads turned toward the kitchen counter to locate the sound.

"It's mine," Raphael said, heading to pick up the phone.

"*Si, mama, si.*" He turned slightly. "Angela Reed. No. *Gracias.*"

Angela turned back to look in Rafe's direction. She'd turned to give him privacy but he'd called her name. Whoever he was talking to knew her. Suspicion mounted and her skin crawled with the knowing. She swallowed and waited while he punched in numbers on his phone. His eyes refused to meet hers, but his clenched jaw was telling her what he didn't. He didn't want to make the call with her there.

"Sir, no sir. I didn't forget that I have an appointment. No, I'll be there on time. Don't worry. No, I don't think I do. Thank you, sir."

She watched as he looked in her direction.

"Angela Reed. Yes sir, thank you, sir."

He flipped his phone closed and turned toward her.

"You want to explain?" Angela asked.

"My mother called to tell me that the commander wanted to talk to me. He'd tried to reach me and couldn't. I have a meeting with IAD this morning. He wanted to make sure I didn't forget."

"Is it because of all the complaints I made?"

Raphael shrugged his shoulders.

"Rafe, have you been sleeping with me to get me to drop the charges?"

"Have I ever asked you to drop the charges?"

"No," Angela admitted. "Why not?"

"Why would I?" he answered. "You hate cops." He dressed quickly. "I'll go home and shower. I have to go to the meeting in uniform," he said pointedly, before kissing her, softly. "I'll see you later, Angel."

"Don't call me Angel."

"Why? You don't object to it when we're making love."

"But we're not making love now. My name is Angela. If you have to call me something else, my friends call me Angie."

"So we're friends now?"

"I don't know what we are anymore," she admitted honestly.

"Neither do I." Raphael smiled. "But I don't want to call you Angie."

"Rafe, I'm not an angel. I'm not even close."

"I'll stick with Angel, *mi amor.*"

Angela shivered. Being called Angel was one thing, but being called his love was another. She stared at him, trying to will him to change the words into a joke. His green eyes blazed with passion, green kryptonite passion. He walked toward her and Angela sat still, waiting for him.

For the past two months she'd done her best to limit his touching her body outside of bed. She still couldn't get used to the electrical current that passed between them.

But last night had changed all of that. They'd not made love. They'd slept in each other's arms simply because they needed to feel the other's presence. There was no denying it. That one act had made her painfully aware of her growing feelings for him. She was falling in love with him. And worse than that, she needed him. She shivered at her admission. Her soul needed him.

He pulled her gently from the chair and wrapped her in his arms and for a long moment she was only aware of the beating of his heart. Then came the heat, and for the first time she gave into it outside of bed. She was drowning in knowledge that she belonged in Rafe's arms. At the moment she could care less that he was a cop, or if he had a dozen sisters that he would object to if they dated a black man. She didn't care. She was falling in love with him.

TWO SIDES TO EVERY STORY

There was no stopping her arms from holding him close, even as her mind screamed for her to stop, to remember that one of them was bound to be hurt in the end.

"Angel," he murmured, and she raised her head. "We can't keep pretending," he said. She closed her eyes.

"Open your eyes, *mi amor*, look at me."

When her eyes remained closed she felt his breath brush across her cheek and his tongue flick her lids. Her eyes popped open.

He smiled. "That's better."

"For whom?" she asked.

"For both of us. We can't go back; last night proved that."

"I don't know if we can move forward. There are too many obstacles," Angela whispered.

"Then we'll stay where we are for the moment. I won't push you," Raphael promised.

No, he wouldn't push her. She was right, there were obstacles. He was one of the cops she was looking for. Only he wasn't dirty, he'd never been dirty. But he had been involved in that entire incident.

Raphael kissed her then, knowing it was wrong, that each moment he held her in his arms he was binding himself tighter, binding her. He was aware that he wanted to make her love him before he told her. He hated lying to her but he hated the iced topaz more. He didn't want her hating him. And until she learned to love him, her hate would win out.

"Angel," he said as he deepened the kiss, losing the need for further words.

Angela heard him moan her name, felt the tremor that claimed his body, felt his need and his love and she no longer wanted to fight it. As his kiss deepened so did her need until it was just her and Rafe. No one else mattered, nothing mattered except the supreme feeling of peace that she felt in his arms. A mental image of her brother intruded. She clutched Rafe to her and pushed the image away.

When the kiss ended they were both shaken. They stood in the middle of the room, their arms around each other, holding on for dear life.

"I have to go, Angel, wish . . ." He caught himself. He'd been going to tell her to wish him luck, but it wasn't necessary. Whatever happened, happened. He would not have her think for a second that he was lying to her, not about his love.

He ran the pad of one finger down her cheek. "Can I call you later?"

"I'll be out at the prison. After that I need to work."

He sighed as he made his way toward the door, taking her with him. "Tonight?" he asked.

"Yes, tonight," she answered.

He kissed her lips softly, smiled and walked out the door.

"Rafe."

He stopped.

"Yes."

"Be careful, okay?"

He eyed her, then leaned back into the door and ran his tongue down the side of her neck. "It's too late for me to be careful, *mi amor*." And he closed the door.

He was right. It was too late for both of them to be careful.

CHAPTER 11

Raphael parked his car at the station, then walked toward the door taking his time. He looked up and down Damen Avenue, noting the people, the churches, and the other officers coming and going. He glanced down, feeling the same thrill that he always got at seeing his badge on his chest.

He'd graduated from college and gone directly into the police academy. Six months later he was a Chicago policeman. That's all he'd ever wanted to be. He stood and watched the little kids running and playing already, thinking it was much too early in the morning for them to be out. Children had played a part in his dream. He wanted to gain the little kids' trust and teach them not to fear the uniform. He wanted to be respected and he would give respect in return.

He'd been born in Puerto Rico, a part of the United States, even though it wasn't treated that way. He'd grown up with the disrespect that most Latinos hated. And he'd watched as many had turned violent or bitter in the face of that blatant disrespect. He'd seen the same disrespect shown to other minority groups and wondered why they battled among themselves rather than banding together.

But none of that had pushed him toward his life choice. It was the fear of cops he'd carried in his heart. They wielded the power. He hated fearing the men with their uniforms and badges and guns. Too many times they'd rolled up in the neighborhood 'just because,' and talked down to Latinos as if they were lesser. He'd seen his friends run and hide. They shared the same fear. They all had too many friends and relatives arrested by cops that spoke not one word of Spanish and didn't care if the people knew their rights or not.

Raphael had become a cop to right a wrong. He wanted respect, not only for himself but for all Latinos. He was determined to stay in the community and be a buffer, to treat each and every person, Latino or not, with the utmost respect, and in turn to be respected.

He'd been on the force for eight years now and this had yet to happen. Even the kids would call him names and give him the finger as he rode around on patrol. And when he entered homes and attempted to comfort the kids, what he received was about a million steps away from respect. And every time there was a question of police conduct, every cop in the department was painted with the same brush. They were all portrayed as dirty, as womanizers, wife beaters, hard drinkers.

Sure, Raphael knew such cops existed; in fact it was rampant. But he wasn't a part of it and neither were a lot of other decent officers. He always felt proud that he'd not succumbed. His plan to never fall in love had taken care of the cheating-cop-that-abuses-his-wife angle.

Now he wondered if lying to Angela made him what he hated, what Angela hated, a dirty cop. He cringed inwardly. He knew he should have told her of his role when she told him of her brother's plight. But he hadn't and there was no way to justify it either to her or to himself.

He was taking away her choices. It wasn't fair to her to let her love him without telling her the truth.

He looked again at his badge. Raphael was still proud to be a part of the department, but he wasn't proud of his actions or the fact that he had no plans to tell Angela of his involvement in the gang war. At least not yet.

He was wrong to allow his wants to overshadow doing the right thing. Still, he knew he would. He was falling in love with her and right or wrong, he wanted to see where it would lead.

Raphael took another look around before going inside. Part of the problem might be taken out of his control. It all depended on IAD. His career was in their hands.

He breathed deeply, not wanting to admit how much he wanted to remain on the force. If he were suspended or fired, he would forever carry that stain. Raphael sighed. All he wanted was to remain an officer, to uphold the law. That and to find some way to make things work with his stubborn angel.

He knocked on the door of IAD and went in smiling, his thoughts on the changes with Angela. She'd told him to be careful. She was falling in love with him also and that thought warmed his heart. Taking a look around the office, he tried unsuccessfully to wipe the smile from his face, to stop thinking of his angel and bring his thoughts back to the outcome of this meeting.

"Officer Remeris, did the captain speak to you before you came in?"

"No," Raphael said, puzzled.

"I thought from the look on your face . . . you seem happy. Never mind," the man said and waved his hand in dismissal.

Raphael glanced at the man dressed in a navy suit. He was short and stubby looking. He then turned his attention to the man seated behind the desk. He couldn't tell much but the men didn't look or act as he'd expected. He sensed a friendly atmosphere, something he'd always been told was non-existent.

"Sit down, sit down," the shorter man said, pointing to a chair. "I'm Captain Smith, and that's Lieutenant Johnson," he said, pointing to the officer still seated.

Raphael sat and waited.

"We wanted to let you know that the investigation is over."

"And?" Raphael asked.

"And you've been cleared of all charges."

"Actually," Lieutenant Johnson interrupted, "the complainant rescinded the complaints."

"When?" Raphael asked. "Did she just call?"

"No, she came in about five weeks ago," Lieutenant Johnson continued.

"Five weeks? Then why were you still investigating me?"

"We had to make sure there was no coercion behind her coming in, you know, no threats."

Threats? Raphael knew he was being told good news but he felt as if he'd still been accused of even more things, and this time by the department. "Threats?"

"Yeah, we didn't want the woman dropping the complaints if under duress. So we investigated what she had to say and we investigated you."

"What did she have to say?"

"She told us her brother was in prison, that he'd accused the police department of beating him, and he'd accused it of a cover-up. When we checked things out in the files, we found your name as one of the officers involved. I guess she must have found out that you were involved and wanted some retribution."

"Did she say she knew I was involved?"

"No, but it stands to reason that she did. Otherwise it wouldn't make much sense, now would it?"

"No. No, I guess it wouldn't," Raphael said. "Why did it take so long?"

"We had to be sure. Anyway, it's over now. Listen, Officer Remeris, we're aware of the reputation that we have in the department and in part it may be true. We have to keep our distance in order to give an unbiased report. But no one is ever happier than we are to clear an officer. It's not our goal to harass officers; we respect them and appreciate the job that they do. And believe it or not, we're on the same team. So congratulations and keep up the good work. From that look on your face when you came in, I thought you already knew."

"What look?" Raphael asked.

"The happy, goofy look. If you didn't know about the outcome, then it must be love. Enjoy it, Officer, and hold on to it."

Raphael walked out of the office, stunned, first that his feelings for Angela had been displayed so that anyone could see. He'd have to work on that. Secondly, that she'd dropped the charges and all this time had not said one word to him, not even this morning when he'd told her of the meeting. He wondered why.

His emotions warred within him. Anger at her that she'd not bothered to mention it and joy that she had done it. He wondered what had made her do it.

TWO SIDES TO EVERY STORY

For the past twenty minutes Angela had driven without her mind on where she was going. She was at the prison so often it seemed as if her car knew the way.

Her thoughts were on Raphael and his meeting with IAD. She wondered if he would be angry when he found out she'd dropped the charges weeks ago and hadn't told him. Then again, he couldn't be any angrier than he'd been when she filed them.

For a long moment she wondered why she'd ever done it. She'd known what she was doing was wrong; still, she'd done it and pretended that it didn't matter if she destroyed the man in the bargain, destroyed his career.

When she'd told her cousin about the complaints, Simone had remained silent. Her silence spoke of her disapproval, as Angela had known it would. She didn't know why she'd told her. Maybe it was her conscience. She only knew now that she wished she'd never done it. Then it hit her. It was in part because of her complaints that she'd been thrown into such frequent contact with Rafe.

She had no idea where they were headed, but she wouldn't deny that she was content to have him in her life. And she'd done nothing to dull the light in his eyes. She rather enjoyed having him look at her as though she was his world, knowing in her heart that he found her special.

Then she shivered again from fear as she remembered her brother's comments. As a car zoomed past her, she glanced at the speedometer and noticed that her speed had dropped to below forty. She laughed, thinking it would be funny to now get a ticket for going too slowly. After all, it was her speeding that had brought Rafe into her life.

She didn't want to think that there had to be a reason for them being together. But she did. She believed him when he said they were meant to meet. He'd not said they were soul mates, but she knew he thought it. And darn if she didn't wonder about it herself. Angela shook

92

her head. She'd better keep her mind on what she was doing, and thinking what she was at the moment was definitely not what she should do when she was driving.

She came upon the Bolingbrook exit, wondering how she'd gotten that far. The trip today appeared to have flown by. Angela made a left turn and headed south on Route 53. Everything seemed so normal.

She passed Arena Auto Auction, remembering when the building had once housed one of the country's first (and only indoor) amusement park—Old Chicago. She'd been there often. Writers had written about the park, placing it in different suburbs, even in the Chicago city limits, but it had never been anywhere but Bolingbrook.

She knew she was wasting time pretending that this was just an excursion, just a drive. As she came into Romeoville, the tension mounted. The prison was just a few more miles.

She observed everything on both sides of the streets, fast food places, stores, anything to take her mind off what was coming up after the next light. Angela took a look to her right at the red brick lining Lewis University and she choked back the sob. Her brother had gone there for nearly a year and a half and now he was literally next door, sitting in a prison. She shuddered with the irony of it all.

She gritted her teeth, preparing to stomach the familiar pat down, knowing that it was a little more each time. But she had to do it in order to see her brother.

She smiled when her brother came to the point of contact. She noticed he broke the hug quicker than usual and she wondered why. They both knew they wouldn't be allowed to touch in the visiting area. She took a seat opposite him as he sat in the elevated seat reserved for the prisoner.

"What's wrong?" she asked at last.

"You haven't been here in over a week."

His voice was hostile, accusing, void of any affection.

"I've been busy," she said. "I have to work, make a living. I have bills to pay for two apartments, I might add." Her tone matched his.

She hated when they snapped at each other, especially now when he was at a disadvantage.

"It's not my fault that I'm not working," Adrian told her.

"I didn't say that it was. I'm just telling you that I have to." Angela sighed. "Look, I'm sorry. You know I try to get here to see you as often as I can."

"You worked before. What's new? Why don't you have the time now?"

There it was again, the accusation. "I've already answered," she replied. "I work."

"You sure it's not that cop you've been screwing?"

Angela glared at her brother, the anger rising quickly at his crudeness. "How would you know what I'm doing? Not that who I care to have in my bed is any of your business."

"Is that how you plan to help me?"

"What are you talking about?"

"You didn't move there to let some cop get in your pants. You're supposed to find Teresa Cortez. How can you do that when you're spending half your time with that immigrant cop?"

As the impact of his words hit her, she wanted to reach out and shake him, erase that smug look from his face. "Are you having someone spy on me?"

"Looking out for you is a better way to put it."

"Why?"

"Because it's dangerous, your asking questions. I don't want you to get hurt." He paused a moment and gave her a smile she knew was fake. "And you don't want that cop hurt, right?" he said.

That sounded and felt like a threat to her. "What are you talking about?" Angela whispered, wanting to see him laugh, make a joke out of it.

"You. Do you think I can allow you to . . . what?" He laughed even more crudely. "Entertain a Chicago cop in your bed? That doesn't look good for me. Looks like I can't take care of my business."

Fear skittered along the nerve endings in Angela's body. She would have to be a fool to miss the brazen innuendo, the deliberate threat. She couldn't believe it. For the first time in two years she had doubts as to her brother's innocence.

"Who are you?" she asked.

"Your brother."

"I don't think so." She attempted to smile, hoping to somehow change things with the quick motion of her lips. "What have you done with my brother? I want him back."

"This is your brother. Maybe you should try opening your eyes for a change and see things as they are, not as you want them to be."

Angela swallowed. "Tell me how you have the power to have me followed. Who are you?" she said again, not surprised when he laughed.

"I sent you in there to do a job. It shouldn't take you that long to get what I need."

"You didn't send me, I volunteered to go. And if you have so much power, these friends of yours you have following me, why haven't they found this woman you're looking for?"

"Your job is not to question me. Just do as you're told. Find that woman so you can get me out of here and stop seeing that cop."

Angela laughed. "What do you think you are, some small-time hood? I'm not someone you can order around. I'm your sister. I'm helping you because I love you and I think . . ." She hesitated. "I think you're innocent. You're not making me do this. It's my choice. As for whoever I'm seeing, that remains my business." Angela's body shook with anger as she watched Adrian shaking his head in disgust.

"I can't believe it. You're selling me out for an illegal."

"I'm not selling you out. I have your back just like always and that will never change. Besides that, he's as much a citizen as you are."

"Now you're defending him?"

"He doesn't need defending, not from bigots."

"You're calling me a bigot? You think I give a damn? I'm telling it like it is. He doesn't want me sleeping with his sister and I don't want him sleeping with mine. Understand?"

"I understand more than you do. This is my body and who I sleep with is my business, not yours. I know for a fact you've slept with more than Black women. What's the deal here?"

Bile filled her mouth and Angela choked on the taste, unable to admit to the full truth of what was happening.

"Listen, I have to go. I have a couple of leads I want to check out. I'll see you in a couple of days," she lied.

They both stood and immediately an officer was walking toward them.

"Just remember what I said," Adrian said under his breath. "What happens next is up to you. I can't protect you if you don't listen to me."

She walked away wanting to believe that her brother wanted to protect her in his own way. Maybe it wasn't what she'd thought. She shook away the feelings she'd had in the prison as she walked to the parking lot.

Angela sat in her car for a full minute before starting the engine. She looked up at the huge prison. It was that place that was changing her and her brother. It bred mistrust.

Adrian was looking out for her, just as he said. The fact that he had people spying on her, that he'd threatened Rafe, that had to have all been a part of that, even him telling her that it was all up to her. It was all some prison-mentality–induced dream. None of it was real.

And if she believed that load of crap she was trying to sell herself, she'd have to be either stupid or naive. She was neither.

Her brother had threatened Rafe, pure and simple. There was no getting around that. And the fact that he even knew she was seeing him gave her reason to worry.

Angela hopped on the Stevenson expressway and headed back to the city, to her new apartment, praying that she would find Teresa Cortez soon. Then she could return to her own life. She looked at the dead trees off to the side of the highway. So much early promise there, she thought, just as her brother's life had once held so much promise.

She thought of Rafe. He was falling in love with her, she knew that. And even though she hadn't told him that she loved him, they both knew that she did. She groaned. Old life or new, she wanted to find a way to make him a part of it. She would have to find a way to help her brother yet not endanger Rafe. If there was a way she could have him in her future, she was determined to find it.

CHAPTER 12

In one night Angela's life had changed. And she knew she would never be the same. One night of lying in Rafe's arms, knowing that she belonged there, that he wanted her there, had changed things. That one night had forged a bond much stronger than all those nights filled with passion.

For the first time since they'd begun their strange dance, she was nervous as she waited for him. A lot had happened. Now that she'd finally admitted her feelings about Rafe to herself, if not to him, she waited with anxious anticipation. She was aware of something that he wasn't.

Seeing him could be putting him at risk. She wanted badly to tell herself that she didn't believe any of the threats her brother had made. How could she and still believe in his innocence? Yet something in his tone had rung true.

She toyed briefly with the idea of not seeing Rafe, of ending it now. Then the knock came at her door and he entered the room. He looked at her for a long moment, searing her with the heat from his gaze. She trembled with the intensity, afraid to move, to speak, to even breathe. He lifted her in his arms and she buried her head against his chest.

"Angel, *mi amor*." he whispered and laid her on the bed. "I've missed you," he moaned.

His lips came down and smothered her with warmth as his hand moved over her body. She looked up into his eyes, wondering if he were going to mention IAD, wanting to know if it was behind them.

But they'd made a promise not to discuss anything real while they were in bed. What she'd done to him was too real, just as real as the possibility that he could be hurt from being associated with her. All of that was too real. All she wanted was to feel his lips on her body and his hand touching her, burning her. She slipped her hands beneath the waistband of his pants and shivered at touching his golden brown skin. He was a couple of shades darker than she was. They blended together perfectly in a play of light and dark.

She reached a hand back up and grabbed a handful of his thick, jet black hair, tangling her fingers in the curls. She yanked harder, wanting to see the surprise in his green eyes.

They were playful and loving, something that had crept into their relationship in the last weeks, catching her unaware. She'd denied it, telling herself that it was foreplay, but it wasn't. It had never been that; it had been their ritual mating dance that was bringing them to this moment, the realization of their inescapable love. She looked at him with awe. He looked back at her with love and she wondered how long he'd known.

They made love tenderly and when they were done he fell to his side, pulled her into his arms and cradled her head on his chest. "Thank you," he murmured.

Angela would not pretend to not know what he was talking about. "It was the right thing to do," she said. "I should have never filed those complaints in the first place. I was wrong."

He kissed her forehead and they both fell asleep.

"I want you to meet my family," Rafe announced as soon as she'd come from the shower.

Angela looked at the food spread out on the table and smiled. "What is this, a bribe?"

"No, I want to make sure you have energy. I have the next two days off."

"I don't," she responded and stood her ground.

"I thought . . ."

TWO SIDES TO EVERY STORY

"I thought you weren't going to push me?" Angela said. "I told you what I have to do. I have some people to talk to today. My brother's counting on me."

Rafe's eyes became shuttered and his glance slid away. She'd known this was going to happen. Love was never easy, even when you didn't admit to anyone other than yourself that it was love. She didn't want to hurt him now or ever.

"Why do you want me to meet your family?" she asked.

He smiled, not answering.

"Who are you going to tell them that I am?"

"My angel."

"Then I'm definitely not going to meet them. No angel, nothing to do with angels, okay?"

"Does that mean that you're going?"

"Who are you going to introduce me as?"

"Do you want me to lie?"

"I want you to keep your word and not push me."

"How is meeting my family pushing you?"

"All men introduce women to their family for one reason only."

"And why do women introduce men to their family?"

She grinned. "Okay, we do the same. But I told you I'm trying my best to be honest with you. This is moving much too fast and if you push me I will have to end it."

"Then end it. I'm a man, you can't tell me what to do."

"*Sagana.*"

"What? What did you just say? Did you call me a jackass? I'm not teaching you Spanish so that you can call me names, Angel."

She shrugged her shoulders. "Why are we fighting?"

He sighed. "Because you're afraid."

"I'm not afraid. I'm just not ready for the things that you want."

"How would you know what I want? You refuse to talk to me. You know nothing about what I want."

"You want commitment and family, babies. I can see it in your eyes."

"I've never wanted those things. I would have never gone into the line of work that I have if I wanted a family. It's too dangerous to get that close to anyone."

"You're saying the right words, but your eyes tell me an entirely different story. You want love, even if you say that you don't. You want a wife and babies."

"And you think I want these things with you?"

A wave of jealousy claimed her; the thought of him touching someone else in the manner that he touched her burned her with a different fire. Angela moved from him, angered that he brought out such emotions in her.

Rafe watched the changes that came over his angel. He saw the flash of jealousy. *Good.* She'd led him around by the short hairs for over two months now. It was time he called a halt. He wouldn't tell her that the thought of having a family of his own had never entered his mind until he'd thought of having that family with her. He turned his attention back to the stove.

"What are you cooking?"

"*Queso, huevos y jamon.* Cheese, eggs and ham," he laughed.

"What are you trying to do, fatten me up?"

He smiled, knowing she was changing the conversation. He wasn't going to let it go that easily, not this time.

"I'm trying to prepare your taste buds for dinner with my family."

"Rafe."

"What? It's dinner, Angel, nothing more."

"No insinuation, no leading them on."

"You mean I won't tell them how I feel about you or how you feel about me?"

"You don't know how you feel about me," Angela answered. "And you definitely don't know how I feel about you." She was trying her best to control her body, to put the brakes on something that would not stop. She was doing her best to protect him. Maybe if she could just keep up even a partial barricade, it could be enough to prevent Rafe from falling for her to the point of no return. If she kept some of the ice and it became necessary for them to part in order to keep him safe, maybe, just maybe, he could forget that he loved her.

"It's much too late too make me change the way I feel."

"That wasn't—"

"Of course it was."

"I still say you don't know how I feel."

"I know how you feel," Rafe laughed, walking over to her. "Even if you don't, I know." He reached out his hand and saw her nipples harden before he even touched her. He grinned broadly. "You can keep pretending, Angel, *mi amor*, but I won't."

Her brother's warning rang in her ears but the intoxicating presence of Rafe overrode her objections. "Just dinner," she agreed. "But not this week, okay? I really do have to finish the project I'm working on."

"I have two days off."

"I'm sorry, I really do have to work."

"There isn't anything I can do to change your mind?" he asked, pulling her into his arms and running his tongue down the side of her neck, feeling the tremble that ran through her.

Angela thought of her work, her brother, then she forgot thinking and gave in to the demands her body was making. She was leaning toward him, her arms automatically going up and around his neck to pull him closer.

"This isn't what I had in mind when I said let's take it slow."

He backed away. "Do you want me to stop?"

She pulled him back, letting her hands do her talking. It seemed that one by one Rafe Remeris was tearing down all her 'don'ts' and turning them into 'why nots.' Sure, she knew that spending the next two days with him when she should be working was going to cost her. She'd have to miss seeing her brother for the rest of the week if she did.

The unpleasant memory of her last visit to him pushed its way into her mind, making her decision easier. And Rafe's lips and hands sealed it.

"Two whole days?"

"Two whole days," he answered.

"We've never done that," she said.

"I know."

He kissed her then, preventing her from asking why, from questioning. Right now all he wanted was her in his arms. He smelled the eggs starting to burn and turned toward the kitchen. Well, maybe he could do with a little breakfast.

"By the way, my taste buds are well acquainted with Latin cuisine," Angela called out.

"Really?"

"Yes."

"Like what? And don't say rice and beans."

"How about, *empanadas, pollo* and *paella*. She laughed. "Want me to continue? I also happen to be well acquainted with a very spicy dish." She smiled at him. "Do you want to know what it's called?"

"Yes, tell me." he whispered softly as his eyes answered the fire she knew was in her own.

"It's called Rafe Remeris," she admitted and succumbed to the kiss that he crossed the room to give her.

Angel and Angel only was on Rafe's mind the entire day. His Angel. Because of that he'd made the people who lived in and around Pilsen happy. He'd only given warnings the entire day; not once had he written out a ticket.

He couldn't wait to see her, to have her finally meet his family. He was smiling broadly. He wouldn't wait, he thought as he took his cell from his uniform shirt pocket and pulled over to the curb to call her.

"Hey, you ready?" he asked as soon as she was on the line.

"Yes. I'm looking forward to it."

"Nervous?" he asked.

"Just a little. Are you going to keep your promise?"

"I didn't make any." He smiled at the phone.

"Rafe," she murmured and her voice made him hot.

"I'll see you in a couple of minutes." He turned left, heading for Angela's apartment instead of the station. He'd take her with him to get his car and then back to his apartment to change. She'd never been there anyway, and it was about time they changed that.

It didn't matter what she said, tonight was a new beginning for them. He no longer cared if anyone from the station saw them together. She was too important to him to keep her hidden.

In record time he was bounding up her steps and pounding on her door. "Angel, open up," he yelled.

"It's open," she yelled back.

Rafe turned the knob. He'd have to have a talk with her about that. It wasn't safe to leave her door open. "Angel, come on, move it." He clapped his hands. "If you're putting on goop you don't need it. You're beautiful without it." He started toward the bedroom and she came out at the same instant. He smiled at her, moving to take her in his arms but she backed away.

Her actions stunned him but it was her look that froze him in place. She was eyeing him warily, her gaze moving swiftly up and down. He watched as the iced topaz returned and she moved even farther from him.

"What's wrong?" he asked, knowing the answer. It was the uniform.

"I don't think I can make it."

"What are you talking about, you can't make it? You're dressed."

"I have a horrible headache. It just came all of a sudden."

"Like in the last two seconds? You didn't have it when I talked to you and you didn't have it when I came in. Why don't you tell me what brought it on?"

Angela stared at him. She steepled her hands beneath her chin and closed her eyes. "I'm sorry. Tell your family that I hope they didn't go to much trouble." She moved past him and picked up the dessert tray she'd bought to take. "Give this to your mother."

Rafe swallowed. He couldn't believe it. She wouldn't do this, not about something so petty. He glared at her. "You can't do this, it's too late. You don't have a choice. I gave you a choice a week ago. You're the one who picked tonight, not me, not my mother."

"I don't have a choice?" Angela spun back. "This is my life, Rafe. You don't run it and you don't tell me what to do. I'm not going."

He stared in disbelief, wanting to beg her to come, wanting it not to mean so much if she didn't. His *madrina's* words came to him. *You will beg her to love you.*

Not tonight, he thought, and headed for the door. With each step he wanted to hear her call him back. He listened for the sound of her footsteps, knowing she wouldn't follow him, hating himself for caring.

Angela held her hand to her stomach. She'd not expected to have the reaction to Rafe that she'd had. Since they'd begun sleeping together he'd not once come to her apartment in his uniform. She'd not even thought about it one way or the other. Her reaction had come out of nowhere. When she saw him standing there, her brother's words hit her like a slap in the face.

She was betraying her brother for a cop. Sudden disgust filled her. She should have known better. Her eyes slid over to the tray of cookies. What had she been thinking? She didn't want to think about the hurt she'd seen in Rafe's eyes or the anger that had flared on the heels of the hurt.

She'd tried telling him that they weren't a good idea. She went to her computer, turned it on, and slipped the earrings from her ears. Losing her thoughts in the technical writing was a welcome diversion.

CHAPTER 13

Rafe walked into his parents' home and pasted a smile on his face. He wasn't ready to share his feelings with anyone. He kissed his mother's cheek and handed her the box of pastries he'd thought to pick up from the bakery.

"What's this?" his mother asked.

"Angela can't make it. She's sorry, but it couldn't be helped, she's ill. She sent dessert."

"When did she get sick?"

Rafe turned away. "I think it started last night. She was hoping she would feel better. She was looking forward to coming but I didn't think she should. I wanted her to rest," he lied.

He walked toward the back of the house, his mother's voice ringing in his ears. She was insulted, as he'd known she would be. *As she should be*, he thought defensively.

The smile dropped from his lips and he rubbed his face with his hand, closing his eyes and sighing. When he opened his eyes his father was standing in front of him.

"She didn't want to come, did she?"

Rafe shook his head, shrugging his shoulder.

"Don't worry, I won't tell your mother. Maybe it's better that she didn't come tonight. You know it shocked everyone that you'd be involved with the woman who was trying so hard to get you fired. Your mother already hates her. Did you tell her that we knew she was the one who'd filed all those complaints?"

"No."

"Why not?"

"She would never have agreed to come."

"What difference would it have made? She didn't come anyway."

"It had nothing to do with you, any of you," he assured him. "It was me. I went over in my uniform and she didn't like it."

His father was observing him with a slight frown on his face. "Why not? Most women get turned on by a man in a uniform. At least Latino women do. Ask your mother," he said.

"She hates cops. I wasn't thinking about that when I went over. I just wanted to see her and I didn't want to wait."

"What are you going to do?"

"I don't know."

"You know, Son, if she doesn't like cops and it's been your dream since you were a little boy to be on the police force, maybe you're making a mistake. Maybe she's not the one for you. I know what Nellie told you. I know she's your *madrina* but sometimes your *titi* Nellie talks too much." He smiled. "Don't listen to Nellie, I don't. Maybe you should just find a beautiful Puerto Rican girl."

"You got something against her being Black, Pops?"

"Nope."

"Then why did you say that?"

"I'm thinking about all the differences between you. Look at your two sisters. Their husbands have them celebrating Kwanza."

"I don't see anything wrong with that. They still celebrate Christmas."

"They both left the church."

"They didn't leave God."

"They may as well have. I don't think your mother can take much more of the family being split in so many directions."

"Is that what you're worried about, that I'm going to leave the church, change my religion?" Raphael laughed. "Pop, do you have any idea how long it's been since I was even inside a church?"

"It's more than that but even if it wasn't, cultural and religious differences are big. Maybe not so much now while you're hot for her body but later it will be. The thing that worries me the most is that she hates what you do for a living. Put that with the fact that you're lying to her and I don't see a future with this girl."

TWO SIDES TO EVERY STORY

Rafe had told his father almost everything. He knew his father wouldn't tell anyone else, including his mother. He'd needed someone to talk to and for most of his life his father had always been that person.

"I never said I was thinking of a future with her."

"You didn't have to. You also didn't tell me that she hated cops. I thought she just didn't like you because you gave her that ticket, and then the two of you started fighting. This is serious, Raphael. Look at you. You're all tied up in knots over this girl. And I'll bet she didn't buy those pastries. You did."

Rafe was stunned. "How did you know that?"

"The box. It's the bakery right down the street."

I should have thought of that, he silently reprimanded himself. "She did buy a tray of cookies. I just refused to bring them, so I got these."

"Yeah, I know, because you didn't want your family to hate her."

Rafe stared at his father. "Why do you think I would do that to keep you from hating her?"

"Because you love her."

"Is it that obvious?"

"It's that obvious. I also can see that you're heading for a lot more pain. It's not over. What do you think is going to happen when she finds out that you were involved in that gang mess that sent her brother to jail? Blood is thicker than water and it's thicker than love."

"If it was Mama would you tell her the truth?"

"I'd like to think that I would have told your mama the truth, and let her make her own decision. If she loved me, she loved me." He shrugged his shoulders. "If she didn't, you wouldn't have been born." He smiled. "Thank God I never had to make that choice."

"I can't tell her, not yet."

"You know what you're doing is wrong."

"I know."

"You know it's going to come back to bite you in the ass. She's going to find out."

"I know, *Poppi*, and eventually I'll tell her, just not yet. I haven't even told her yet that I love her, not really. I call her *mi angel*, or *mi amor*."

"If she has eyes she knows that you love her, you don't have to say the words. But make no mistake, Son, women want to hear that you love them. I'm sure your angel is not any different."

"I don't know. She doesn't even like it when I call her *mi amor*. You should have seen the way she looked at me tonight. It was like it was the very first time, like nothing had happened between us to change anything."

"You still want to continue with this? What are you planning on doing, quitting the force?"

"Never. As for what I'm going to do, I have no idea what I plan on doing. Right now I'm so angry with her that I'm wondering how I can be talking so calmly with you about this."

His father laughed. "That's when you're good and hooked, Son, when women have you doing things you don't want to do, things that you know will kill you in the end. And all we do is say give me more."

They laughed together and went to the dining room to eat.

Rafe stayed at his parents' house until after ten, pretending to be interested in the conversation of his family, the squabbles between his sisters and brother. He tried hard not to watch the clock. But his father caught his eye once when he was taking a peek at his watch and grinned. He said goodnight at last, ignoring his mother's offer for him to sleep over.

"Goodnight, *Poppi*." he said to his father as he began to walk down the stairs.

"Rafe, if you're heading to see her you'd better go home and change."

Rafe looked down at his uniform. He'd almost forgotten. "Thanks," he said and walked to his car. He should just ignore his father's warning and march back to Angela's and demand that she talk with him. But facing the iced topaz of her gaze was not what he wanted to do tonight. He'd let her get to him, and just as he'd always known, falling for a woman was going to be disastrous. He was sure as hell going to have to reclaim his stones.

—m—

"Angela, we need to talk," he said through the closed door, wondering if she was going to keep him outside and wondering what he would do if she did.

The door opened and she stood there, one hand on the frame, one on the door, still keeping him out. "I don't want to fight with you, Rafe," she said quietly.

"I don't want to fight with you either," he answered, realizing that he meant it. "Can I come in?" he asked.

"I don't think you should. It's not going to solve anything and we're only going to make it harder in the end."

"I'm willing to take my chances."

Angela opened the door wider. "How did it go?"

"Not so good."

"Are you still angry?"

"Yes."

"And you came anyway?"

"Yes."

She licked her lips. She wanted to tell him that she was sorry for what had happened, that she would never let it happen again, but she couldn't be sure.

"Rafe, we're not a good match." she said instead. "We should call a halt to this before it's too late."

"It's already too late." he answered and lifted her in his arms.

"How long do you think this will solve things?"

"I thought you didn't want to fight," he answered her. "I know that I don't. I want to make love to you," he whispered into her ear. "I want to take you to bed."

"But eventually we'll have to leave the bed." Angela laid her head against his chest.

"We don't have to worry about that tonight. Maybe you were right. Maybe we moved a little too fast. I'm sorry if I pushed you," Raphael said into the soft flesh of her neck.

And she was sorry that she'd pushed him into saying that, into apologizing when he had no reason to. Rafe wasn't the sort of man who would easily kowtow to a woman's whims or demands forever. She was aware of that. But now, now what they had was new and fragile and he wanted it to work. A single sob tore loose from her throat. "Rafe."

"Hush, baby," he said walking into the bedroom and laying her on the bed.

"Tu eres tan hermoas. No quero luchar con contigo, solamente tequero hacer amor contigo."

"What did you say?"

"I said you're beautiful. I don't want to fight with you. I only want to make love with you."

His head bent and he kissed her neck. As he lowered her to the bed, she moaned. This wasn't the way for them to solve the problems between them. But for now she'd accept it.

She was glad that she had on a gown; it made it so much easier. She closed her eyes as his hands made their way under the flimsy material and he began caressing her. "Rafe," she whispered, "I'm trying."

"I know you are, baby. Don't worry, *mi amor*. We'll get it right."

She wrapped her arms around him, her heart breaking over what she knew wasn't the end of pain for them. "Rafe," she said, the pain in her voice evident even to her own ears. Angela stopped herself from saying more. There were no promises she could make. She could only offer him now.

"Touch me," he moaned in her ear.

This she could do. She pulled his pants from his hips and ran her hand down his torso, loving the feel of him, as she always did. She felt the shiver as she touched him, and smiled. Angela never tired of the feel of Rafe's body. She begin kissing his shoulder, working her way down his arm, finding his muscle firm and hard. She ran her fingers over the indentations, over all of him before she cupped him, giving him what he wanted. She caressed him as he caressed her and together they moaned and found their way toward heaven when he entered her.

Tears slid beneath her closed lids, and she held in the words she so wanted to say to him. She didn't want to end this and make her words into a lie. And so far they had not found a way to make it work out of bed. They'd stolen two days and even those had been fraught with problems.

She woke with kisses on her face and his hand between her legs and she smiled before turning to face him.

"Will you go out with me?" he asked.

She thought of the words had brother had used and hesitated. If they took their relationship to the streets, people would see them. She shivered. If anything happened to him she would never be able to forgive herself.

"Have you tired of me so soon?" she laughed, attempting to turn his request and her answer into a joke. "I thought we could maybe watch a movie on television or something."

"Are you ashamed of me?"

"No, of course not."

"It feels that way."

"It's not.

"Then what is it?"

"Things are happening that we agreed in the beginning we wouldn't allow, going out just makes it more . . ."

"More what? Like a relationship, like we're not just using each other for sex?"

She cringed. "Rafe, I have to finish what I came here to do. I haven't lied to you about my reasons for moving here.

"I'm only asking you to go out with me. I haven't asked for a lifetime commitment."

She wanted to do as he asked but subconsciously Angela wondered if she would be placing them both at risk if she did. She wished she could tell him that they were being spied on but wondered if that would make things worse. What would happen to her brother?

"Forget it, Angel."

She witnessed the hurt in his voice, saw it on his face, and she didn't want it there. "I'll go," she said.

"Don't do me any favors."

Oh yeah, her life was becoming more complicated by the day. She knew she was about to plead with a man she'd hated a few weeks ago to forgive her. She should be running as far away from him as she could get before one or both of them got hurt.

"Rafe, I'm sorry if I hurt your feelings. I didn't mean to. I just don't want either of us to get hurt. We both have a lot at stake here. I don't want us to cloud things just because of sex."

She saw his disparaging look and laughed. "Okay, I'll admit it's incredible, out-of-this- galaxy sex. Still, I don't want us getting confused about what's happening between us."

"No, *mi amor*, let's not confuse things."

"Rafe."

He stood glaring at her. "What? Isn't this what you wanted, for me not to care about you, to think of this only as our having a good time?"

She groaned inwardly before answering him. "I thought we had decided that we could at least be friends."

"You're right, we're friends."

"And as your friend," she allowed her voice to underline her words, "as your friend I would love to go out with you."

Raphael stared at her. At least his *madrina* had told him what he was in for. He would indeed have to work for her love if he wanted it.

She smiled at him.

He wanted it.

"So where do you want to go and when?" Angela asked.

"Next week I get three days off in a row. I can request my two off days for the following week, put them together and we can have five whole days. Maybe we could take a trip somewhere."

"There's a big difference in that and going out to a movie or to eat. Besides, I'd miss too many days seeing my brother." When she glanced in Rafe's direction, his green gaze caught her, then snagged her heart. Yes, he was in too close but she couldn't stop it.

"Where do you want to go?" she asked.

"We could drive to Branson."

"Don't think so."

"We could fly to Vegas."

"No."

"How about Wisconsin Dells?"

Angela tilted her head sideways to better observe Rafe. He was getting what he wanted, the two of them as a couple. "The Dells would be nice," she said. "I can afford it," she added, trying to hold on to a measure of control by paying her own way.

"Good, I'm glad to hear that," Raphael answered, kissing her at last, knowing that they both knew he had no intention of letting her pay. But if she needed to believe that to agree to go, then why fight?

"I know what you're thinking, Rafe. I'm serious."

"Of course you know what I'm thinking. You can feel me, Angel," he said and reached for her hand and placed it on his erection.

"You're trying to be cute. I'm talking about the trip. I'm paying for half."

Raphael arched a brow and looked at her but didn't answer. He'd let her think she was paying for this vacation if that was what she needed, but no way in hell would a woman pay his way.

"We're going dutch," Angela warned.

"I don't understand. What do you mean by dutch?" he grinned. "I'm Puerto Rican, not Dutch." Then he grabbed her and began tickling her, not allowing her to formulate a response. This would be the start of some thing bigger than he'd ever dreamed possible. He kissed her, thinking that would be the perfect moment to tell her that he loved her.

CHAPTER 14

Finally lady luck was smiling down on her. Angela could have kissed the woman right there in the grocery store. She was the first person who'd admitted to knowing Teresa Cortez. However, the woman had said something really strange, that Teresa had been going with a Black man who was in jail for dealing drugs. She'd have to ask her brother to look into that, maybe the man was someone he knew. At least it was worth a shot.

That little bit of information gave her hope. She now had something positive to tell her brother. She hoped he would concentrate on that, and not on the fact that she was going to be out of town for a week. She wasn't going to deny that she would be with Rafe, but she was hoping that it wouldn't come up.

From the moment she hugged her brother at the point of contact, she'd sensed his anger but now she knew why. She waited until they were seated.

"I think I may have good news for you."

The silence was so thick she wondered if the guards might come over just to check on them. "I've made some progress and I have a lead on Teresa."

"And you found this lead in bed with the cop?"

"Don't start."

"I warned you."

"Yeah, I know. I didn't like it any more the first time you did it. You can't tell me who to date."

"Maybe I can't but you're going to wish you had listened to me."

"He loves me."

"He's using you."

"I think I'm falling in love with him."

"I hope for your sake you're not."

"Don't do anything to him."

"How can I? I'm locked up."

"If you have someone hurt him, I swear . . ."

"You swear?" Adrian interrupted. "What do you swear? We're blood. Are you going to go against me? If he gets hurt, blame yourself. I warned you. You had no business going to bed with a cop in the first place."

"Do you think I went looking for a cop? It just happened, Adrian. I didn't ask for it. We fought for months. It just happened. Let it go. He's a good guy. He really is." She glanced away, then back at her brother. "Adrian, I care for him, I don't want anything to happen to him."

Angela watched a change come over her brother. He went from a snarling fearsome man back to the older brother she adored, without batting an eye.

"Hey, I was trying to look out for you, but you're right, it's your life and believe me, I'm happy for you. I'll do whatever it takes to make you happy." He laughed, "I think I'm going a little nuts being in here. Forgive me. You know me, I would never think of doing anything to anyone. Even if I wanted to, I don't have that kind of weight. You know, after awhile you start behaving just like everyone else in here."

He was right. Angela glanced around at the other prisoners and visitors. They all appeared guarded and distrustful. Their eyes were constantly surveying the place and the people in it. There was definitely something about the atmosphere, the *prison mentality*, she'd heard it called. Her gaze landed on her brother and a tiny shiver touched the base of her spine.

Angela had felt the same thing happen to her lately when she came into the prison. She was guarded also, viewing each person she saw as potential danger. She stared at her brother. It was happening even with

Adrian, the brother she'd always trusted and believed in. Now she was beginning to feel doubt creep in and she didn't like it. She no longer had the blind trust in him she'd had her entire life. She was beginning to think of things her cousin Simone had said to her about Adrian not being innocent. Staring at her brother, listening to his words, she'd begun wondering if he'd been involved somehow, just as Simone wondered. Angela now found herself unsure of her brother's innocence. She saw the way he was behaving and, as a cop would do, she doubted. It had to be the prison that was affecting her trust. She thought of Rafe. *Maybe not.*

Adrian was staring at her so she reached her hand out and gave his fingers a squeeze before hurriedly pulling away, knowing she'd broken the rules of contact. Maybe the lack of touch was the culprit, the reason she doubted. Whatever it was, she wanted it gone. Her brother was innocent, had always been innocent. Angela had to remember that. Of course her brother would never harm Rafe. As he'd said, she should have never gotten involved with a cop. Only it was much too late to back out of it now. She was in love with Rafe Remeris. And their upcoming vacation would be the perfect time to tell him.

For perhaps the hundredth time Angela rechecked everything. She recognized it as her nerves but the awareness didn't stop her.

She was going away with Rafe for five days. She was looking forward to it as much as he was. He'd been bouncing off the walls with excitement the night before.

There was only one thing left to do and that was to let someone know where the heck she was, just in case. She smiled inwardly. Just in case Rafe turned out to be some maniac. There was only one person she would tell and that was Simone.

A quick glance at the clock told her she'd better hurry. Rafe would be by to pick her up in less than an hour.

"Simone, I just wanted to check in with you. I'm leaving in a few."

"I can't believe you're really going," Simone answered.

"Why?"

"You haven't been anywhere since Adrian got in trouble."

"I know." Angela smiled to herself. She knew her cousin had a ton of questions that she wasn't asking.

"Does Auntie know you have a boyfriend?"

"He's not my boyfriend." Angela laughed at her cousin's curiosity. "I was wondering how long it would take you to break down and ask me. You're been so proper I was beginning to think someone had invaded your body and I wanted my nosy-ass cousin back."

Simone shrieked. "I was trying to give you space. You've been so closemouthed since you got a boyfriend that I don't know what I can and can't say to you anymore."

"I told you he's not my boyfriend," Angela insisted, knowing that she was lying, and also knowing that as well as Simone knew her, she also was aware of that fact. Still, she persisted in keeping up the false façade.

"I don't know what else to call him. You keep telling me you're not dating, that you're just hanging out, but you don't go on vacation with someone that you're just hanging out with and you don't have that sound in your voice that you have in yours."

"What sound?" Angela couldn't help asking even though it would probably lead to another debate.

"That happy sound, like you're in love. Are you falling in love with the cop, Cuz?"

"What if I told you yes?"

"I'd say good for you."

"What if I said no?"

"I'd say too bad. You need someone in your life. You're too young to give up your life because your brother was stupid enough to get involved with that dumb-ass shit."

"Simone."

"Don't Simone me. You're not stupid. I could slap him for screwing you over. And I could slap some sense into you for wasting your time feeling sorry for his ass."

There, it was out there between them. Simone didn't believe that Adrian was innocent and she did. At least she wanted to.

"Simone, why did you have to bring that up right now? I just wanted to tell you where I'm going to be just in case something happens, so you'll know how to reach me."

"That's a lie. I know you're taking your cell phone with you. You may not want to admit it, but you called because you want someone who will be straight with you. You wanted me to talk about the cop. And you wanted me to tell you not to feel guilty that you're falling in love with him."

"I don't feel guilty."

"Then you are falling in love with him?"

"I didn't say that."

"Then what aren't you feeling guilty about?"

"What do you think?"

"Yeah, yeah, I know all that shit the family keeps saying. We hate cops, yada, yada. Look, I know there are a lot of rotten cops out there. There are enough dead brothers to prove that fact. But I also know that you wouldn't be sleeping with the guy if you thought he was a dirty cop. And I know for sure you wouldn't be getting ready to go on vacation with him if you even thought he so much as knew your brother. So have a good time."

"Thanks, Simone. Rafe really is a nice guy. He's so sweet and tender yet at the same time I've never known a more masculine man."

"Of course he's nice. Like I said, you're a smart woman. So how does he feel about you?"

Angela could feel herself blushing. "He loves me."

"Has he told you that?"

"Not in so many words. But you should see the way he looks at me."

"In bed or out?"

"Why?"

"Don't be a fool; you know there's a difference."

"I know." Angela stopped and thought about the way Rafe looked at her, both in and out of bed. She thought of all the reasons he shouldn't love her, all the horrible things she'd put him through. Then she thought again of the look that would come into his eyes when he'd first see her when he came into her apartment and she thought of the way he cradled her in his arms as he slept. He loved her. That was one thing she didn't doubt. And just as she was, she assumed he was waiting for the perfect moment to tell her.

"Are you listening to me?"

Simone was screaming at her and she gathered from the ferocity of the words she'd been screaming for quite awhile. "I'm sorry, I guess I was doing a little daydreaming."

"About Rafe?"

"Who else?"

"Okay, tell me about the look. Is it in bed or out?"

"Both."

"Both."

"He even forgave me for getting him in trouble." Angela heard the snort on the other end of the phone. "You don't have to tell me, I know. I never should have tried getting him in trouble."

"He should have filed charges against you."

"Simone," Angela laughed, shocked, her laughter choking her. "You're going against family. You're a traitor."

"So what? Who the hell cares?"

"Yeah, who cares?" Angela answered and for a moment they were both silent, both reading the other's thoughts.

"It's okay for you to be in love, Angela," Simone said softly. "It's okay that he's a cop, and it's okay that you're going away with him for a vacation. You're not a prisoner; you've done nothing wrong. You've given over two years of your life for your brother. Go with Rafe and have fun. Don't throw the chance of love away, Cuz. It's not that easy to come by."

Angela wished she could tell Simone about the threats that Adrian had made against Rafe. Maybe she'd be able to help her put it in focus. But then again, Simone was hard on Adrian. She had been from the moment it had happened.

Even when they'd all been at the hospital, Simone had been the only one who'd said things looked fishy to her. Only she hadn't dared to say it to anyone other than Angela. She would have been kicked out of the family for so much as thinking it. Nope, Adrian was the good guy and the cops were the bad guys and that was exactly what Angela had believed. Until Rafe. Now, like Simone, she knew all cops weren't bad.

"Will you go out to the prison to see Adrian while I'm gone?"

"Yes, I'll go, but to tell you the truth he's pissing me off. When I go he acts like he's some big-time thug."

"He has to act like that in prison if he wants to survive," Angela said, feeling as though she had to defend her brother, even though inwardly she agreed with her cousin.

"I don't know."

"It's an act, Simone. Trust me, he has to save face."

"So what? I'm getting tired of it. He treats me like dirt."

"He knows you don't believe him," Angela answered her cousin, a bit miffed that Simone had never bothered to hide her disbelief.

"He knows I'm not you," Simone huffed indignantly. "He can't put one over on me so easily."

Angela shouldn't have been shocked and in actuality she wasn't. However, her feelings were hurt. Simone was the closest thing she had to a sister and her best friend. She didn't like Simone thinking that she was a fool. So yes, she was offended.

"What are you saying?" she asked. "First you said I'm not stupid, now you're saying I'm too stupid to see through Adrian if he were lying."

"There it is again, Angela, that little word—*if.* You're right, you're not stupid, except when it comes to family. Then you turn your brain off and act like you don't even have one. I know Adrian is feeding you a lot of that and I can't blame you for wanting to believe him. After all, he's your brother. But come on, one day you're going to have to listen to something other than what he tells you. I can't believe that as much as you go out to that prison you haven't noticed a change in your brother."

"I've noticed a change."

"And you haven't doubted?"

"Look, Simone, let me give you the phone number. I can't keep talking about this. I have to go."

"Yeah okay, give me the number but I know you feel something's wrong. That's why you're in a hurry to get rid of me."

Angela gave her cousin the number to the resort and hung up knowing that she was partially right. Maybe she had called Simone for validation, to hear someone tell her that she deserved to be happy. Maybe guilt had lurked somewhere near the back of her mind.

Guilt that she was going away with a cop and worries that her going away with Rafe could possibly endanger him. She couldn't talk that over with anyone. Simone would go running straight to the authorities and Adrian would be in even more trouble. She couldn't risk that; her parents would never forgive her if that happened. And she would never forgive herself if something happened to Rafe and she'd done nothing about it.

"Ready, Angel," Rafe said, kissing her as he took the luggage from her hand.

She gave him a smile before looking up and down the street, then back up at her apartment. As she climbed into Rafe's car, strangeness overtook her. This was the first time she'd ever seen his car, the first time they'd been outside together besides his stopping her for some traffic violation. Today was the beginning of a lot of firsts for them. And while she was excited, there was a hint of fear that hung on to her. Rafe was watching her and she pretended not to notice.

"What's wrong?" he asked.

"Nothing," she replied and glanced out the window.

"Something's going on. You're looking around as though you're waiting for us to get arrested." He attempted a smile. "You weren't like this when the possibility was real."

He was trying to make her comfortable, she knew that, but it wasn't working.

"It's not illegal for us to be together, Angel."

"I know." She smiled, this time a real one. She didn't want to ruin things. She would put her guilt away for the next five days. She would take the five days for herself and deal with the consequences when she returned.

"I'm okay, Rafe."

She reached for his hand and when he gave her fingers a squeeze she felt the heat. This was the reason she was in the car with Rafe. He did something to her that she'd never expected. He'd stolen a part of her heart and in the process he'd claimed her soul. She needed to be with him as much as he needed to be with her. If only she didn't feel the guilt it would be perfect.

"Baby, I'm not going to push you. That's not what this is about. Stop worrying. I'm not trying to define what we have. I just wanted us to spend some time away from everything that interferes in our lives."

"I guess that's what has me worried, Rafe. We haven't talked about anything. We started out with our rules and then we broke them. And now here we are heading off for five days and neither of us knows quite what to make of our relationship."

"It can be whatever you want it to be."

"It's not up to me, Rafe."

"Sure it is. You made the choice to be with me. I know it's hard for you not to see your brother but I promise we're going to have a good time."

Angela looked away. She didn't want to take her family with her but somehow they were intruding. She didn't blame him for mentioning her brother. Actually she found it rather sweet that he was aware how important her family was to her. Still, she didn't want to discuss them now. She'd been accused of being a traitor by her brother.

As she looked out of the window knowing that she would be missing time with him, she felt like one. And she didn't want to. Angela wanted to be like any other young woman and explore the possibility of being in love. She didn't want to carry the weight of the entire African American race on her shoulders, nor did she want Rafe to carry the burden of the entire Latino population.

She wanted to forget that he was a cop and that she'd had a long-time feud with anyone in uniform. She wanted this time to be about the two of them. And she didn't want the guilt that was continually clawing at her. She wanted to make it go away.

Raphael had noticed from the moment he'd picked Angela up that something was wrong with her. She'd smiled at him but still he sensed worry underneath and he'd done his best to put her at ease. He wondered if it were the fact that she would not be seeing her brother or the fact that for the first time they were truly making their relationship public. He glanced at her as she looked out of the window. She was so far from him that she might as well be in Siberia.

This was like swimming through a pool filled with cold mud. Rafe sighed. He wanted this trip to be perfect.

He'd never told a woman that he loved her, never expected that he ever would. His angel was not making it easy on him. While he admired her family loyalty, he didn't want her thinking of her family while they were together. He'd spent way too much money to make this time special for her. He'd asked his four sisters for advice, taking each of their romantic fantasies and combining them into one huge fantasy for his angel. He sure hoped she liked it.

Raphael looked sideways at her, wondering what she would do when he told her. He knew she was falling in love with him. He also knew she didn't want to. A twinge of guilt pushed at him for the things he didn't plan to tell her in the next five days and he pushed it back. He'd tell her . . . later. First, he had to tell her that he loved her.

Glancing toward Angela, Raphael pushed the button on the radio, thankful that within a matter of minutes he heard Angela humming along to the songs. When he joined in with his croaking, out-of-tune voice, she laughed and just like that the mud was gone. All he could see was clear sailing ahead.

CHAPTER 15

Angela stood in the lobby of the new Pentar Hotel in the heart of Wisconsin Dells. It was magnificent. Her stomach fluttered once, then twice. She felt as though she were taking a giant leap into a void, into a situation she might not be able to control.

She patted her pocket, feeling the bulge of her wallet. *I'll pay my own way*, she thought. That would give her a measure of control. She knew Rafe thought she was kidding; his macho attitude wouldn't permit him considering anything but the man paying for things. But she needed to maintain a sense of balance. She had to pay for something and she'd find a way to do it.

"Why are you standing so far away from me?"

Rafe came up to her, slid his arm around her waist and nuzzled her neck. "You don't want anyone to know that you're with me?"

For the first time Angela believed Rafe meant the words said in a teasing fashion. "Why do you keep asking me that?"

"Look around you. How many Latinos do you think are checking in as guests?"

She looked around, then smiled. "About the same number of African American that are checking in." She watched as the corners of his lips twitched and he smiled. Despite her qualms against public displays of affection, Angela stood on tiptoe and kissed Rafe smack dab on the lips right there in the lobby, and she didn't care who saw them.

"I'm very proud to be seen with you."

"No matter when or where?"

"No matter when or where," she answered, knowing he was speaking of the future, of family meetings, and she was answering him honestly. It wouldn't be the fact that he was Latino that would bother her family. Despite the slurs her brother had used, she knew it would be Rafe's being a cop that would bother them more than anything.

"Listen, I thought you told me I was going to have a good time."

"You're not enjoying this?" he said and blew on her neck, causing the hairs to rise and a tingle to slip down her spine.

She grinned like a fool. What did he expect her to do in the lobby? He pulled on her hand and she followed, for once meekly, not complaining. He had a bad habit of turning her into mush with his touch.

The scent of flowers filled her nostrils moments before Rafe turned the key and they walked into the room. Angela stood for a moment in shock. The room was filled with vases of flowers of differing varieties. The perfume from the blooms captured her senses. She spotted a card with her name leaning against one of the vases and opened it. Smiling, she turned toward Rafe, who was grinning madly.

"Rafe, this is so romantic," she said softly, loving it, wondering how on earth she could pretend it wasn't what it was meant to be. She felt again for her security. Only this time the wallet did not bring her comfort.

"You like it?" he asked.

She saw the question in his eyes, the wondering. She went to him and threw her arms around him. "Yes, I love it." She kissed his cheeks, his forehead, then his lips. "I love it."

"Good," he said in a voice filled with his usual warmth tinged with a swagger.

Things were moving along faster than Angela had intended. She wanted to back away for just a moment. She needed to not be so close to him, to his masculine power.

"Give me a minute," she said, then headed for the bathroom. She broke away from him, entered the bathroom and gasped in surprise. The bathroom was also filled with flowers and another card. She read the card and tears came to her eyes. He was going all out. She wasn't blind; she knew he was waiting for the right moment to tell her that he loved her. Rafe had planned this just as she had. Only now she didn't know for sure if she should go through with it. If only she could get Adrian's words out of her head.

It was only so long that she could stay in the bathroom. She pasted a smile on her face, caught sight of herself in the mirror, and pegged her smile as phony. She took another look at the flowers filling the bathroom, then walked out.

"Rafe," she said, unable to say anything else. Her heart was hammering like crazy, her legs had suddenly gone weak, and her need for oxygen prevented speech.

He stood there for a moment grinning at her, devouring her with his eyes. "You are so beautiful," he said, then repeated it again. "*Tu eres tan es hermoas.*"

His eyes raked over her before returning to her face and Angela saw the burning need within him. Rafe's love for her was evident. She didn't need to hear the words. But for once she wanted to hear them and that was dangerous. Once they said it, there was no going back. She waited, trembling, her eyes glued to his lips, waiting to hear him tell her that he loved her.

A bell rang and Angela blinked. The moment gone, she looked toward Rafe. "What's that?"

"A doorbell."

"A doorbell in a hotel?" She grinned. "Who's at the door?"

"Open it and find out."

A ring, Angela thought, *someone is bringing me a ring*. He was going to propose. Her heart beat even faster as she opened the door.

"Hello, Mrs. Remeris. We need you to come with us. Something has been prepared for you."

Angela turned toward Rafe, wondering why he'd signed them in as a married couple. Wishful thinking or him protecting her virtue? *Probably a little bit of both*, she thought as she turned toward Rafe. "Just me?" she asked.

"You're ready to ditch me so soon?" he smiled back at her.

"No. Where are we going?"

"Let's just follow him."

And they did, into the elevator and down a corridor and into a small room filled with more flowers and scented candles. A fireplace was in the center of the room and couches were placed strategically around it. There were two other couples, she noted, each near the fire yet seeming to be alone. They were led to the couch directly in the center. It was then she noticed the high back and side arms that added extra privacy, cutting them off from the other couples and enclosing them in their own special cocoon of romantic warmth.

Angela glanced down at the table positioned in front of the couch, at the wine chilling in the bucket and the cheese and fruit set in a bowl on the table. She saw another card with her name on it propped against the ice bucket.

Rafe's arm was around her and his breath was teasing the hairs on the back of her neck. *This must be costing him a fortune*, she thought. Chicago cops didn't make that kind of money, at least not honestly. She shivered and pushed the evil thought away. Rafe kissed her earlobes and the thought was gone permanently. Her fingers trembled slightly as she pulled the card from the envelope and laughed. It was completely in Spanish.

"You keep that one until you can read it," Rafe teased.

"You don't want to tell me what it says?"

"That would spoil it."

A tingle of wanting started from her toes and traveled upward until she was consumed with it. Her blood burned in her veins, making her more aware than ever of the source of the heat. At that moment she gave up any pretense of being able to stand on her own and slid rather ungracefully to the waiting sofa, laughing as Rafe grinned at her knowingly.

As the wine was being poured Angela wondered at what point she should tell him that she really wasn't a wine drinker. She brought her glass to her lips. *I won't*, she thought as she sipped on the wine.

When she put her glass down, he dipped a strawberry into it and held it to her lips. She bit into the fruit, her eyes locked on Rafe. Her hand reached for the napkin to wipe away the juice but he was quicker. His tongue shot out, licked her lips clean, and she shivered again. She didn't know how she could continue staring into his green gaze without kissing him.

Her hand reached for a strawberry. She dipped it into Rafe's glass and fed him as he'd done her, then she repeated the act and licked away the juices. And that ever-present tingle ravished her inside, making her burn with a heat so intense she didn't know if she'd survive.

"We'd better stop," Rafe moaned. "You're spoiling my plans."

Angela smiled, dipped another berry into the clear wine and slid it between his lips. This time as he bit into it, she pressed her lips against his and eased her tongue into his mouth a fraction of an inch. Her eyes darted down and she spotted the bulge and withdrew. "You're right; we'd better cool it."

"Just for now, *mi amor.*"

For over an hour they sat holding each other, gazing into the fire, nibbling the fruit and cheese, kissing, touching and making it damn impossible to go back to being two people with no connections, who had sex in an apartment. They both knew this was the beginning and the end. The end of their pretense, the beginning of a relationship.

Angela's heart was beating faster. Never in her life had she been more consumed with emotions. She wanted to cry out for him to stop, to push him away, but at the thought of his heat leaving her, she leaned in even closer.

The same smiling man in black tux was standing at the table beside them. "If you're all done here, I'll escort you to your room," he said.

Angela caught the look the man threw to Rafe and she quivered inwardly, wondering what was next.

They followed behind the man in the tuxedo. *So elegant,* she thought. She felt Rafe curling his hand around hers, squeezing her fingers. The feelings he produced in her made it hard for her to even breathe, let alone think.

"This is too much," she said at last. "This has to have cost . . ." She paused. "That was rude of me. I feel so pampered."

The door to the suite was opened and they stepped in. Angela immediately sensed a change. She glanced at Rafe and saw the smile he couldn't suppress if he tried. She stepped in and saw the room had indeed been changed. Rose petals adorned the floor and led, she was sure, to the bedroom. And a different trail went the way of the bathroom. A quick glance and she spotted even more flowers than there had been on their arrival, and more cards. She reached for one, feeling shivers of anticipation claim her.

"Thanks," she laughed, able to read the first card.

"You're not learning Spanish as quickly as I'd hoped so I thought I'd better give you at least a couple that you can read now."

Angela spotted another card across the room and walked toward it, laughing when she pulled it out and saw that it was also in Spanish.

"Just a couple huh?"

"For now?"

"Ahem."

At the sound Angela turned. She'd forgotten that they were not alone.

"There are robes and slippers on your bed. If you'll put those on and go downstairs, the masseur will be waiting for you. Enjoy your massage."

Their escort smiled broadly at them and to Angela's surprise, didn't even wait for a tip. Once again the thought came that Rafe had to have dropped a bundle on their little vacation.

Angela waited until the door to the suite closed before turning and grinning. "Both of us?"

"Of course. Do you think I'm going to have you naked and not be around?" he answered with a leer.

And this is day one, she thought, as she followed him into the bedroom, changing quickly in order to have the massage.

The terrycloth felt warm against her skin. As she rubbed her cheeks along the material, her eyes connected with Rafe's. The heat between them simmered like a smoldering fire. As he raked his eyes over her she backed away.

"I really want that massage," she laughed, and took another two steps backwards.

"More than . . ."

"Right now, yes." She smiled to take away the slight sting of her refusal. "We have all night for that."

"I'm crushed. I must be losing my touch."

"You're not losing it but since you went to so much trouble to set this up, I want to enjoy it." Angela practically ran from the room as the look in Rafe's eyes intensified and she knew if he came near her the only massaging she would receive would be from his hands caressing her into submission.

What a crazy plan, Raphael thought as he followed Angela out the door and to the elevator. Here he'd paid to pamper her and all he could think of at the moment was how much he wanted to make love to her, to bury himself to the hilt in her hot moistness.

Yeah, he had it bad. He laughed to himself and stuck a hand out to swipe the back of his angel's behind. He didn't expect the smoldering look of lust she bestowed on him, and forced a groan up from his chest. His flesh hardened and his robe tented. He shook his head in amusement. It was much too late to worry about that now. He'd just have to hope that the massage would cool him off. But how could it? It had never been meant to cool him off but to heat up his angel. He groaned again, thinking what a stupid plan he'd devised. He shouldn't have listened to his sisters. There was no way on God's green's earth that he could participate in giving Angela her massage without jumping her bones.

In the massage area, Angela did as instructed and lay on the table, peeping over to her right at Rafe as he did the same.

"Put your head here," she was directed by a huge bear of a man.

She did as instructed, turning her head to the left as she was told to do. For a moment she wondered how on earth Rafe was going to stay there and allow a man to touch her naked flesh. She didn't think he could, but, hey, it would be worth it to see his face later if she faked a moan or two.

"Ouch, that hurts."

"Sorry."

A noise that Angela couldn't decipher blasted through her but before she could raise her head to investigate she was being pounded again.

"Not so hard," she said to the bear of a masseur.

"Sorry."

The tempo changed as did the texture of the man's hand. She was filled with heat as he worked the muscles in her thighs. From the moment the man's hands touched her flesh she'd known the difference. It was Rafe. For a moment she thought of moving, of telling him to stop. Then she thought better of it. She sighed, allowing her muscle to relax and soften.

His hands began probing, searching, moving between her thighs, rubbing with an erotic touch that could close the hotel down in a flash. He was trying to get her to move and the best she was giving him was her sighs of pleasure.

Rafe was a bit annoyed that Angela had accepted the switch that the direction her massage was taking with not so much as a sound, other than the sighs of pleasure that would be driving him wild if he knew for sure that she knew it was him. She had to know that it was him. He was insane and his angel was the culprit. She was driving him insane, making him jealous of the pleasure he was giving her.

"That feels good but could you move to my back for awhile?" Angela moaned.

Without a word he moved his hands from the silky heat of her thighs and lingered for a moment on her rounded derriere before moving to her back. He was hard. His annoyance hadn't prevented his arousal.

The little witch, he thought as he began to pound on her back with the same intensity as the professional masseur had done.

"Rafe, stop that."

He did.

"You knew it was me?"

"Of course I knew it was you," Angela said, turning to face him. She grinned. "Did you really think I couldn't tell your touch?"

"I don't know, you never said a word."

"Do you think I would let just anyone do the things to me that you were doing?"

Rafe could feel himself growing ever harder as he watched his angel. Her brown eyes held a hint of mischief. He allowed his eyes to rake over her body that was no longer covered by the huge white towel but simply soft shimmering brown skin. She followed his gaze before her eyes traveled over him, stopping at his crotch. Then she laughed deep, throaty and hot, and he melted.

A knock sounded on the door and stopped what he'd wanted to do for the past three hours. He couldn't make love to her here. Besides, her day wasn't done. He would give this day to her if it killed him. The painful erection warned him that it just might.

"Mr. Remeris, are the two of you still in there?"

Rafe leered at Angela, then walked to open the door.

"I think I want him to finish the massage," Angela announced.

"Not a chance in hell," he grunted, pointing a finger indicating that Angela should cover up. No way was this guy going to touch his woman, not now, not ever.

When the massages were done, the brutal male for him, a masseuse for her, they went back to their suite.

"Rafe, this is wonderful!"

"If you had a fantasy would this be a part of it?"

"Maybe."

"Maybe?"

"I haven't thought much about it but that look on your face when you thought I didn't know it was you was priceless."

"You like playing with me, don't you?"

A hand slipped around him and he groaned as she squeezed. A tremor shook him and he grabbed her roughly, shoving his tongue into her mouth and pulling her close. "Angel," he whispered, breathing in the scent of the massage oil lingering on her skin. He licked her neck and felt her shiver at the same moment that his own flesh quivered in her hand.

"I want you," he moaned, "now."

"What are we waiting for?"

His eyes closed and he sighed. "My surprise isn't over."

"Skip it."

"What about dinner?"

"I want dessert," Angela replied and gave another squeeze.

Raphael thought about the dinner he'd planned, the bath after. Then he thought about the warm hand kneading him and his own hand began its search, pushing into her hot moistness, feeling her juices flow over his hand. Dinner or her? There was no question.

A knock that he ignored only served to bring about a louder, more insistent one, followed by a voice bellowing for them. Damn it, he should have taken into account how hot he would be by this point. But no, he'd listened to four women tell him what his angel would want.

"You didn't have to go to so much trouble."

He glanced at her, moving his hands. "What do you mean?"

"All of this. You don't have to seduce me. Our arrangement means you don't have to try."

A lump of pain twisted in Raphael's gut. Their arrangement? Seducing her? Hell, that wasn't what he was going for. This was meant to make her love him. She was running hot and cold, confusing the hell out of him.

Raphael pulled away, disappointed. Closing his robe he made his way to the door. How could she even think this was just to get what he already had? If he'd just wanted to get into her pants, he could have done that without driving for hours and depleting his savings by a hefty amount. He glanced back over his shoulder and caught her watching him, a wary expression on her face. *She knew*, he thought. She knew what he was doing and she was still afraid.

CHAPTER 16

Angela felt a prick of conscience as Rafe's look of pain rolled over her. He wasn't used to being vulnerable, not like this, and she'd thrown what he was trying to do back in his face. It was unintentional. The words had just sort of tumbled out of her mouth.

She shivered, suddenly afraid of her emotions and of Rafe's. There would be no turning back once they'd said the words. Angela had never felt like this about anyone. She remembered the first time they'd met, the hatred and the fire, now the love. He made her want things: him, love, home and family. The same things she'd accused him of wanting.

The knowledge that to love Rafe would create future chaos and dissension in her life colored her decision slightly. She could get over her brother's anger but she didn't know if she could get over the hurt that he thought she wasn't doing her best for him, that her relationship with Rafe was clouding that. She knew in the back of her mind that the thought of her parents, her entire family, thinking she was a traitor was holding her back from admitting her love to Rafe.

Still, there had been no need to throw his love for her back in his face and she was ashamed of her actions. She'd have to make it up to him.

Angela watched as he walked toward the door. She looked at the way he moved, the sinewy muscles of his thighs, the way his backside moved. She loved his tight butt. She loved his body and she loved him.

A tingle of awareness touched lightly at her scalp and she knew then what the burning was about, what it had been about from the moment they'd first touched. He was right. They were soul mates.

"We have to get dressed for dinner," Rafe said when he returned to the room. She noticed that there was a coolness about him; the playfulness had vanished. She sat on the bed as he disappeared into the shower without even asking her to join him.

Latin men and their macho BS, she thought, then cringed that she'd even thought such a thing. It wasn't that he was Latin; it was the simple fact that he was a man. She'd hurt his feelings and like a man he had to prove he didn't need her, even if he did. He knew it and she knew it. They needed each other.

Two could play the same game, Angela thought as she went silently into the shower that Rafe had exited. The steam from his water lingered, fogging the mirror, while the clean scent wafted across the room and wrapped itself around her. She might not cave entirely, but she would definitely bend, Angela thought as the steam filled her head and thoughts of Rafe touching her filled her heart.

When she came from the shower, she purposefully let the towel drop from her body and pool around her feet. She propped her leg on the bed and rubbed her body with lotion, giving him a clear view of all her secrets. She resisted the temptation to smile. She kept her head turned away as she put on each item of clothing.

Angela knew without a doubt Rafe's eyes were glued to her body, watching as she went through her antics. By sheer force of will, she prevented herself from turning to see how he was handling her little floor show.

One thing was certain: There was no need to face him in order to know the effect she was having on him. She imagined how hard he was and could barely keep from laughing out loud. *This should be fun*, she thought. *He wants to ignore me, let him try.* She gave her behind an extra wiggle, pulling the nylons up slowly. She heard a low guttural moan and laughed deep in her throat. He would not ignore her, of that she was positive.

"I'm ready." She turned. "Are you?"

Fire and ice greeted her. A salacious grin spread across Rafe's face and he turned from her and waited for her to pass. A swat on her behind meant to make her turn startled her.

"That's for playing with me."

"I thought you liked it when I played with you?"

"Not with my feelings, Angel, *mi amor.* You're evil, do you know that?"

"Yes," she answered. "I've tried telling you that *angel* doesn't fit." Her breath caught in her throat at the look in his eyes.

"Let's go and eat, Angel."

Two hours later, Angela walked back into the suite with Rafe. A nice glow filled her; she was more than ready to accept the pampering he had provided.

"Give me a minute," she called out to him as she made her way to the bathroom. But he came behind her, kissing her senseless.

Angela stood looking in the mirror, looking at Rafe behind her, holding her, kissing her. It was an erotic image that had been held at bay since their arrival.

"Rafe," she murmured.

"Not yet."

"Why?"

"Look around you, Angel."

She did as he asked, laughing, wondering how on earth she could have missed the huge tub filled with water. She moved from Rafe and dipped in a finger. It was hot. This was definitely well orchestrated. She noticed a huge bowl of fruit and cheese perched on the wide back of the Jacuzzi and another filled with chocolates. Rose petals floated on the water. There was a television descending from the ceiling and positioned for the bather.

Unless they were showing erotic movies, Angela couldn't imagine sitting there watching it, not with the way Rafe was watching her. Anyway, he was the only thing on her mind at the moment.

Her skin burned with the trail of kisses he laid and she shivered in his arms.

"This can wait, Rafe."

He drew back.

"Not you, this." She said pointing to the tub.

"Wouldn't you like to soak, Angel?"

"Yes, but there are other things I'd like more."

"I'd like to bathe you," he insisted, pulling at the zipper at the back of her dress, running his hand down her back over the lace of her bra.

She watched him undress her in the mirror, finding the picture strangely riveting. Angela had never thought of herself as an exhibitionist but she couldn't tear her eyes away, not even when the one expensive dress she owned slid to the floor. She remained where she was, waiting for him to take the bra from her shoulders. When he slid down to his knees she trembled and closed her eyes.

His lips were pressed against the silk of her stockings and he peeled them from her legs with his lips. His hands cupped her butt as he used his teeth to tease the silk panties away from her skin. Angela opened her eyes, expecting to be embarrassed by the image. She wasn't.

Instead, she watched fascinated as Rafe's dark head moved downwards, slowing as he continued taking the panties from her hips. His mouth lingered at the juncture of her thighs and she heard him groan, but he continued. The juices from her body now ran freely down her legs and she sagged involuntarily against him. His touch was filling her with desire.

Unexpectedly he came up, lifted her into his arms and plunged her into the water.

"Rafe."

He didn't answer. His green eyes, darkened by his passion, blazed with heat. His hand trembled against her skin as he rubbed her with a cloth and she moved away from his touch.

"No."

He glanced up, his vision clouded by lust, not understanding what it was that she wanted.

"If you want to bathe me you will do it from inside the tub," Angela whispered. She watched as a smile of understanding filled him and he rapidly peeled away his clothes and jumped unceremoniously into the tub, spilling water in his haste.

"I thought you would want to have the tub to yourself."

"Are you crazy?"

"My sisters thought it would be romantic."

TWO SIDES TO EVERY STORY

"So this was all your sisters' idea?"

"Yes, they all told me their fantasies."

"It's all nice, very nice," she amended, "but since this is for me, my fantasy is now fulfilled: to have you in the tub with me, not me alone. What's your fantasy?"

He grinned.

"That's going to be your reality. What's your fantasy?"

Raphael's fantasy was the wish that he could undo the past, his own and their combined one. There were many things in Raphael's life that he wished had never happened. Taking part in that gang war over two years ago was one of them. But that that been his job. He'd done nothing to be ashamed of. Still, if he was talking fantasy, he wished that the woman he loved would not judge him by the past.

Raphael pulled her close, resting his head on her back. In his fantasy the things that had made him a cop would have never happened.

"Rafe, don't you have any fantasies?"

"Yes," he murmured against her skin. "You're my fantasy." Then he pulled her around to face him and he looked at her with the intensity of his feelings. "I love you, Angel."

A lump formed in his throat. He'd not planned on telling her tonight. He'd wanted to wait until the end of their trip. "*Te amo,* Angel," he couldn't help repeating. He'd never before said those words and for some strange reason they now wanted to burst out of him.

"I love you, Angel," he repeated for the third time. "*Te amo,*" he said, this time softer. She'd not answered. He took her face into his hands and kissed her lips, her eyes, her hair, pain welling in his chest with the need to do something other than look at her face. He'd been wrong. She didn't love him as he'd thought.

"I know you love me, Rafe," Angela suddenly whispered back.

He crushed her to him. He would not ask; it had to be freely given. He held her tighter, wishing he'd waited, that he'd not said it, not yet, not until she was ready to say it back to him. Damn, he'd ruined everything.

"Rafe."

"Yes," he answered.

"*Te amo.*"

"You love me?" Raphael asked. "You're not just parroting me, saying it to be nice?"

"I wouldn't tell you that I love you to be nice."

"It would be rude if you didn't. You sure you don't just want to not be rude?"

"Has being rude ever been a problem with me?"

"No," he laughed. "You've never had a problem with being rude. Do you really love me?" He held her chin with his finger. "Don't lie, Angel."

He felt her shiver, saw her eyes veiled, unreadable, her lips curving gently into a smile. Then her eyes cleared as if she'd fought some inner demon.

"*Te amo*, Rafe Remeris."

The demon had been destroyed and Rafe had won; his angel loved him.

"*Te amo,*" she repeated.

"You're learning," he whispered. "Welcome to my world." Then he took her lips between his teeth and bit down, causing her to flinch just a little, but as she did so, her lips opened and he was in. He was no longer waiting for her to grant him her favors. She loved him and he was taking his pleasures from her just as she would take hers from him. They were now in a relationship. They had love.

He sucked on her tongue, tasting the sweetness from the wine and the tartness of the key lime dessert they'd had at dinner. He deepened the kiss, drawing on her essence. He wanted to lick away all but the taste of her, the sweet, sweet taste of the woman he loved. His hands roamed over her body and he groaned, feeling himself growing harder with each breath. His erection was pressing against her abdomen, jumping without even so much as a touch, wanting to be inside her.

Raphael looked at Angela's closed eyes, her writhing body, and went to his knees, stooping to lave her chocolate drop nipples with his tongue.

She smelled wonderful, all woman, all tantalizing softness. He was determined to lick every drop of that damn massage lotion from her body. He pulled one puckered breast into his mouth and held her firmly. She was so close to his body that not even the water in the tub could find a place to go. She moaned and he suckled her harder.

He positioned his body lower, raising her hips upward. He dipped his fingers into the wetness and pulled her closer as she tried to pull away.

"Rafe," she moaned and he ignored her, knowing that she knew what he was going to do, knowing that she didn't want him to. For some reason he couldn't fathom, she'd never allowed him to bring her fulfillment in that manner. Now all of that was over. She was his, and he was going to bring her satisfaction in every way.

"Rafe, no," she repeated and attempted to squirm away.

"Hush, Angel. You asked if I had a fantasy. This is it, to make love to you in every way possible. *Te amo,* Angel, every inch of you. And I want to taste you from bottom to top."

With that he dipped his head and tasted her. The hot water sloshed over them. He tasted the soapy water, the rose petals, then he tasted her and he continued tasting her until she cried out her pleasure. Even then he tasted her until her body went limp and she sagged in his arms, moaning low. Then he worked his way back up, kissing her thighs, nibbling on that little dimple on her belly, swirling his tongue over the crest of her mound, swooping down and back again. All the emotions they'd tried to deny in the beginning had built up in the weeks between them. It had now culminated in this moment of acceptance of their love.

It was done.

Angel was his.

Angela lay limp in Rafe's arms. It had happened so fast. He had ignited a fire in her and quenched it. The orgasm had taken her completely, making her weak with the release. She'd known it would be like this from the first time they'd made love and he'd attempted to taste her inner core. She'd pushed him away as the liquid fire from his tongue had threatened to consume her.

It had been bad enough that a man she hated made her burn with his touch. But they'd not loved each other. She couldn't give him the ultimate power over her, so she'd held back, always letting him go so far and no farther, and tonight he'd not allowed her to hold him at bay. He'd pushed on and taken her as if he had the right and he did. She'd given him that right. She'd told him she loved him.

Aftershocks of her climax continued to rupture through her. She'd never felt so naked, so vulnerable. Rafe was the first man she'd told she loved him. He wasn't the first man to make love to her in that fashion but he was the only man she'd known who would have the power to possess her. Angela didn't want to be possessed, but it was too late now.

"Open your eyes, Angel."

"No."

"Open your eyes, Angel, you belong to me now."

That was just what she was afraid of.

"Last warning."

"And then?" she asked.

In the space of a breath Angela was pulled beneath the water. Her eyes popped open and she sputtered, choking a little in her surprise. Then just as suddenly she was pulled upward and she sputtered this time indignantly, hitting out. Her legs were pulled from beneath her and she screamed out, laughing, "Stop it. Have you gone crazy?"

"Yes," he answered. "I've gone crazy. I'm crazy in love with you." He pulled her close to his body. "And you love me. That, Angel, is my fantasy."

"Hmm, I've never been a fantasy."

"You are now. For the first time in a very long time, Angel, I'm happy."

There was no need to tell his angel that he'd wrestled with his own demons, that he'd slain them and that it had been because of her, her love. The one thing he'd always thought he couldn't have, the one thing he never believed he deserved. Every question he'd ever had about himself as a man had been answered here in this tub in his angel's arms. He was a man and she was his woman. The past was the past; it would remain dead and buried. He had his angel.

He pulled her into a kiss, playing along when she attempted to push him beneath the water, only rising up to kiss her again. They were acting like children, splashing water over each other and the floor. He knew they were both relishing the freedom, letting the water wash away their fears.

He reached for the soap and bathed her as he'd promised and she bathed him in return, her eyes soft and brown, turning liquid with desire, with fire, with passion.

Raphael held still as she climbed on him, taking him into her body, riding him as if she had the right. She did. He'd given it to her. He loved her. He held her close, watching her face, her look of total abandon as she rode toward her orgasm, bringing him along. He forced himself not to control things, not to take over. This was her show and she wanted to be the emcee. He saw her face twist, felt her muscles tighten and he couldn't resist pushing upward, stabbing away at the last restraint.

She came then, falling on him, all tightened muscles, and he caught her scream of surrender in his mouth and continued plunging into her until her scream became his own and his own orgasm shook him to his core. He was gripping her so tightly that her tiny moan of pain finally pierced through the fog his brain had become and he eased the pressure.

"I'm sorry, Angel," he whispered. "We've made love so many times but it was never like this."

"That's because we never made love," she answered back.

"I did," he insisted.

"I said we, Rafe."

"So this is how it is when you're in love?"

"I guess. I've never been in love."

"Never?" Rafe asked her, surprised at her answer.

"Never."

"Neither have I. How are we going to know what's normal and what's not?" he grinned. "What if we're going about this all wrong? I think we're going to need lots of practice."

He grinned again, feeling her heat, feeling himself harden again. He couldn't believe it. Finally his famed Latin blood was proving useful.

He turned her back to him, then eased her over his shaft, groaning as she slid downward. He crushed her to him, laying his head on her back, cupping her breast with one hand, the other slipping between them to rub her mound. He felt tremors through his entire body, felt his own hard flesh pulsing and pounding, felt the slickness of the two of them as he attempted to touch her in places that he wasn't already filling. *There was no room*, he thought proudly, and just continued with his trying. She seemed to liked it.

A roar burst loose from his throat and he thrust upwards again a moment after he'd felt her own orgasm happening. He wanted to join her, for them to experience it together, and they did.

They both lay panting for the longest time, unable to be cooled by the now tepid water. Rafe breathed in and out, his breathing rough, his throat raw with his passion.

"Never tell me you're not an angel. You just took me to heaven," Raphael whispered, licking the back of her neck. His gut was still twisting from the power of their combined orgasm.

"I saw heaven with you also, Rafe. But I could swear you were the angel that took me there."

Raphael laughed at the thought. He'd never told his angel that his full name was Raphael not Rafe. He was named for an archangel. Before he'd always hated that. Now, well hell, it tickled him.

He eyed the bowls of fruit and chocolate. After that meal they'd had he didn't think he'd be hungry again for a month, but he was starving; he needed more energy for the things he had planned. He was going to make love to his angel all night long and he couldn't very well do that without some nourishment.

He pulled the drain from the tub. "It's getting cool," he said to the question in her eyes. "I like this tub. I think I'd like to stay for awhile if you don't mind."

"I don't mind," Angela answered, settling herself over him, lying against him. She smiled at the look in his eyes. This look she also knew.

"You want some of the food, don't you?"

"How did you know?"

"When have we ever . . . when have we ever made love," she said, admitting that it had been more than sex for her, "and you didn't want to eat?" She grinned.

"I can't help it, you deplete me." He laughed, replugging the tub and refilling it with warm water.

"That's supposed to be 'complete' you."

"It is, but it's also true that you deplete me," he mocked, reaching for a piece of fruit with one hand and the remote with the other.

It was then Angela knew the tub was never meant to be just a woman's fantasy. This was definitely meant for a man: food, television and a willing woman. What more could any man ask? She smiled to herself and cuddled with Rafe as he nibbled her between bites of food. He'd stolen more than her heart. *He's stolen my soul,* she thought as she fell asleep.

CHAPTER 17

Four nights of passion and now they were down to their last night. There was a subtle change in everything. There was a possessiveness in Rafe that Angela had not noticed before. Now whenever they were in the hotel, if she so much as spoke to another man she could hear him growling low in his throat. He kept her glued to his side. At first it had been romantic and amusing.

But when they woke in the morning, this fairy tale would be over and they would both be returning to reality. She had no plans to allow him to control her life. She needed to take back some measure of control before they left, and she knew just the way to do it.

"What's taking the waitress so long with the check?" Rafe looked at Angela. "I've asked for it three times."

"The check has been taken care of."

He frowned and she saw the curiosity and anticipated his questions. "You?"

"Yes," she replied.

"Why?"

"I wanted to."

"Angel, I think it's a little more than that. I think you're trying to send me a message."

"Maybe I am."

"Why are you trying to ruin a perfect trip?"

"It's not the trip I'm trying to ruin. I'm just paying for dinner. I told you before we made plans that I would pay my own way."

"And you knew that was never going to happen."

"I know, but I can treat you to dinner."

"Why didn't you tell me at the beginning that you wanted to treat?"

"Because the last few days you've turned into the macho Latino, glaring at guys if they so much as look in my direction."

"Latino?"

"Remember the conversation we had about stereotypes? We both agreed they were there for a reason, that at least some of the things prove to be true. You're doing all the things my brother said that you would."

"And I wouldn't do this if I were Black?"

Angela cringed. She really didn't know. She'd never allowed any man to get so close. She thought about it for a moment. Yes, Black men did the same thing.

"Okay, I'm sorry about that. But I can't deal with your thinking you have a right to control who looks at me."

"And you think that's because I'm Puerto Rican?"

"If it's not, then why is it that you've changed?"

"Tell me something, Angel. When have we ever gone out together? You're my woman now. I'm in love with you and you said that you love me. Do you think I want men looking at you as though you're available?"

"You don't have the right to make that decision for me."

"I have every right."

"How do you think that?"

"I love you."

"Love doesn't give you that right."

"Then tell me what does?"

"Nothing, Rafe. You don't have the right ever to tell me what to do."

He dipped his head and glared at her before looking away. "And if a woman comes up to me and tries to hit on me right in your face, how are you going to react?"

"I'll let you handle it."

"Right."

"You don't believe me?"

"Hell no, I don't believe you. When the waitress smiled at me you ran your foot up the side of my leg to let me know that I was yours."

Angela stopped fuming. She hadn't known that Rafe had even been aware that she'd seen the waitress flirting with him. The fact that he'd answered her in Spanish was something else that had pissed her off.

"I didn't glare at her," Angela insisted.

"You didn't have to. I told her I wasn't interested."

"In Spanish?"

"In Spanish."

"Why?"

"Because there was no need to embarrass her."

"But you chose to embarrass me?"

Rafe cocked his head. "How did I embarrass you, Angel?"

"The waitress spoke English, she took our order in English, yet she purposefully spoke to you in Spanish and you answered her the same. I find it rude and disrespectful when a person that can speak English speaks another language in front of people that don't understand it. I told you that before and you promised you wouldn't do it."

"Sometimes it's necessary, Angel."

"I disagree."

"How did this get around to being my fault? I was talking about your paying the bill. You're getting me off the track. I wanted to know why you're trying so hard to push me away after we've had such a good time."

"I don't want you misunderstanding our relationship. I'm not yours to own or to possess and before we get home I need to clear that up."

"You've cleared it up, Angel. Now let me clear this up for you. You will never do it again. You will not pay my way. I am a man. I don't need a woman to pay for me. And I don't need anyone to think they will have my favors for money."

"What are you talking about?" Angela asked, curious that he'd said such a thing. She saw his eyes darken, saw a flash of pain, and stopped, deciding not to pry.

Rafe closed his eyes and counted silently to ten. He'd said too much. He understood what Angela had done, that she was afraid of their love and was trying hard to maintain herself separately from him. It was just that her paying for dinner had brought about memories that had no place in this hotel, no place in their relationship. Loving his angel had stirred more than his passion. It had stirred memories that were best left in the past.

They lay in the bed, each turned away. The argument from dinner lingered between them, filling the bed with ice. Raphael groaned to himself, wishing he'd not reacted so violently to Angela paying for a simple meal.

"*Te amo*, Rafe."

He turned and wrapped his arms around her, the fear receding as he said a prayer of thanks that she loved him still.

"I'm sorry, baby, tonight wasn't all about you."

"I got that feeling. What was it, Rafe? What made you go off like that?"

"Not now, Angel. It has no place in our bed. It was just a memory, one that shouldn't have interrupted us."

"Can't you tell me?"

He hugged her close. No, he couldn't tell her that before loving her he'd doubted his very manhood. Yes, there were certain things Latin men prided themselves on and that was one of them. There was no need to tell her she'd dispelled all of his doubts without knowing it. He didn't want to see the look of shame or pity in her brown eyes. And if she hated him because of it, that brown would turn again to that iced topaz that he hated. No, this was one memory that he would bear alone.

He made love to her as if his very life depended on it. He wanted to seal their love, for nothing to come between them. Raphael didn't want it to end when they returned home. And he wanted her to feel the same.

He suckled her, nibbled her skin, felt her heat and rejoiced. Her nails clawed at his back, her legs gripped him around the waist, holding him firmly to her. Raphael looked in her eyes, saw the fire, and he shook with the knowing. The fire was for him. When they came together he refused to let her go. They were one. She belonged to him whether she wanted to acknowledge it or not, and he belonged to her.

—ɷ—

"Cassie Williams, check again," Angela said, frantic. "My name has always been on the list. You've frisked me enough times to know that something has to be wrong." Panic began to creep in on her as she wondered if somehow it had been found out that all this time she'd been using a fake name and fake identification.

The surly guard looked again, then leered at her. "There's nothing wrong. The prisoner had you removed from his list of visitors."

She didn't believe it. Adrian didn't want to see her. A lump formed in her throat and she forced the tears back from her eyes. She would not cry, not here in this place. She caught one or two people staring at her, knowing more than likely they thought she was being shunned for a new girlfriend. She walked back toward the exit. She'd rather that be the case. It would be so much better than being shunned by her blood.

She walked out into the parking lot wondering why he'd gone to such lengths. She'd told him that she would be out of town. Simone had visited him for her. Angela knew without a doubt that her cousin had kept her promise.

This time the ride from the prison seemed to take forever. Angela couldn't prevent the tears that slid beneath her lashes, wetting her face and leaving a trail of salt. She swiped at her eyes with the back of her hand. She'd have to make it up to Adrian. She'd have to spend the next few days doubling her efforts. She ignored the tightening in her gut, the knowledge that her work had piled up and she had three deadlines waiting. It didn't matter. Although she'd done her best to find something to help her brother, nothing had worked. She'd just have to work harder.

Adrian didn't believe that she had done her best. She knew that was the reason he'd taken her name off the visitors list. He thought she'd traded him in for Rafe. She hadn't. She'd have to find a way to make it work, to show her brother that being in love would not interfere with her helping him. At the same time she'd prove to the entire family that Rafe was not a dirty cop. He was one of the good guys. He had to be. She wouldn't love him if he weren't.

"Simone, what happened? I was gone only five days, but Adrian took my name off his visitors list. Did he say anything to you?"

"Yeah, he said he was going to. I didn't believe him."

"But why, and why didn't you call me? You had my number for emergencies."

"I didn't think it was an emergency."

"My brother not wanting to see me? You didn't think it was an emergency?"

"No, I didn't. You haven't had anyone in your life in all this time. I thought you deserved to enjoy yourself. Look, I know he's your brother and that you love him, but he's a jerk and a big crybaby."

"He's in prison. What do you want him to do?"

"Stop acting like it's everyone's fault that he's there and grow up."

Angela looked at her cousin, glaring at her. "Did you say anything to him about who I was with?"

"Yes, I told him that you had a boyfriend."

"Did you tell him that it was Rafe?"

"He already knew."

"How do you know?" Angela asked, fear simmering just below the surface as she remembered Adrian's warning.

"He asked me if it was that cop. I assumed you had told him, so I said yes. I mean, how else would he know about it? You okay?" Simone asked. "If it were me I wouldn't worry about it. I'd make his ass beg me to come back. You're letting Adrian blackmail you. You all are and it pisses me off. He walks around that prison like he thinks he's a big deal. He's got two more years; I'd let him do them. Maybe it'll knock some sense into him."

If Angela ever needed her cousin it was now. But she couldn't tell her that she was afraid, that Adrian had threatened Rafe. If Simone had her way, her brother would spend the rest of his life behind bars and that Angela didn't want. His being there was killing their parents and putting a strain on her relationship with her brother.

"Simone, I have to go. I have to keep looking. I think I'm getting close."

"To what? You know Adrian was involved. I know you do."

She couldn't listen, not now. "I'll see you," Angela said, and headed out the door. She drove home and spent the next five hours combing the streets, hoping to find a tidbit that would be the next piece to the puzzle.

She worked every hour that she could, barely making her freelance deadlines, putting Rafe off, telling him she was swamped. Her heart ached. She wanted to see him, to hold him, to feel alive in his arms, but her fears kept him at arm's length. She wanted him safe.

She should have known that wasn't going to go over too big with Rafe. Within five days of returning home he was ignoring her pleas that she was busy. He was at her door and she had no choice but to let him in.

"Hey," she said, avoiding his eyes.

"Hey yourself. I've missed you," Rafe said.

"I've missed you too."

"Is that why you haven't picked up the phone and called me, or why you won't return my calls? And better yet, is your missing me the reason you won't let me come over?"

Damn. He'd told himself that he wasn't going to do that, that he was going to play it nonchalant, pretend that she hadn't hurt him, that he wasn't bothered by her refusal to see him. But something had happened the moment she opened the door. He was overcome with wanting her. His need for her to love him tightened painfully across his chest and he wanted her to throw her arms around him, remind them both that they had admitted they were in love.

He stood in the center of the room biting his lips, almost wishing that he'd stuck by his vow not to become involved emotionally with a woman. It never failed; they changed your life forever.

She grinned at him.

He changed his mind. Loving her was worth the pain.

"I had to make up for all the work I've missed and I had to go out and get some leads. I'm not having a lot of luck," Angela confessed.

"Oh, I thought it was me."

"What are you talking about?"

"Well, I thought it was possibly the romance of the hotel, that you'd been in the moment, and said things that you now regret."

Angela walked toward him. "Things like what? I don't recall doing anything that I regret except maybe trying to buy you dinner." She stopped an inch from his face. "*Te amo.* That's not going to change."

She pressed her body next to his, her lips so close that her breath warmed him, then sent chills he couldn't explain. That had never happened.

Not wasting time thinking about it, he reached for her. "*Te amo,* Angel, and that will never ever change." He kissed her, the loneliness of being without her the past five days receding, replaced by the memories of their five nights of passion at the Dells.

Her hands were suddenly on him, in his pants, and in the blink of an eye he was inside her. They came quickly, as though an urgent need pushed them. They'd not bothered to lie down; he'd merely entered her where they stood and taken his pleasure as she took her own.

"You did miss me, didn't you?" Angela moaned as she sank against his chest.

"I see you missed me too." Rafe laughed. And I'm glad to know it."

"What did you think?"

"I thought you wished you hadn't said you love me."

"Do you regret telling me?" Angela whispered.

"Are you kidding? I planned that whole trip to tell you that I loved you. I wanted to make everything right, to share my life with you. I want you to know everything about me, why I became a cop, what I've done since becoming one. I want you to know everything."

"Are there secrets you've been keeping from me?"

She was running her tongue across his lips, pressing even closer, and he could feel himself getting hard again. The quickie had been just that, a quickie. She was backing away from him, teasing him, making him want her even more.

Raphael was painfully aware of his arousal. His erection was straining against the zipper of his jeans, begging for release, begging to be buried in the one woman who could crush his dream. He watched Angela as she took another step away from him.

"Don't even think about it, Angel," he said softly. "No more games."

"Was I playing games?" Angela asked.

"You were," he answered.

The deceptively soft voice was laced with steel. Angela stared at the green eyes that were holding her gaze. A shiver claimed her, running down her spine and settling in her toes, only to start the journey in reverse in a matter of seconds. She started walking back toward him. "Are there any secrets?"

"Secrets can wait," he growled, lifting her in his arms and taking her to the bedroom. This time they would do it right. He would make love to her as an angel deserved. He would make sure that she saw heaven again; then he would tell her.

TWO SIDES TO EVERY STORY

The blinding sun streaming through the window woke Rafe and he glanced at the clock in alarm. *Oh shit.* He had less than twenty minutes to get to work and he had to go home and change.

"Angel, wake up." He bent and kissed her eyes. "I have to go." He dashed into the shower, making it short and sweet. He was out in under two minutes, putting his clothes on and rushing out the door to his own apartment to change into his uniform. The commander would have his ass if he showed up late for roll call. "See you tonight, Angel. How about I take you to dinner?" he called over his shoulder, not giving her time to answer before leaving.

CHAPTER 18

Angela stayed right where she was, sated from the night of passion. She knew she should get up and get moving, go out, get clues, but she didn't want to budge. She thought about Rafe's words as he left her apartment. This would be their first real date. This would be their real beginning.

But before she could get to that she had to try and make things right with her brother. She called her parents. She knew Adrian had not taken her off the list without telling them.

"Angela," her daddy said after taking the phone from her mother, who'd barely said hello to her. *Angela?* This was serious if her father wasn't calling her *baby.*

"Hey, Daddy, what's going on? Are you mad at me or something?"

"Do I have a reason to be?"

"I don't think so."

"That's a matter of opinion."

"Daddy, don't do this. Just spit it out, tell me what's got you with a bug . . ." Angela blew out a breath, knowing not to finish that sentence. "He called you?"

"You talking about your brother?"

Angela sighed. She no longer had to guess. They knew. "Yeah. Adrian took me off his visitors list."

"He told us that it was dangerous for you to see him. He said that you're dating a cop and he's afraid that you might give him some information that would hurt him."

"He really thinks that I would do something to hurt him?"

"Are you dating a cop?"

"Yes, but how is that hurting Adrian?"

"You know how much this family has been hurt by the Chicago police. I can't believe that you would do this."

"I didn't do this to hurt you. I didn't do it to hurt any of you. You told me I should live my life. You said I deserved it. Don't I deserve to have someone love me?"

"The only one you could find to love you was a cop?"

Her father's voice was filled with disgust, making her want to cry. "I didn't fall in love with him because he's a cop."

"Who is he?"

"His name's Rafe Remeris."

"He's Mexican?"

"No, he's Puerto Rican. What difference does it make?"

"Your brother said a Spanish cop beat the shit out of him and you're asking me what difference does it make?"

"It wasn't Rafe."

"How do you know?"

"I know."

"Have you asked him?"

"I told him what happened to my brother. He would have told me if he'd been involved."

"Dream on. Listen, I'll tell your brother to put your name back on the list and you can go and try to sell this to him. You don't have to worry about Adrian anymore. Your mother and I already made our decision and this time you're not talking me out of it. We already put the house on the market."

"Daddy!"

"Don't *daddy* me. Someone has to stand by your brother. I always thought you would, that being a part of this family meant something. But I see the first chance you got to show what family means, you showed us. Too bad it wasn't what I thought it would be. I was always so proud of you. Now . . ."

His voice trailed off and this time the tears came. "Daddy, I am loyal. I have done nothing but help Adrian. I moved into the Pilsen neighborhood to help him. Didn't he tell you that or did he forget?" Angela asked angrily.

"He told us that you had met this cop and moved into the Pilsen area so that you could be with him. He told us that you went on vacation with him. So Adrian took your name off the list. And I can't say that I blame him, not after you lied to all of us."

"Daddy, I'll go and see Adrian. He's just mad at me. When you go again he'll tell you the truth. I was doing all of this to help him."

Angela was shocked her brother had lied and had turned everything that she had tried to do to help him into a lie. Now her parents doubted her intentions. "Simone knows the truth," she said weakly.

"Simone would tell us whatever you tell her to say. She and Adrian fight all the time. You think I would believe what she has to say about your brother? She's always made it known that she doesn't believe him. Look, you do what you have to do. You're right, it is your life, and I hope you're happy. I hope you can live with yourself for lying to us and for betraying your brother. If that cop is more important than your family, then go for it."

Her father hung up the phone, leaving Angela shocked and dazed. Five days, she'd only taken five days for herself and this was the result. She couldn't believe all that she'd given up for her brother. All her time, not to mention almost every dime she made, went into something for his benefit. She had no idea why he needed so much money in prison, and she hadn't questioned it. She just put it in his account.

Angela couldn't help the anger that was now claiming her. The things she'd done for her brother she'd done willingly. Still, she'd paid a high price to help him and now to have it made into a lie . . .

She took a pillow from her rented sofa and threw it against the wall in frustration. She hated the sofa. In fact she hated every piece of furniture that she'd rented. She'd done it all for her brother and for no other reason. She'd given up her home, taking on the expense of another apartment in the Pilsen community as Adrian had asked her to do.

The whole crazy plan had been his scheme, not hers. But when he'd said he thought it would help, Angela had readily volunteered. Adrian had been the one who'd told her not to tell their parents. He'd suggested she lie to spare them the worry and she'd agreed. Now he'd turned on her.

For a moment she hated him and for that moment her eyes were clear and she saw in him the same things that Simone had pointed out. He wasn't the innocent victim that she'd championed for the past two years. An innocent person wouldn't have destroyed her so thoroughly. He'd done it all deliberately, all because she'd defied him and fallen in love.

Well, she wasn't going to cry. She'd come here to do a job. And if there really was information, which she truly doubted at this point, she would find it. Now there was more to consider. There was the possibility of her parents' selling their home and of something happening to Rafe.

Angela grabbed her purse and attacked the streets of Pilsen like a commando. Although her Spanish was a tad better, for some unknown reason the people that she ran into were speaking English. She made a connection and soon was talking freely with a group of women that knew Teresa Cortez. One said that she'd moved to México. Angela didn't know if it was true but if so, it would answer why she'd had such a hard time finding her.

"I know Teresa."

Angela turned around. "You know her?" Angela asked, surprised that the woman was speaking to her so freely.

"Yes, I know her. She was dating this guy who went to prison. Since then lots of people have been looking for Teresa. I think she ran off with a lot of money."

"Do you know where she got the money?"

"I don't know. I think it belonged to her boyfriend."

"The guy in prison?"

"Yeah, him. Someone told me that she was scared that he was going to try and kill her."

"Kill her?"

"Yes, I heard it had to do with drugs. If you want, I could take you to her brother's house. He'd be able to tell you more."

The hairs on the back of Angela's neck stood up and for some strange reason she didn't trust the woman who was speaking. She'd lived in the community for several months now, and no one knew anything. In the past week clues had been coming much faster than they should have. Now without even knowing her, this woman was telling her more than she needed to know and was offering to take her to the woman's brother.

"Thank you. I can't go right now but if you would give me your number I would appreciate it."

"Tell me, why are you needing all of this information?"

"I'm doing a story about the Chicago police and I hope to get some things changed. I heard about this big gang fight a couple of years ago and I've been working on it. Someone happened to mention that Teresa Cortez would have some inside information.

"I heard that some of the men that went to prison had been set up. It happens too often and I want to see if I can make a difference, maybe help some of the families. If enough noise is made, it's possible that someone will try and fix it." Angela smiled. "I'll be willing to pay for any information."

She pulled a twenty from her wallet and thanked the woman, reaching for the torn piece of paper with the woman's number on it and wishing that for once she could ask Rafe's advice.

She turned to pay for her items and saw the women she'd been talking to earlier look away quickly as though they no longer wanted to talk to her. Something was wrong. All of her instincts were screaming that warning at her. Getting information was what she'd moved to Pilsen for but it had come too easy.

Angela pasted a smile on her face and walked out of the store, walking in a different direction than her apartment. The feeling that had come over her was fear. She didn't like it, never had, but she realized it was there for a reason, to warn her against rash movement.

For two hours Angela roamed the community, this time not asking questions, just taking pictures, pretending to be the reporter that she'd portrayed herself to be, hoping that somehow she would be believed.

At last she felt safe enough to return home. Despite her misgivings, she felt the information was true. Something had nagged at her from the moment her brother had concocted this scheme.

Money, she thought. Could this all be about money? And if so, who was the Black guy that Teresa was dating? Had the woman really come into a large sum of money and taken off? Either way she had something she could tell her brother and gauge his reaction. She'd tell him that she'd tried and had hit a dead end, that the woman was gone and she sure as hell wasn't following her out of the country.

Angela checked her watch. Rafe would be picking her up soon. Their first date, she thought, and this nonsense with Adrian and her parents wasn't going to ruin it. He had already doubted that she'd meant it when she said she loved him. She was not going to have him doubt her again. Her family was already angry. They could remain angry until after her date with Rafe. It would serve them right.

Rafe was watching Angela. Something was wrong. He'd tried to ask her about it but she had been evasive. He wondered if somehow she'd discovered his secret on her own. But he doubted it. She wasn't angry at him or disappointed; she was preoccupied and sad. He'd done nothing to make her sad. At least not yet, he thought.

"*Que paso?*"

"Nothing."

"You understood what I asked?" Raphael said in stunned surprise. Angela blinked. "I guess I did. I'm not sure. Say it again."

"*Que paso?*"

"What's the matter?" she repeated. "Yes, I understood." She smiled, then stopped as the waitress approached the table and began talking rapidly to Rafe. She frowned, ignoring that he said *excuse me* to her before continuing his conversation.

She heard him say *pollo* and knew he was ordering chicken. She heard *arroz* and knew it was rice. Still it irked her. And made her feel guilty. She didn't want to give up either her family or her heritage for Rafe.

Rafe watched the iced topaz return. *This was going to be a long night*, he thought. They had both chosen to make loving harder. He shrugged his shoulders and looked hard at her. "We're in a Spanish restaurant. What did you think they were going to speak?"

"What if I had come in here alone? Are you saying they wouldn't have been able to take my order?"

"Why are we fighting? It seems if we're apart for a few hours something happens. Why don't you tell me what it is, because I don't know what the hell we're fighting about."

"Neither do I," Angela answered honestly, then turned to watch a young mother comfort her child. "It's okay, *poppi*. You don't have to eat that," she heard the mother say to her child.

A lump formed in her throat. "We're so different, Rafe."

"I know," he answered. "I'm a man and you're a woman."

"It's more than that. I don't like being out with you and not knowing what you're saying half the time. Sure, I can learn the language but why should I have to? I'm not in a foreign country. This is America. Why can't everyone that comes here speak English?"

"I thought you didn't have a problem with me being Spanish?"

She looked again at the mother and child. "I don't, I just don't understand."

"I told you why mothers call their children *poppi*. It just means that she loves him. It's no big deal."

"But it is. I didn't think it would be," Angela whispered as tears slid beneath her lashes. It wasn't Rafe's fault that her family wasn't speaking to her or that she actually liked to hear the young mother saying *poppi* to her son as she comforted him.

It was just that now it seemed that she only had Rafe in her life and it frightened her that there were some parts of his world that she didn't share or fully understand. She knew for a fact that their religions were different. She wasn't changing hers for anyone, not even him. The more she thought about it, the more it seemed that they should stop before it went any further, while they could still call a halt.

He touched her hand; then the pad of his finger slid up her cheek and she burned, burned with wanting him. It was already too late. For better or for worse it was too late to call a halt.

"Angel, if you want to stop loving me, then do so now because I'm done with this. I'm Puerto Rican, I speak Spanish. I'm American, Angel, a citizen of this country just as you are. You're going to have to believe it when I tell you that I would never do anything to hurt you. I know how you feel about not understanding what I'm saying, and I'll make you a promise. Unless it's absolutely necessary I'll talk in English when you're around. And if not I'll tell you what was said. So tell me, have you changed your mind?"

"No."

"In that case this nonsense is over. I'm not going to put myself through it. This ends tonight. You've been in charge of our," he smirked, "I'll use the term loosely, you've been in charge of our relationship but that's over. No more."

"And who's in charge now?"

"Guess."

"Rafe?"

Raphael laughed. "I think I see the problem. Angela Reed, meet Rafe Remeris."

"What are you talking about? I know your name already."

"Ah, my angel, you don't know the real me." He smiled. "I guess it's not all your fault, is it?"

"Should I be scared?"

He laughed then, deep, rich and throaty, before pulling her into his arms. "Maybe you should be. Listen, I'm not trying to get into your pants," he leered. "I've already been there. I'm going for something much more important. I'm trying to get into your heart."

"You are in my heart."

"Not as deeply as I want to be."

"Rafe, I can't."

"And that's what I mean to change. I need you to trust me, trust that I won't hurt you."

"It's not myself I'm worried about. You're a cop, Rafe; my brother is a con. He thinks I'm going to tell you something that will hurt him. My parents think the same thing. He even went so far as to take me off of his visitors list. You can't promise me that if you found out information that would harm my brother you wouldn't use it."

"How could you think I would hurt anyone that you loved?"

"Rafe, I don't want to talk about this now. You're right, we're in a Spanish restaurant, you ordered in Spanish. I shouldn't let it bother me."

"You're changing the subject, Angel. That's not what's bothering you. Let me in. I know how much you love your brother. I know it has to be killing you that he doesn't want to see you. I remember how we met, you were coming from visiting him."

"I think the subject needs changing."

"I don't."

"I do, Rafe. We're still trying to figure us out. Just give me this one night, this one date. You promised. When we're done here I just want to go for a walk, arm in arm, pretend that we don't have any problems."

Rafe refused to let up. Angela was too important to him. He was tired of being her toy. He was a man and they needed to set boundaries now. If they didn't, when he told her the truth they wouldn't survive it. And come hell or high water he'd decided that he would tell her when they returned to her apartment.

And he would tell her before they made love. He wouldn't, couldn't, keep taking advantage of her in that manner. It would be with her having full knowledge of what he'd done before he made love to her again.

They argued through dinner and continued the argument out into the street. He wasn't going to let go of it.

CHAPTER 19

"I can't believe it; the slut is still with the cop."

"Why don't we just pop a cap in her ass?"

"I don't think her brother would like that."

"Who cares what he'd like? I think I'll do him a favor and get rid of his tramp of a sister. She's not loyal anyway. This cop beats the shit out of her brother and she screws him."

Raphael turned away from Angela, wishing he'd paid more attention to the two men who'd eyed them angrily as they passed. His mind had been only on Angela, on the fact that he would soon be telling her something that could tear them apart and keep them from becoming a couple.

Damn, he thought, his attention now on the men, knowing it was probably too late and feeling immense guilt that he hadn't done a better job of protecting her. It wasn't like him to be so unobservant. Now look what it had gotten them. He had only seconds to react but it seemed as if the world slowed down as he made his decision. He could either attempt to tackle the men or he could push Angela down and behind him, out of the way of the bullet that he knew would be coming. There was no choice. In less than the time it took to take his next breath Raphael yanked hard on Angela's arm and forced her down on the ground behind him. He blocked her body. Before either of them had a chance to think, Raphael felt the gunshot hit him. It stung like hell. The burning wormed its way through him, making him hot while at the same time chilling his blood. His blood. He noticed the red color staining his chest.

"Shoot her," the short Black guy said to the taller Hispanic. Raphael fell backwards, turning as he did so, determined to protect Angela.

"You're crazy, man. That's his sister. I'm outta here."

"We should at least kill the cop."

"We weren't supposed to kill him. It was only to be a warning."

Raphael was trying to will the pain away and not having much luck, not with Angela squirming beneath him. "Its okay, baby," he moaned, softly keeping his eyes on the men, covering her. His main concern was that she not be hit. The Black man sucked in his cheek, alerting Raphael to his intentions, and he turned his head slightly to avoid it. As he'd known he would do, the man spit on him, then turned from him and ran away. Raphael sighed, taking in a painful breath.

"They're gone," he said raising his body from Angela, reaching in his jacket for his cell, cursing himself for not having a gun. He'd promised Angela a normal date and it had almost gotten them killed.

Angela was screaming. He had to keep her safe, calm her down. He thought about this woozily as he felt his body slowly going into shock. It still wasn't safe for Angela and he couldn't pass out until he made sure she was safe. He flipped open his cell, punched in 911, and managed to say, "Officer down" and the street address. His eyes shifted toward Angela, and followed her gaze. Huge with fear, her eyes were glued to the spot on his chest that was oozing blood. "I'm okay, Angel," he managed in a shaky voice hardly more than a whisper.

"They shot you," Angela said in shock. "Why would they do that?"

Tears were raining down her cheeks and she felt disoriented. Then out of nowhere she knew what to do. She screamed out for help, reached for the scarf around her neck and pressed it against the hole. Using her left hand to press the makeshift bandage tightly against Rafe's wound, she cradled his head with her right arm. She would remain calm, do what she had to do. She was scared as hell but she couldn't do a thing about that. She knew he saw her fear and probably thought it was for herself. It wasn't. It had never been. Rafe had gotten shot to save her. And to think that a few minutes before they had been arguing about him being too macho, about him speaking in his native tongue. It all seemed so stupid now. If only she could go back in time. But she couldn't. Rafe had been shot and she couldn't undo it.

She watched as his eyes closed and she kissed the lids. She thought of the mother and child in the restaurant and what Rafe had told her about the purest form of love. She finally understood.

"Hold on, *poppi*," she crooned, "hold on."

Angela alternated between pacing and sitting in the hospital waiting room. She'd been questioned by the police several times and each time she'd dissolved in tears as she relieved the incident.

What information she'd given the police hadn't been of much use and she was aware of that. But now that she'd had time to think, to remember the words, every instinct in her screamed out that her brother was involved. Angela shivered from the fear of knowing. She thought of her parents' anger, believing she'd thrown her brother over for a man. If she told the police what she actually remembered, she knew without a doubt she would never be forgiven. She would have no family.

Tears continued to pour down her cheeks as she wrestled with the dilemma. She loved Rafe. She couldn't let the people who'd shot him get away with it. And then the nagging doubts would start over anew. She'd also heard the men say clearly that Rafe had beaten the shit out of her brother. She trembled, feeling ice all the way to her soul.

As she waited for news, she thought about Rafe's family. She didn't know anything much about them, she hadn't wanted to. Now she regretted that decision. They should be here at the hospital. If anything happened to him . . . She shuddered and felt the sting of still more tears.

Angela saw the doctor coming toward her and prayed harder. "Please, God, please," she moaned as the doctor stopped in front of her.

"He's out of surgery and doing fine. He's going to be okay. Luckily the bullet didn't hit any major organs," the doctor said.

Angela couldn't believe it. For a moment she thought she'd heard wrong. "You're not just saying that?" she asked. "When the ambulance got to him, he was unconscious."

"It looked much worse than it actually was."

Angela looked at the doctor, hearing his words, wanting to believe him, not knowing if she did. "The gunshot sounded so loud. I've never heard a gun up close. Was it one of those bullets that I've heard about?" She felt the shudder in her inner soul. "Was it a cop killer?"

"Actually I think that bullet is a myth, but I know what you're asking. I'd guess he was shot with a .22. That's a small gun," he explained. "They probably used that particular one because it's easy to conceal or the fact that it doesn't make as much noise. Whatever, it was lucky for him."

"It sounded loud to me."

"I'm sure it did, but believe me, a larger gun would have sounded even louder."

"Are you sure he's going to be okay? I mean, all that blood, and he was so cold."

"He lost a lot of blood, but he's going to be fine. Matter of fact, he's awake. I really shouldn't let you in but he's in such a state worrying about you that I think he'll rest easier if he sees you for a second."

"I can go in?" Angela asked.

"Just for a second. I don't want him excited; just let him know that you're here."

"How long before I can . . . before he can talk?"

"Give him a few hours. I want to make sure he's stable. I'll leave word with the nurses, don't worry. Now come on, I want to check on him again anyway."

Angela walked in the room, her eyes landing on the medical equipment. Rafe's eyes were closed and his skin color wasn't normal. She shuddered. It was her fault that he was lying in that bed.

She inched closer, staying behind the doctor until Rafe's eyes opened. She was at his side in a flash.

"Rafe."

"Are you okay, Angel?"

"I'm fine. Don't worry about me." She kissed his cheek, his forehead, squeezed his hand, and glanced in the direction of the doctor.

"Okay now, Officer Remeris, you have to get some rest. She can come back in a little while."

Rafe squeezed her hand and looked at her. "Are you going to stick around?"

"Of course," Angela answered, a little embarrassed that he'd even had to ask. "Where else would I go?" She kissed his lips as he drifted off. She looked at the doctor. "I'll be in the lounge waiting if you need me."

She returned to the waiting area and paced the family lounge for hours, trying not to think of her brother or his warning. He couldn't have had anything to do with Rafe's getting shot, he couldn't have. But she knew he had. She'd heard the men.

And for the first time in two years Adrian wasn't her primary concern. Rafe was. All this and her mind kept going back over dinner and the fact that she'd spent two hours fighting with him over what language he spoke.

Angela watched as the room filled with people. She heard them talking in rapid Spanish. Then she head them mention Raphael Remeris and she looked toward them. They had to be talking about Rafe.

"He's going to be okay," she volunteered.

She felt the chill as all eyes turned toward her. She saw the question in their eyes and she didn't know how to answer it. Who was she to Rafe? He loved her, she knew that much, but they didn't officially have a relationship. What they had was something that had begun because they couldn't figure out any way to not kill each other. They were on their first date trying to determine what it was they would be.

"Who are you?" a cold feminine voice finally asked.

"I'm Angela Reed. Rafe and I are friends."

"Rafe?" Angela licked her lips. Maybe they weren't talking about the same patient. The people gathered in the room appeared to have no idea who Rafe Remeris was.

"Do you mean Raphael?" a man that strongly resembled Rafe asked. "Raphael Remeris?"

"I think so," Angela answered, feeling embarrassed for the second time that night. "Officer Remeris."

"I'm his father." He glanced around the room. "We don't call him Rafe."

"I'm sorry."

"No need to be. Were you with him? What happened?"

Angela looked down when the same sense of panic that had claimed her earlier in the evening returned. "He was shot," she said hoarsely.

"Do you know who did it?"

"I talked to the police and I gave a description but I didn't know them." Her stomach knotted. No, she didn't know them but she was pretty sure she knew who'd sent them.

"You saw him, Raphael, I mean. Is he really okay?"

"His color wasn't so good, but the doctor did let me see him. He squeezed my hand and said a couple of words. He's strong."

A woman came to stand alongside Rafe's father. "I'm his mother. You're the woman he was supposed to bring to dinner, the one who tried to get him fired."

Angela tried to think of words to say but nothing came to mind. Rafe's father took his mother by the arm and pulled her away. He was talking so rapidly that she could only catch a word here and there, and that was that Rafe, Raphael, loved her. That she knew. But his family did not. His mother hated her and if she really knew what Angela had done, she'd hate her even more.

She glanced up, grateful that the doctor was back. He was watching her. She glanced around and noticed an older woman smiling at her.

"Ms. Reed, we're having a heck of a time keeping Officer Remeris immobilized. He's awake and he's still worried about you; he wants to make sure you're okay. Can you go in and see him for a minute?"

"I'm his mother. We don't know this woman. Why should she go in before us?"

"He wants her and I have to do what's good for my patient."

Angela followed the doctor. The hostile looks made the air vibrate. She wanted to tell his family that she was sorry, but sorry for what? That Raphael loved her? That he'd gotten shot trying to save her? That more than likely it was done deliberately because of her brother? How was she to say any of that to them when she could barely admit the truth to herself? Angela pushed open the door to the hospital room, steeling herself for the worst. By now Rafe had had time to remember.

"Are you really okay?" he asked the moment their eyes connected. She walked toward the bed. She'd expected him to be sleeping for some time yet. She definitely hadn't thought he'd be in any condition to talk to her, let alone worry about her. As she approached the bed she tried desperately to keep the tears from falling. He was staring at her.

"Did you get hurt?"

Her eyes followed his to the blood on her blouse. "No." She shook her head, not wanting to tell him that it was his blood. "You scared me," she said and took his hand.

"I'm sorry, I didn't mean to." Raphael smiled at her, seeing the worry in her eyes, seeing the tears. He didn't want her to cry. His mouth was dry and his body felt heavy as lead, but in spite of all that, Raphael could never remember feeling such joy. His angel was safe for the moment; that was all that concerned him.

"It's my fault," Angela whispered. "I'm so sorry."

"Baby, wanting to go for a walk is not your fault," he said, deliberately misunderstanding. "How can you be sorry for doing what I asked? I love you, Angel, now stop looking so sad."

He wanted to rub the tears away. Make love to her, hold her close, keep her safe, but right now he couldn't. He could hardly keep his eyes open. Angela's heart was hurting with the knowledge she possessed. She was not going to allow her brother to get away with what he'd done. She trembled as she thought of her parents and what they would do. It didn't matter. Her gaze swung toward the door as she heard the commotion outside and wondered what was going on. A nurse came in and put to rest her questions.

"His family's pitching a fit to get in here. Do you mind?" The nurse looked at Raphael. "We can't keep them out much longer," she added.

"Let them in or my mom will start throwing things." Raphael smiled and closed his eyes.

"But everyone can't stay, not all at once." The nurse nodded toward Angela. "She needs to leave."

Raphael opened his eyes. "No." He shook his head. "No, baby, you stay." He was gripping her fingers tighter. "You stay, Angel."

Angela looked down at Raphael, then up at the nurse. "Can I?" She stood motionless as the woman sighed, shrugged her shoulders and left the room.

Something deep inside Angela was telling her this was the wrong move, but she stayed. Raphael's mother and father came in. The man smiled at her but his mother glared and rushed to the bed. Her tears were mixed with anger, and her Spanish was spoken so rapidly that even if Angela had spoken more Spanish she wouldn't have been able to follow what his mother was saying.

"*Habla ingles, Mama,*" Raphael said, turning his head toward Angela. "This is Angela Reed."

Angela watched while the woman glared even more viciously, then turned her head.

"We met," his mother snapped.

"Mama, *ella me amo.*"

That Angela understood.

"You've had nothing but problems since you met her, Raphael. Look at you. You never got shot before."

Angela was wishing that he'd not bothered telling his family to speak in English. She'd rather not understand that they blamed her for his getting shot; she already blamed herself.

"Don't, Mama, I love her," Rafe repeated, squeezing Angela's fingers.

"Does she love you? She didn't even know your given name. She calls you Rafe. I haven't heard her do any of the talking. You're doing it for her. Can't she talk for herself?"

"You're glaring at her. You think she's going to talk now? She's been through a lot tonight. Leave her alone. I can answer your question because I know the answer. Yes, she loves me. *Ella me amos.*" Raphael answered, looking at Angela, knowing that she'd understood.

Angela didn't dispute him nor did she say yes. It wasn't the time, not with them glaring at her. She wondered if he'd heard what the men said, if he knew she was the reason he was lying in the bed. She wondered if he'd love her when he remembered. She looked down at him, saw the way he looked at her. *No,* she thought, *he had apologized for the walk.*

He beat her brother, now she's screwing him. A shudder went through her entire body. It couldn't be true. She couldn't know these things about the two men in her life in the very same night. Rafe was staring at her. He'd risked his life to save her. What did she do now?

Angela stayed close to the bed, trying to remain unobtrusive, trying to pretend she wasn't there while one by one Raphael's family came in to see for themselves that he was fine, then left. And one by one they glared at her as he admonished them to talk in English.

When the old woman who'd smiled at her outside in the lounge entered the room, Angela sensed a difference. She wasn't glaring. Instead, she was smiling warmly at her. Angela looked away as the woman talked with Rafe, noticing that he did not restrict her Spanish. Angela suspected they were talking about her.

"So Raphael didn't tell you his name?" The woman smiled. "He hates it," she grinned. "He was named for the angels. Archangel, our Raphael. And you're his angel, he tells me." She grinned. "That's why we don't call him Rafe. Raphael is an esteemed name."

Surprised at the woman's friendliness, Angela smiled back the first smile since Rafe had gotten shot. "Is everyone mad that I wasn't treating him like an angel?"

"You could say that. Raphael is very special." She leaned down and patted his cheek. "He is an angel." She whispered some words to Raphael, then smiled at Angela.

"She is my angel, Nellie. I love you, don't I, Angel?" he switched to English. Then back to Spanish. "*Te amo*, Angel."

Angela blushed at the endearment that he used in front of the woman, wondering why he was behaving so differently with her than he had with his family.

"Angel, this is Nellie, my *madrina*, my godmother. I call her *Titi* Nellie, Auntie Nellie," Raphael explained.

"Hello, Angela. I guess like Raphael's mother I also didn't hear your answer. Do you love Raphael?" the old woman asked.

Angela didn't answer.

The old woman continued smiling. "There's no need to answer, it's there in your eyes. Is your love as strong as your hate?"

"Nellie!"

"What?"

"Stop that," Raphael said, then lapsed into Spanish. Angela attempted to walk away but he held her hand even tighter. "This is one of those Spanish times," he said, holding her gaze.

"*No la asuste.*" Raphael said.

Angela watched while the old woman patted Raphael's cheek, and then smiled as she left the room.

"What was that you said to her?" she asked.

"I asked her not to scare you. I told her we were no longer fighting, that it had been a long time since you hated me. I told her not to worry, that you love me. You do love me don't you, Angel? You don't hate me any longer, do you?" he grinned.

"There was no way you said all of that. But I'm not going to call you on it. And to answer your question, I don't hate you. *Te amo.*" She bit her lip. "Is that why the rest of your family was giving me the evil eye, they know about our feuding?" She was trying to keep it light. Now was definitely not the time to say anything about what she'd heard.

"Of course they do, but don't worry," he grinned. "In time they will come to love you. Just as I do, Angel." Then he fell asleep.

Angela held onto Raphael's hand. She was trembling. She couldn't blame his family for their coldness. After all, she'd tried to get him fired. A relationship between them had been the last thing on either of their minds months before.

She looked toward the door. If his family hated her before, she wondered how they would feel when they learned that she was in part to blame for Raphael being shot.

Angela looked down at the man she loved, not wanting to believe that he was one of the cops involved with beating her brother. But why had the men said what they had?

Tears seeped beneath her lashes as she looked at her bloodied shirt. The picture of Rafe shoving her out of the way to protect her flashed before her. Would a man that would beat a man senseless risk his own life to save the woman he loved?

Angela wasn't sure and she had to be. She couldn't afford to make any more mistakes. Too many people were counting on her. She hated being forced to wait to see her brother but right now she wasn't leaving Rafe's side. She owed him that much. Besides, she didn't know if she was back on the visitors list. It was a good thing because the way she was feeling as she looked down at Rafe, she would be tempted to go to the district attorney herself with the new information.

CHAPTER 20

Three days after Raphael had been released from the hospital, Angela received word from her father that Adrian had restored her name to the visitors list.

Despite the hostilities of Rafe's family, she'd packed a small bag and stayed at his side, knowing he'd not gone to his parents' home because of her. She wasn't welcome there, that much was obvious.

She wasn't welcomed by them at his home either, but he wanted her there, so they had no choice but to tolerate her, as she in turn tolerated them. After all, she had more knowledge of the situation and believed some of their anger toward her was justified.

When the call came from her father, Angela anticipated the reaction of Rafe's family. She played it out in her head. Though they didn't want her around, they would most assuredly balk at her leaving, if only for a short time.

But this was something that couldn't wait. Angela had no intention of wasting time in confronting her brother.

She ignored the looks of Rafe's mother as she sniffed and asked her if she was leaving Raphael to fend for himself. That had almost made her smile. If Raphael so much as sighed, three or four people would be immediately at his side, pushing her away. *Fend for himself?* What a joke.

Angela's attempt to explain that she was only going to be gone a couple of hours had meant nothing to the woman. In the end it hadn't mattered. Angela had to go and see her brother.

"Don't worry, I won't be long," she assured Rafe and kissed him, ignoring the looks his mother tossed her way. She saw doubt creep into his eyes, but he didn't verbalize it. "I'll be back," she repeated and left.

Neither the sneer nor the overly long pat down bothered Angela. She had one goal in mind: to see if her brother had had anything to do with Rafe being shot.

She spotted his cocky long-legged walk before he even reached her. He didn't reach out to embrace her and she didn't move toward him. This wasn't a social visit.

"So what do you want?" Adrian asked the moment they had entered the common room.

"I want to know if you had anything to do with what happened."

"You're talking in riddles. I don't know what you're talking about."

"Don't be cute. The warning you gave me, did you do something?" she asked pointedly, looking around the room, trying to keep her voice low, still not wanting to be overheard.

"What are you talking about?" Adrian asked.

"Rafe, I'm talking about Rafe."

"The only thing I have to say on that subject is what I already said. If anything happens to him you have only yourself to blame."

"Why you . . ."

"Watch it, little sister."

Adrian stood and grinned at her. She couldn't believe it.

"I think it's time for you to leave now." He laughed. "Don't look so surprised. You're smart, I'm sure you have sense enough to do the right thing now." He walked away from Angela and after a moment she had no choice but to leave.

Adrian had warned her before Rafe was shot. Now he'd warned her again. She couldn't keep playing with Rafe's life no matter how much she wanted to be with him.

"How did everything go?" Rafe asked her when she returned to his apartment.

"Not so good," she admitted honestly but refused to say more.

Raphael had been home for a week and was still constantly surrounded by friends and family. Angela felt in the way. Not only that, she received glares and heard curses muttered at her in Spanish. She knew enough dirty words to know them in any language. She'd put off what she had to do long enough. After the talk with her brother she knew she had to break things off with Rafe. It wasn't safe for him to continue being with her.

"What's on your mind, Angel? You look as if you're about to do something really awful," he peered into her eyes, "like break up with me."

He ran his fingertips down her bare arm and she felt her skin burn as it always did when he touched her like that.

"So tell me, what is this really about, Angel?"

"Stop calling me that." She turned from him wishing she didn't have to do what she was about to do, but knowing it was the only way to keep him safe. *God, if there's any other way to protect Rafe without my leaving him, show me. Please.* She sighed. There was no other answer. She had no choice but to break Rafe's heart and break her own in the process. He'd saved her life. Now she intended to save his. With her arms folded across her chest Angela looked around Rafe's apartment. She closed her eyes and shook her head. There were too many people there. For what she had to do they needed privacy. "We need to talk . . . alone." He tried to touch her but she moved away and waited until he went to his family. She heard the raised voices. Comprehension of Spanish wasn't necessary to know they were pissed off on being put out.

"Okay, my family is gone," Rafe said a few minutes later, coming back into the room. "What is it that you wanted to say to me, Angel?"

"I'm serious, Rafe. I don't like your calling me Angel, so stop it."

"No, *mi amor.*"

"I'm not your love, you're infatuated, that's all." Angela attempted a smile. "You're just glad I'm not filing complaints and trying to get you into trouble anymore. After all of that anything would look like love."

"Why are you doing this?"

"I moved to Pilsen for a purpose. You've made me forget that. I moved here to get information to clear my brother, to show that he'd been framed, to find the cops that beat him and make them pay. I love you. But tell me, how am I suppose to forget what we both heard?"

"So that's it. You think you may have found one of the cops. Am I right?"

For a moment Angela stared at Rafe. She'd been talking about the men who had shot Rafe and their connection to Adrian. She blinked as understanding of what Rafe was saying dawned on her.

"Do you think I'm a dirty cop, Angel?"

"Yes." She shifted her gaze on seeing the pain in his eyes. She'd never intended to hurt him like this in order to protect him, but he'd given her the perfect pretext. "Yes, Rafe, I think you're no different from any other Chicago cop."

"Then I guess you're right. If you don't trust me what's the point?"

"Did you beat my brother?"

"I don't know."

Despite wanting to protect Rafe, since he'd brought it up, she now wanted to know the truth. "How can you not know? Either you did or you didn't."

"It was crazy that night. Two officers were injured, and we were getting the worst end of that deal, Angel. Did I hit anyone? Yes, Angel, I did. Was it your brother? I can't say. Did he deserve it? Probably. Would I do it again? Yes. It's my job. What would you have had me do, Angel? When I ran in on that scene it was crazy, gang bangers all over the place. They weren't going down easy. They were firing on cops. People were swinging on me and I was swinging back. I don't know if your brother is innocent. He says he was just in the neighborhood when everything went down, that he wasn't in on the drug deal that went bad."

"He wasn't."

"So he said, Angel. But all of the bangers that went to jail that night said they were innocent."

"You knew why I was in this neighborhood. I confided to you. Why didn't you ever tell me that you were involved? You lied to me."

"You said you didn't want to know anything about my job, that we were not to discuss anything real. You told me to stay out of what you were doing."

"You're using my words against me. You lied to me."

"Yes, I lied by not telling you everything. I lied because I couldn't stand the way you looked at me, the hatred in your eyes. I couldn't take it anymore."

"Is that why you wanted to sleep with me, to make me stop hating you?" *Please, God let him say no.*

Raphael groaned. He should have told her. He had been wrong not to. "I was wrong for lying to you but none of that had anything to do with what happened between us. I made love to you, Angel, because I wanted to. I had to," he amended. "I had to know if I would incinerate from your touch."

Angela fought to keep from shivering. She prayed for the courage to leave the only man she'd ever loved. Regardless how she felt hearing of Rafe's involvement in the gang war, it wasn't Adrian she was concerned for now. It was Rafe and she'd protect him in the only way she knew how. She'd leave him. "Rafe, I have to go."

"You're being a coward."

"I don't want to fight with you. But can't you see after everything that's happened our being together is a bad idea? What kind of future do we have, Rafe? Too many unanswered questions still remain."

"I was going to tell you, Angel. Don't you remember? I told you I had secrets I wanted to share with you. I wasn't planning on keeping it from you forever."

"No, maybe not forever, just until you thought there was no turning back. After you knew for sure that I loved you. I'm not stupid, Rafe. I know now that's why you did that whole romantic trip. It wasn't to seduce me; it was to make me forget that this has to end, that I was right to hate the police department. It's probably part of your oath to lie to the public. How can I believe you now? How can I believe anything that you say?"

But she did. She didn't doubt his love for her. Angela wanted badly for Rafe to say something that would fix what had happened. It had taken all of her life to get here to this point where she loved someone as much as she loved him. She didn't want to let go of it so easily, but what could she do? Her family had been right. Her brother, for all his arrogance, had been right also. Her falling in love with a Chicago cop had led to trouble.

"I have to find the answers," she continued. "I promised my brother that I would. He said there is a woman who can clear him. I have to find her."

"Have you asked yourself why, if there is a person that can clear him, why he wouldn't give the name to the police? Why didn't he give it to the detective your family hired? Why only you?" Raphael saw her quizzical look.

"Yes, Angel, I know about the detective. Why did your brother think you could do what the professionals can't? Why isn't he worried about your safety here without protection? And ask yourself this, if you already haven't: Why did those guys want to shoot you for being with me? They knew your brother, Angel, and it wasn't what he told you. There was no Black against Hispanic thing going on. One was Black and the other Hispanic. They were gang members but they were on the same side. At least in that you're not blind. I know you heard everything they said."

"Yes, I heard them." She sighed. "How can you still think you love me after what you heard, after knowing that it was my fault?"

"Your fault, Angel?"

"Yes, my fault. If it hadn't been for our involvement . . ." She sucked back a sob, remembering her brother's warning to her, a warning she'd ignored, a warning that had almost gotten Rafe killed. She had to be careful. She'd almost confessed to him her real reason for leaving him. If he knew he'd never let her go. He was too stubborn for his own good. He wouldn't think about protecting himself. He was too macho to worry. And he loved her too much to let her go because of a threat. She'd have to be the sensible one. She couldn't let him love her. It was too dangerous and she didn't want something more happening to Raphael.

As for whether or not he'd beaten her brother he hadn't denied it. He'd even admitted that if he had it all to do over again he would. Her family might think she was being disloyal for loving Rafe, but she didn't. She did know she wouldn't be disloyal to Rafe by staying with him knowing that Adrian's threats were all too real.

"Angel, I know that you love me. I'm not just going by the fact that you told me you would love me forever. I've seen your love in your eyes. I feel it in your touch when we make love. I'm not in it alone and believe me, *mi amor,* we both know it's not just sex. I heard you call me *poppi,* Angel. You love me."

"I do love you Rafe, but you lied to me." *Just as I'm lying to you now,* she thought.

"I admit that I was wrong to lie to you. But you have to believe I was going to tell you. I always planned on doing that from the moment I knew the truth," Raphael confessed.

"You once asked me what I would do if I found the man responsible for beating my brother." Angela sucked in a deep breath. "I told you it wouldn't make any difference. I couldn't allow it to make any difference. But you saved my life. I guess that makes us even."

"Even." He walked toward her, a deadly glint in his eyes. "Is that what it makes us? Even? You want someone to bring down? Do it. You think I'm a dirty cop? Prove it," he said, his voice rising more with each word.

"I'm not going to beg you. I don't care what my godmother said. You either love and trust me or you don't. And if you don't, then I don't want you. Leave, Angel. Leave now before I forget how much I love you and throw you out."

Tears threatened to spill but she couldn't let them, not if she wanted to convince Rafe of her reasons for leaving him. His anger permeated the room but it was his pain that did her in. She wanted to throw herself into his arms, beg him to go away someplace with her where Adrian couldn't carry out his threats. Daring a glance at Rafe, she knew it was no use. He would never run from a fight. She moved around the room gathering her belongings, not wanting to leave, knowing she had no choice. She blinked and wiped her eyes with the back of her hand, then walked out the door without looking at Rafe. If she did she was afraid she wouldn't be able to go through with it.

He'd watched while she gathered her things and left. Even, was that what she'd called it? He'd known from the moment he'd met her that she would be trouble. He'd also known from the dozens of screwed-up relationships of the cops on the force that falling in love was the worst move he could make. But damn if he hadn't gone ahead and done it anyway.

And he'd put aside all the little bits of information he'd dug up on Angela's brother. From where he sat her brother didn't look so damn innocent.

Raphael cursed loudly. He knew how family could twist you around their little fingers, especially if you had to go to prison to visit them. He shuddered, pushing away the dark memories from his past.

Someone had to free Angela from her brother. He closed his eyes. The thought of going into another prison made sweat break out on his body. He'd promised himself that he would never set foot inside another prison for as long as he lived. Too many visits, too many memories. Fear seeped in around the fringes of his memories and Raphael pushed it away.

It wasn't up to him. He owed Angel nothing. She wouldn't believe him anyway and it would serve no purpose.

The more he attempted to talk himself out of going to the prison, the more he was aware that he would go. He would not allow what had happened to him happen to Angela. The thought of men pawing her filled him with rage. He would do what he hadn't done in twenty years—he would voluntarily go to the prison.

Raphael felt sick to his stomach. The last thing in the world he wanted to do was walk into Statesville and it had nothing to do with him being a cop.

Disgust filled him as the memories rolled in.

CHAPTER 21

Angela waited until they were in the common room before turning to her brother. She swallowed, deciding to give him the information she'd been sent into Pilsen to get.

"I got it." She watched as her brother's eyes widened and he sat down at an empty table and motioned for her to do the same.

"You found her?" Adrian asked.

"Not exactly," she answered and waited.

"Then what the hell are you talking about?"

"I found people that know her. They say she went to Mexico, that she had a great deal of money and she split."

"That bitch, that stupid, dumb-ass bitch!" Adrian hit the table with his fist, his eyes glowing with anger. "Damn it! I don't believe it. If you'd done what I told you to do to start with you would have found her." He jumped up from the table and looked angrily at Angela.

"There's more," she said, looking up at him.

"What?" he yelled, and shook his head as he tried to rein in his emotions. "What more could there possibly be? You let the bitch take off with my money."

"Your money? Is that what this has all been about, money? You told me she had information that would free you."

Her brother glared in her general direction and she could tell he was having a difficult time controlling his anger. He looked away from her, turned back and said between gritted teeth, "Your job isn't over. Bring me proof."

"How do you expect me to get proof?" Angela watched as her brother changed once again into a man that she didn't know. "Adrian, were you the one she was involved with?"

"I was screwing her, big deal."

Her heart ached. "Rafe saved my life." She waited for him to ask how or why she'd needed saving, but when it became obvious that he wasn't going to say a word, she laughed. "Someone tried to kill me. Rafe pushed me down and lay on top of me. He got shot." Her brother shrugged his shoulder.

"They called me a slut, said I was disloyal to my family, that they should kill me."

Still her brother said not a word.

"Did you send them to kill me?" she asked, her breath coming out so slowly that she thought she would pass out.

"No."

Angela wanted to believe him. She pushed the tears away. "Did you tell someone to shoot Rafe?" There, it was out. She hadn't just insinuated, she'd come right out and asked him. For a long moment Adrian stared at her with the eyes of a stranger.

"What are you looking for, a confession? Are you going to run to that cop boyfriend of yours and sell me out?" he finally said.

Angela felt like a fool, a blind trusting fool. She didn't want to ask Adrian any more questions. The answers were all plain as the scowl on his face. She decided to try a new tactic. She had to see if there was so much as a trace of her brother left in the stranger who sat smugly in front of her.

"Dad's putting the house up for sale."

Her brother didn't answer.

"I'm not going to let them do that. You're not going to take everything from them."

"I didn't ask them to do it. It was their choice."

"Yeah, you've got them fighting to free you when you know that you're not innocent. I'm not going to let them go broke. I'm going to stop them from shelling out any more money to that detective."

"What are you going to tell them?"

"The truth."

"What truth, that you're still sleeping with that cop and that you now believe him over your own brother, or that you've decided to hell with family?"

"I haven't done that. I've just opened my eyes."

"You think they're going to believe you? I bet the rest of the family doesn't even know about the cop, do they?" He laughed. "You're embarrassed to tell them about him, aren't you? If I hadn't told Mom and Dad, even they wouldn't know."

"I don't have to make an announcement to the family that I'm in love." She looked her brother in the eye. "And I do love him."

"So why are you keeping it such a big secret?"

"It's my business," Angela insisted.

"Maybe you're not so sure you have the story right. What if he's shagging you to make you forget about the fact that you have a brother rotting in prison?"

"Stop trying to make it what it isn't, Adrian. You make it sound so dirty. It's not like that. He loves me. You need to understand that."

"I'll tell you what I don't need, and that's for you to visit me or to do anything else for me. But I'll tell you something and I'm only doing it because you're family. Watch your back."

"If anything else happens to Rafe I'll make you a promise." Angela had her brother's attention now. "I'll make sure that I spend all my time making sure you stay here right where you are."

His mouth dropped.

"I'm not kidding," she added, allowing the coldness to color her words.

"Then you are choosing him over me."

"You can put it any way that you want. Rafe didn't do anything to put you in here. He was only doing his job that night. And to answer your question, no, all of the family don't know about him but that's going to change. I love him. I'm not going to keep denying it to you or lying to him." She sat at the table while he stood.

"I'm outta here. You made your choice," Adrian snarled.

"Just remember what I said," she said softly. "I meant it."

"Now you're threatening me?"

"Fair's fair. You did it to me. And I think I have a lot more weight behind mine. How do you think any law enforcement agency will react to what I have to tell them?"

He glared at her and she smiled. "If I were you, Adrian, I'd tell my friends to watch out for Rafe, make sure he doesn't get hurt."

"Excuse me?"

"Adrian, I know what you did."

"You're psychic now?"

"Don't act cute." She was shaking in anger. "I know what you did and I'm not going to let you get away with it."

"First off, I have no idea who Rafe is, or what you're talking about. You can check with the warden or the guards. I haven't left the prison. What's wrong, little sister, are you hallucinating?"

Angela was angrier than she'd ever been, angrier even than when she'd gotten the call from her father saying that Adrian had been hurt and was at Northwestern Hospital. She'd never known she was capable of such rage. And for two years the rage had grown, turning into a bitter hatred. Now that rage was turned on her brother.

"Don't play with me," she muttered through gritted teeth.

"Or what?"

"Do you really want to know? I'll go to the police and I'll tell them you were behind this." She smiled at him in the same manner he was smiling at her, anger stretching her lips, not joy. "That was a dumb move you made having Rafe shot."

She watched while her brother's eyes turned hard and cold, his features no longer his own. A sense of evil settled around them.

"He's still alive, isn't he?"

Angela didn't answer.

"I hope he stays that way." Adrian smiled.

"Who the hell are you? When I leave here, I'm going to tell Rafe."

He laughed. "Do that and I guarantee you he's dead."

Angela sat back in her seat, all the air gone from her lungs. No matter what she'd said, what threats she'd made, she'd wanted her brother to tell her that it was all her imagination, that he'd had nothing to do with Rafe being shot. But he hadn't. He'd admitted to having Rafe shot and now he was threatening to kill him.

"I'm leaving Pilsen. I'm not looking for this woman anymore. She's gone. I don't know what you're into but I'm out of it."

"You're leaving when I tell you to leave, is that clear?" Adrian cocked his head to the side.

"And if I don't, will you have me killed?"

"I'd never hurt you. You're my sister." he smiled. "I can't control things from here and I can't help it if that cop of yours finds himself without a father . . ." He paused. "Or a mother." Adrian laughed, "Maybe a sister or brother. I wonder how much he will love you when he knows that you set him up to have his family slaughtered."

Terror rode her blood. This had to be some horrible grade B movie. This couldn't be real. "I didn't do anything."

"But he'll believe you did."

"He won't believe it, he loves me."

"And he knows just how much you hate cops, that you moved into the neighborhood to take them down. You think with his family's blood all around him he's going to believe you love him?"

"Were you ever beaten by the cops?"

"Of course," he answered without missing a beat.

"Were you beaten by Rafe?"

"I didn't take names if that's what you're asking," he laughed. "What does it matter? You're done with him. When you go back to the apartment you're going to break it off with him for good. Is that understood? And then you're going to do the job I sent you into there to do and then you're done."

"I hate you," Angela whispered.

"No, sweetie, you love me, remember. I'm your big brother." He laughed louder and rose from the seat to leave. He cocked his finger at her as though it were a gun. "Remember what I said," he smirked and walked away.

She saw the guard coming and got up from the table. "I'll see you later," she said, pretending for the sake of the guard watching that nothing was wrong. She wondered why she even bothered. As she walked out of the prison and to her car, she didn't cry one tear until she was headed back on the Stevenson. Then and only then did she allow the tears to flow. She had to do what she'd been too cowardly to do before. She had to go in person and confront her parents.

——❧——

Walking through the door of her parents' home, Angela stopped for a moment and sighed. This could be the last time that she did this. They'd put so much money not only into keeping the home in good repair, but in fixing it up, adding on. It was the nicest home on the block. It would go fast. Angela had no doubt about that. And her parents would throw every dime of the money down a sinkhole.

Adrian didn't care. He only wanted out and it didn't matter to him what the cost would be. It mattered to her. She didn't want her parents to lose everything they'd worked so hard to achieve. It had taken years for them to get to this point in their lives. They should have it easy. They shouldn't have to struggle all over again, and for what?

Her mother came to the door to see who'd entered, took one look at her and backed away.

"Your brother just called. He told us what you've done."

"Did he tell you what he did?" Angela asked.

"He's not the one who's being lying to us. All this time you made us think you were away for your job. How could you do that?"

"I was doing that for Adrian. I wanted to help him."

Her mother was looking at her sternly. "And now you don't want to help him anymore, is that it?"

"No, that's not it. But what he wants me to do isn't the right thing."

"Will it get him out of jail?"

"Mom, I don't think that's what he's worried about. I think this whole thing is about money. And what he's doing to you, to all of us, is wrong."

Her father was shaking his head. The disappointment reached out and grabbed her and wrapped around her.

"I never thought I would live to see the day my kids would turn against each other. I never thought it would happen, not to my kids."

Angela saw his eyes become glassy with tears. In her entire life she'd seen her father cry only once and that was the day that her brother had been sentenced to prison. Then they'd all cried; now he thought she was a Judas.

"I haven't turned against Adrian."

"That's not how it looks from here."

"Don't sell the house," she whispered softly.

"We'd do it for you. What makes you think we wouldn't do it for your brother?"

"You're going to have nothing."

"Do you think we care about that? What we want more than anything is to have your brother home where he belongs," her mother shouted.

"He'll be home when he serves his time." Angela was crying softly. Somehow, she didn't feel as if she had to right to cry when they were in so much pain. But so was she. It hurt to know what she knew.

"He did it," she whispered. "He's not innocent.

"And you think I care?" Her mother was now hysterical. "Do you think that makes a difference to me? That's my baby in that cell with those criminals. He's not used to being around that kind of trash. We didn't raise him that way."

"No one who's in there had parents who raised them that way. It's not the fault of parents for the acts adult children choose."

"Are you really going to continue dating the cop that beat your brother? It was bad enough that you were dating any cop but one that did this to your brother? Adrian told us that he was involved. He said you knew it and didn't care."

Adrian had meant his threats to her just as she'd meant the things she'd said to him. He'd done a first-rate job of poisoning their parents against her.

She stared at them, wanting to tell them that Rafe had had nothing to do with beating her brother. But even he didn't know if he had.

"Rafe isn't a dirty cop; he was doing his job."

"They sent him out there to beat my baby?" her mother screamed at her.

"No, they sent him out there to protect the neighborhood, to protect the people and that's what he was trying to do. I don't know if he hit Adrian. But I can tell you he wouldn't have done anything to him if he hadn't been provoked. He's not like that."

She was near hysterics, knowing that the more she talked the worse she was making the situation. Angela couldn't begin to give an explanation her parents would like. Hell, she didn't like it.

"Adrian tried to have Rafe killed."

"He told us you would say that."

"You don't believe me?" Angela looked across the room at her father. "I wouldn't lie about this. I wish I had a tape but I don't."

"You're listening to the cop and you're trying to help him. It's your life," her father said, coming to face her. "Do what you want to do."

"Daddy, you know how much I love Adrian. I haven't thought about myself for over two years, no shopping, no going out to movies, no dating, nothing. I've devoted myself to being miserable and hating. I'm tired of hating and nothing anyone can say will make me hate Rafe. I broke up with him, but that doesn't mean that I don't love him."

"Did you tell him that your brother tried to have him killed?"

Her parents were glaring at her and for a moment they looked like strangers. How could they possibly think she would have done that?

"Of course not," she answered. "You don't even have to ask me that."

"We don't know you anymore. We have to ask. A couple of weeks ago I would have bet my life that you wouldn't lie to us, wouldn't betray your brother, but you've done them both. I have to ask."

Angela moved toward her mother. Her mother moved away, sobbing, breaking Angela's heart.

"You're not doing any good here, you're only making your mother more upset," her father said, coming to stand between Angela and her mother.

"We don't care about you dating this guy anymore so you may as well do it. Heaven forbid that you should put your life on hold. You're right, forget about your brother, go have your affair, do what makes you happy. You don't need your family; you have Rafe Remeris."

The last her father spat out with such disgust that it felt as if she'd been physically hit. Her heart clenched within her chest, the pain almost unbearable, and she thought of Rafe and wondered if he had felt this way when she'd not trusted him, when she'd left.

"I told you I broke it off already. I can't just walk back into his life. I hurt him."

"That's why you're here. He doesn't want you, now you want your family."

She saw the sadness in her father's eyes and was aware of what he was going to do. His eyes swung toward the door and he walked toward it. "I think you should leave," he said and refused to look at her.

Angela agreed. There was nothing she could do at the moment to regain her parents' trust. She walked out the door and called the one person who would be happy to hear of her fight with Adrian.

She laughed bitterly as she waited for her cousin to answer. For more than two years she'd fought Simone. Now she was agreeing with her.

"Let me guess," Simone began after hearing her voice. "Your brother beat you to the punch. He turned your parents against you."

"I guess he did. When I talked to my dad earlier I thought I would be able to see them in person and convince them of the things I'd found out. But they think I did all of this because of Rafe."

"You told them about the cop?"

"Adrian did."

"Wow, I can just imagine what you went through. Did they order you to stop seeing him?"

"They can't. I'm an adult and I take care of myself."

Simone laughed, "Yeah, but I'd bet they wanted to."

"Maybe, but they did ask me to leave."

"Ooh, that must have hurt."

"More than you could ever know. I forgot to tell you that I broke it off with Rafe."

"How did he take it?"

"He told me to get the hell out of his life."

"You're kidding?"

Angela sighed. "Maybe that wasn't exactly what he said but it was what he meant. I hurt him. I don't blame him but I did it for him. I don't want him getting hurt."

"What are you talking about?" Simone's voice was alert. "Did Adrian have something to do with the cop getting shot?"

Angela wished she could take back her words. She didn't want to add to her brother's time. "No, that wasn't what I meant," she lied. "I mean, I don't want him hurt by the family. I know my mom's going to be on the phone with your mother in a minute or so, if she's not already, telling your mother that I've gone crazy, that I'm dating a cop."

Simone laughed again. "You can bet on that. I'll probably get lectured just because of you. Now my mother will be all in my business and you know I don't like that."

"No, but you sure know how to stay in mine."

"You needed me in yours."

"Why?"

"Because you didn't have any. Girl, it's been so long since you had a man that I was just trying to help."

Angel laughed despite the painful truth in her cousin's words. "Let's hope it won't be that long again."

For an hour after she'd returned home Angela had paced the rooms wondering what she was going to do. The thought of anything more happening to Rafe or his family because of her was more than she could bear. The thought of not being able to tell him to be careful hurt like hell.

She closed her eyes in angry frustration as the tears rolled down her cheeks. She loved him and once again she'd made the wrong choice. Giving him up for her brother was a choice she hadn't wanted, but one she felt forced to live with. Now, after talking with Adrian, it was crucial to keep up her deception. She had to pretend that he meant nothing to her. She wondered if he would believe her. Part of her prayed that he wouldn't.

CHAPTER 22

Her car seemed to lurch into the air and fall down with a thud. Angela shook her head; she knew what it was. She had a flat. She pulled over to the side of the road and cursed. She didn't need this today.

Five minutes later she cursed again. It was going to take the tow truck two hours to assist her. They were busy, they'd said, get someone else to help, they'd said. "Send me back my money," she'd said.

She screamed out of frustration and pounded on the dashboard. *Forget it*, she thought, *I'll change the tire myself*. She knew what to do. True, she'd never actually changed a tire, but she knew what to do.

She got out the lug wrench, placed it over the first lug and tried to turn it. Nothing happened. She tried again, but the lug refused to budge.

Angela was becoming more frustrated by the second when she noticed a cop car halfway down the block put on his lights and come toward her.

That's all I need, she thought, *another cop. What's he going to do, give me a ticket for having a flat?* She attempted once again to turn the stubborn metal and once again nothing happened.

The cop approached her and she barely glanced over her shoulder at him.

"Having any luck with that?" He pointed at the lug wrench in her hand, making her want to ask if he saw the tire off the car.

"Not yet," she answered instead, "but it's coming."

"Mind if I give it a try?" he asked, coming toward her and holding out his hand for the wrench.

Angela held the wrench for a moment and looked at the officer, wondering what his angle was. "Are you from the Damen station?" she asked.

"No, I'm not."

"Do you know Officer Rafe Remeris?"

"No. Is he a friend of yours?"

He still held his hand out for the wrench. Angela handed it over. "He used to be." After answering the officer's question, she stood back watching as the officer took the tire off so easily that that in itself angered her.

"I've never seen the Chicago police help anyone change a flat," she stated in a matter-of-fact manner.

She couldn't see his face but she could hear the smile in his voice. "Serve and protect," he said. "That's what we do." He started putting the spare on.

Angela still was unconvinced. The man had to have an agenda. All she had to do was wait and it should become clear enough. More than likely he would hit on her when he was done.

"All done." He tossed the wrench and the flat in the trunk, slammed it, and smiled at her

Here it comes, she thought, *the let's-have-a-drink or how-about-coffee line.*

"You have a good day now."

He started to walk away. "Thank you," Angela stuttered. She stuck her hand out. "I really mean it. You surprised me by helping me. I don't know what to say. Is there anything I can do for you?" she asked. If he was going to hit on her, now was the time.

"Yes," he said.

Here it comes, she thought.

"Don't forget to get a new tire or at least get that one patched."

Angela stood speechless for a moment. "Why did you stop and help, really? And please don't say it's your duty to serve and protect."

He grinned broadly. "Okay, it was obvious you weren't going to get that tire off and if my wife had a flat somewhere, I would hope someone would come along and give her a hand. Take care now."

He got in his car and Angela stood by the side of the road and waved at him. She climbed back into her car, glanced at the visitor pass and chewed on her lips. She wasn't supposed to get help from the Chicago police. That wasn't how it went. Maybe if it had been a Black officer she could accept it, but it hadn't been.

Things were going screwy. Her brother was not the man she'd thought he was. At the same time she'd met at least two Chicago police who were not what she'd thought.

She didn't want to think about it. She didn't want to think about Rafe. She'd lost him, and she certainly didn't want to think that she'd lost him because of a lie.

For days there had been nothing in Angela's life but work, work and more work. She hadn't talked to her parents or even to Simone. What could any of them say? They had gone over it all. Besides that, there was only one person she really wanted to talk to and the fear of putting his life at risk prevented her from doing so.

She'd taken to driving, pretending that she wasn't hoping that maybe, just maybe, she'd spot Rafe driving by in his squad car. She thought of the many times she'd come out of stores in the neighborhood to find him giving her a ticket. Even that was preferable to now. At least she got to see him. Now she didn't even get a glimpse of him.

Angela wanted Rafe Remeris. She wanted to talk to him, she wanted to watch him scrounging around in her kitchen for ice cream, she wanted him to make breakfast for her, and she wanted to make love to him.

But she'd sent him away. She'd hurt him and she didn't think he'd ever forgive her.

Her foot pressed the accelerator and she took a look around. She was only a couple of blocks from where they'd first met. She pressed a little harder, aware of what she was doing, praying that he'd returned to work and he would be working today.

It didn't take long for the sound of sirens to come behind her. She looked in her mirror and saw the flashing lights. The sight brought the tears she'd been fighting. She watched the officer approaching her and the tears came faster. It wasn't Rafe.

"License and insurance."

Angela handed them over, blinking away the tears. She didn't lip off, didn't utter a word, merely looked at the man that was frowning at her.

"You okay?" the officer asked.

"I'm okay."

The officer peered in at her for a moment, then handed her back her license. "Take it easy," he said. "You were speeding."

Instead of his kindness helping, it completely unhinged her and the tears became sobs. The man was looking at her as though he were afraid she was going to go completely insane. He asked again, "Are you able to drive home?"

Angela stopped her tears. It had been her decision to send Rafe from her life. She just needed to hear his voice to know that he was alive, make sure nothing had happened to his family. If she could ever stop trembling she would call him. In the state she was in now she knew she would break down. No, she had to wait until she could pretend that all was well in her world. She couldn't ask for his help for fear of signing a death warrant for him or his family.

"I'm okay," she finally managed.

Raphael sat in his car in the prison parking lot. He'd broken out in a cold sweat and it preventing him from opening the door. He couldn't do it. He couldn't go inside the building; he'd promised himself he'd never, ever go back.

Memories flooded him, pushing at him, bringing back the horror that he thought had been long buried. With the horror came his shame and a doubt that he'd not worried about for years.

He was shaking so badly that he put his hands on the steering wheel to control them, hating the tremors that were wracking his body. His eyes closed tightly as bile rushed up to choke him.

In the nick of time Raphael wrenched open the car door and puked. He couldn't do this. He couldn't go though with it. Turning the key, he backed out, ignoring the look the guard gave him. He didn't care; he couldn't go inside that building.

Angela had waited as long as she possibly could. She had to hear Rafe's voice just to assure herself that Adrian had not harmed him. She dialed his cell and waited, her heart pounding in her chest, praying that he wouldn't hang up on her.

"I just wanted to check on you," she said quickly, the moment his voice came on the line. She breathed a sigh of relief that he was alive. A moment later the anger in his voice almost had her wishing that she had not called.

"Don't do me any favors," he snarled. "You made your decision. You don't love me and I'll soon stop loving you."

Raphael gripped the phone, wondering how long that lie would take to become reality, if ever. He didn't think it would happen but he was damn tired of lying down and allowing her to walk all over him. He wasn't doing it anymore.

"Rafe, you understand about family. Tell me you wouldn't do the same. Tell me if you had family in prison you wouldn't do anything you could to get them out, that you wouldn't spend every moment you could visiting them, making sure they wouldn't go crazy. If you'd ever been in my situation . . ."

"I've been in your situation. And to answer your question, hell no, I wouldn't spend every minute of my time in that place. I pray to God that I never have to go into a prison again in my life."

He was screaming at her, knowing that it wasn't really her that he was yelling at. She'd come so close to something he'd tried to keep hidden.

"How can I worry about myself when my brother is rotting away in Statesville? I don't have a choice. How can I even be thinking about being with . . ." Angela hesitated and sighed, wishing she could tell him what she really wanted. "Rafe, I'm sorry. I'm sorry about all the things I've done to make your life miserable. I'm sorry that you were shot—"

"Are you sorry that your brother had someone do it?" he asked, interrupting her pitiful litany. Raphael was in no mood to hear that she was sorry. There was only one thing that he wanted to hear from her and sorry wasn't it.

"My God! Rafe, you never said anything about what those men said. I didn't know if you remembered . . . of course I'm sorry . . . I wish . . . I wish I could take that night back," she sobbed.

"Why didn't you say anything?"

"I couldn't."

"I want you to tell me, Angel, did your brother confess to you?"

Dead silence. What had he expected? "What do you think I'm going to do with the information, Angel?"

"Rafe."

"Why did you call, Angel?"

"I can't."

"You can't trust me not to hurt you?"

"I can't do what you're asking."

"You can't trust me not to hurt you? Don't call again. There's no use." Rafe hung the phone up. He'd meant it when he told her not to call again. He'd rather not have her in his life if she didn't trust him. It hurt like hell, but in time he hoped that hurt would go away.

"Officer Remeris, I'm glad to see that you're doing okay."

Raphael smiled at the woman, surprised that anyone in the neighbor gave a damn. "Thank you," he muttered.

"The woman that you were with when you were shot, is she okay as well?"

Raphael's tightened his jaw. "She's fine."

"Good." The woman smiled at him, then turned slightly as though she didn't want to be seen talking with him. She was fidgeting, pulling at her hair, her clothes. She opened her mouth as though to speak again, then stopped and a painful look that he could only assume was meant to be a smile registered on her face.

There was something not right. Raphael watched as the woman looked around as though she thought someone was watching her. "Is there something that you want to tell me?" he asked.

"I don't think that it's safe for her to be in the neighborhood. She's asking too many questions. Is she your girlfriend?"

"No."

"If she's your friend, you might want to tell her to leave."

"Is something going on?"

"I don't know, just rumors probably." But the woman shrugged her shoulders. "There were a few bangers in the store I was in the other day and they were talking about retribution, something about making the," she hesitated, "making the sister pay."

Raphael felt instant fear, fear for his angel. "What are you talking about? Making her pay how, for what?"

"Something about money and Teresa Cortez. Her brother, he can't find her and some money. I don't really know what they were talking about but it was like a sister for a sister. I just thought you might want to tell her to leave before something happens to her."

"Who is Teresa Cortez?"

"I don't know her but I think she must be a sister of one of the bangers. And I think it has something to do with your friend. There are people who don't believe that she's a reporter. They are looking for this Black guy's sister. They don't know for sure, but they think she might be the one they want or that she can lead them to the woman. I don't know exactly what it is but I know it's something to do with a woman, something with her brother." She looked behind her. "I've talked with your friend a few times and she seems nice. I don't want to see her get hurt."

"Thank you," Raphael answered, pretending a calm he didn't feel. "I can assure you, she is what she claims. She's a reporter. If anyone asks, you can tell them to see me. I'll vouch for her." He thanked the woman again.

"Don't worry," Raphael patted the woman's shoulder. "I'll do my best to get her to leave."

He walked away wondering if the woman was being truthful or if she was fishing. Either way, he wasn't giving anyone any reason to think that Angela Reed was not what she claimed to be.

He wished he believed that having told the woman that Angela was a reporter, protecting her cover, he'd assured her safety. He hadn't and he knew it. He had to talk to her.

Raphael rubbed his hands across his face. Damn it, he didn't want to see her, but he couldn't just not tell her. He had to give her the information and give her the chance to leave. He hoped to God that she took the chance. He needed her out of the neighborhood. He didn't want to know that she was a few blocks way, within touching distance, yet he couldn't touch. *Damn.*

"Angela." He rapped on the door. "It's me, Raphael. We need to talk." At first he thought she wasn't home but remembered he'd seen her car in the parking lot. So he knocked again. "Angela," he bellowed. "You may as well answer the door because I'm not leaving."

As he'd intended with all the pounding, she opened the door. "Was it that easy to get you to stop calling me angel?" she asked.

He didn't smile. There was nothing funny happening. "Close the door," he barked. "I need to talk to you."

"What is it?" she asked, subdued.

"Do you know Teresa Cortez?" He saw the expression on her face, saw her blink, yet she said not a word. It hurt that she didn't trust him with that information.

"Don't play games with me." He stalked over to her. "What the hell have you gotten yourself into?"

"I told you I came to help my brother."

"How?"

"I can't tell you."

"Why?"

"Rafe, you're a cop."

"I thought I was more than that to you."

"Rafe . . . I . . . I . . . I can't tell you."

"What you're doing is dangerous. You can get hurt, Angel."

And so could he. Her brother's words rang in her ear. The thought of anything more happening to Rafe or his family was more than she could stand. Angela swallowed several times trying to stop herself from crying, from just throwing herself into Rafe's arm and telling him everything. She glanced toward the window, wondering if someone was watching him even now, wondering if he'd be safe when he left her apartment. She felt the tremble of fear and hugged her arms around her body. She had to keep Rafe safe.

"Leave, Rafe, this isn't going to accomplish anything."

"I want to know what you're doing out on the streets. What name are you using when you're pretending to be a reporter?"

"This is Chicago, Rafe, getting false identification has never been a problem."

"Angel, don't you think I know that? But think about this, Angel. Eventually, everyone gets caught. Look at the truck driver scandal. Even Governor Ryan had to answer for the phony driver's licenses. The department has busted thousands of people using fake driver's licenses. I know they're out there. I'm asking you what name you're using."

"You can't afford to know all the things I'm doing, and I can't afford for you to know. It's your job . . ." she sighed. In a way it was his job. Adrian had him shot because of it. She wasn't going to give her brother the opportunity to kill him. She intended to do just what her brother said, get the information on Teresa and get the hell out of Pilsen. All she had to do was that and Rafe and his family would be safe.

"My job?" Rafe glared at her. "Do you think I came here because of my job?"

"I don't know," Angela lied.

"You still don't trust me, do you, Angel?"

Silence.

He ground his teeth together, sighing audibly as his eyes closed. How the hell did he make her understand this was not just about loyalty to her family, this was about her life?

Before he knew it he was holding her arms. He'd sworn not to touch her ever again, but now he was. He wanted to shake some sense into her. He wanted to kiss her. He did neither.

"Your damn brother is going to get you killed."

Her eyes darkened and he thought she was going to cry. He knew she was remembering what had almost happened. He pressed on, "And that bullet was from his homies. What the hell do you think is going to happen when someone that doesn't like you well enough to call you a bitch comes looking for you. What if someone wants some payback and you're it? What if Teresa Cortez's brother wants revenge?"

"You don't know what you're talking about."

"Maybe not," Raphael answered with disgust. "But I don't think you know either. There is something more going on here, something that I'd be willing to stake my life on that your brother didn't tell you."

He yanked her hand and placed it on his chest. "I'd say I've already put my life on the line."

"No one is after me," Angela said softly. "You don't have to worry about me."

"You don't know that."

"And neither do you," she countered.

"I know this entire thing doesn't feel right to me. I want you out of the neighborhood. Go back to Naperville. You don't belong here. You're only going to get yourself killed if you stay in Pilsen."

"I can't leave until I finish what I started. It's too late for me to just walk away." Angela continued to argue.

"Then you might be leaving here in a body bag."

"I don't care as long as . . ." Tears filled her eyes, and she longed to tell him that as long as he was safe, it wouldn't matter what happened to her. One tear fell and she wiped it away. He'd had a fit when she'd tried to buy him dinner. She could just imagine his reaction if he knew she was attempting to save his life. "I don't care," she repeated.

"Damn you, Angel. I care." He grabbed her and kissed her long and hard, ignoring her struggling. "I care, don't you understand? I care. I don't want anything to happen to you."

Angela was crying. "I can't leave, Rafe, not yet."

"I want you out of this neighborhood. I want you to go back to Naperville where you belong."

"If you want me gone, then maybe you can help me. If you hear anything about Teresa Cortez, just tell me where to find her. I just need to talk to her. I can't leave until I talk to her."

Angela was shivering; at least that much of what she was saying was true. If she wanted to keep Rafe's family alive she would do exactly what her brother said. And she couldn't allow the fact that she might be putting her own life on the line to dissuade her.

"Do you know this whole thing may just be about money, no dirty cops, just some drug money? Your brother is not innocent. Open your eyes, Angel. Why is he having you look for this woman? Why put you in a Spanish neighborhood playing at being a reporter? I told you before that you were going to get into trouble. And you don't have the slightest idea why. You're just going blindly along, not even bothering to question the bull that your brother has given you. You're a smart woman. Why don't you at least act like it?"

"He's my brother."

"He's going to get you killed."

"No he's not," she said. *He's going to get you killed if I don't do what he says, you and your family,* she thought. She couldn't let it happen.

Raphael backed away; there was no need to keep repeating the same thing. She had been there when he'd been shot. She'd heard the same words he had.

He closed his eyes. If only he'd told her earlier that he'd been on the scene that night when things went down with her brother, maybe his words would carry more meaning. Maybe she would allow herself to trust him.

"I can't leave, Rafe. I have to do what my brother asked. I don't have a choice."

"What do you mean, you don't have a choice?"

"Nothing . . . I just meant he's family, that's all." Angela couldn't continue looking at Rafe and lying to him, so she looked away.

"Then let me help. Tell me the truth. Tell me everything your brother told you."

"Just give me the name of the person who gave you this information. Tell me how I can contact them."

"You're crazy, do you know that? You're loco. I'm not about to help you commit suicide. You want information, then you let me help you. Let me go with you to see this woman."

"I can't."

"Angel, do you really believe in your heart that I'm a dirty cop?" This time her silence hurt more than the bullet that had ripped into his chest. This pain he didn't think he'd ever get over.

"At least ask your brother for the truth. If you're going to die you may as well know the truth of what you're dying for. I don't think money is worth your life, Angel," he said and looked at her before he walked to the door.

Nothing had changed for him. He loved her still; some part of him probably always would. He'd tried again to get her to trust him, but he couldn't force that. It had to be freely given and she didn't want to give it.

"Oh God," Angela moaned, rolling herself into a tight ball on the couch. She'd never known she was such a good actress, that she could say words in defense of her brother when she knew what he was, what he'd done.

She couldn't allow anything to happen to Rafe, no matter how much she wanted him, or how much she wanted him to hold her, to protect her. He didn't have the advantage of knowing what she knew. She had to be the one to protect him, to keep him safe. She had no other choice. She loved him too much to let more harm come to him because of her.

CHAPTER 23

"What am I going to do? I can't watch her twenty-four hours a day." Raphael ran his fingers through his hair. "I don't even know if it's true."

His father patted him on the shoulder as he'd done when he was a small boy.

"You did all you could. You told her to be careful, you told her to move."

"Do you think that's going to help me if something happens to her?"

"But you two are no longer together."

"And you think that means I don't still love her? I love her, *Poppi*. I can't let anything happen to her, but she's so damn stubborn, so independent. She thinks she can do it all on her own. I've been looking into this mess with her brother. I don't know all the details but what I do know, I don't like. From what I can tell, it's a crazy plan. I can't believe she went along with it. She doesn't even know what she's gotten herself involved in."

"Neither do you."

"I was thinking of going to the prison to talk to her brother, see if he could talk some sense into her or maybe he could call her out of the neighborhood. She won't listen to me; maybe she'll listen if he does it. He seems to be the only one she will listen to."

His father's face paled and Raphael knew the reason. His father was the only one he'd told about what had happened to him years earlier in the prison. His father had been the one who'd told him he had no reason to feel shame. His father had also been the one whose shoulder he'd cried on and the one who'd given him back his self-esteem.

"Raphael?"

"What else can I do?" he replied in a low voice, not wanting to cause his father worry but knowing he couldn't leave Angela alone.

"You cannot go."

"I have to help her."

"You've never been back, Raphael. I could go to the prison and talk to her brother for you."

"This is something that I have to do, *Poppi*." He smiled. "I tried once. I couldn't make myself go in."

"You don't have to do this, Son. You don't have to put yourself through this. It's not your fault if the girl won't listen. You tried."

"But I have to try everything. I can't just give up. I can't let anything happen to her."

"She doesn't want you, Son."

"Don't you understand that it doesn't matter? I never thought I would ever fall in love. I didn't want anyone touching me, not my heart. I've played it safe most of my life, just sex, casual relationships. Didn't you ever notice when I was younger I never dated a girl more than once or twice, afraid that you hadn't told me the truth, afraid that maybe it was my fault what had happened, that maybe I really wasn't a man. It took a long time to let go of that, *Poppi*."

Raphael shuddered and thought of his angel. He thought of the times he'd been to heaven with her. Any lingering doubts from his youth had all been erased in her arms. He'd given her possession of his heart and his soul. She'd made him forget his vow never to become vulnerable. His father would never understand any of that. Angela Reed was the one thing in his life that Nellie had been right about. He knew his father didn't place much stock in Nellie and her fortune telling. Neither had he. At least he hadn't until he'd found his soul mate, his angel. She was important to him. It didn't matter how she felt about him. He would help her or die trying.

"Raphael, you didn't need her in order to know that you're a man. You're listening to Nellie about her being your soul mate. Don't listen to Nellie. This girl has brought you nothing but grief."

"None of that's true, *Poppi*. I love her. Even if she doesn't want to be with me, I owe her. I know you don't believe it but this time Nellie was right. Angela is my soul mate. She touched my heart, and I never thought that would ever happen to me. She made me love her and she proved to me that I am a man."

"She also almost got you killed, and don't forget about the fact that she almost got you fired. I think you would be better off without this girl."

"I'm not trying to win her back." Raphael sighed, resigned that his father wouldn't want him to go the prison for any reason. He stared at his father for a moment and he saw the memories flare up in his father's eyes, memories that he'd brought back with his decision.

"I'm not looking for her to change her mind about us," Raphael offered.

"Aren't you?"

"No, *Poppi*, I'm just trying to protect her."

"But the prison. You don't have to go there."

Raphael smiled. "We both knew one day I would have to conquer that demon."

"But you don't have to. It's a choice you're making; you don't have to take yourself back into that hellhole."

His father was getting angry and agitated, and Raphael knew that he blamed himself for what had happened.

"It wasn't your fault, *Poppi*." Raphael said softly. "I'll be okay. I'm not a little kid anymore. I can take care of myself." He looked at his father for a long moment. "You're right about one thing. It is a choice. And I choose to do everything I can to keep her safe. Trust me to know that I'm doing what I have to do."

"I trust you," his father answered.

At least there was one person he loved that trusted him. Raphael had always known his father trusted him the same as Raphael trusted his father. If he hadn't, he never would have told, and his father would not now be looking at him with so much pain and misery in his eyes.

"I can't just sit back and not try to get her brother to talk to her. If he loves his sister, maybe he can get her to leave the neighborhood, keep her out of danger."

"Do you think it's going to work?"

"I don't hold out a lot of hope. I mean, if he was worried about her he never would have sent her into the neighbor alone."

"Raphael, you think I don't understand, but I do. I do understand why you have to go. I just wish that you'd let me go with you. It worries me also that you're a cop going in there."

Raphael laughed. "That's the least of my worries." He saw the frown crease his father's face and stopped kidding. "Don't say it, *Poppi*, I will be careful. I promise."

The next day found Raphael repeating his journey to the prison. Regardless of what happened, he would go inside the walls and he would try and talk some sense into Angela's brother. Then with any luck, he'd talk some sense into her.

As he neared the prison, trepidation made the pounding in his head intensify. He ground his teeth together and rubbed his forehead against the arm of his shirt.

The one place he'd avoided for most of his life loomed before him. Raphael walked into the building with sweat pouring down his body. For a moment he paused, wanting to turn around. Then he saw Angela in his mind, took a deep breath and pushed it out. She was the reason that he was going in. He had to find a way to free her.

Their lives were tied into his going inside. He needed her to trust him. He had promised that he wouldn't push her into telling, and he wasn't going to. But he was going to the source, he was going to talk to her brother.

A shiver traveled down Raphael's spine and disgust filled him. Heads turned in his direction and he wondered if they knew he was a cop. No way, it was impossible.

Rafe gave his name and told the guard who he wanted to see. Then he sat down and waited, rubbing his hands down the legs of his pants. He tried to not let his disgust overcome him. He'd joined the rank of the criminals; he'd paid someone to put his name on Adrian Reed's list of visitors. Now he had to wait to see if curiosity would make the man come. Then again, Raphael figured, if nothing else, Angela's brother should at least want to get at look at the man he'd tried to have killed.

His eyes scanned each man that came to the point of contact, looking for something of his angel in each one. At last a man came that he knew without a doubt was her brother.

His eyes met Adrian Reed's and Raphael stood.

"You're the cop?" Adrian asked.

"I am." Raphael answered, not giving a damn that several people stared at him and whispered. "Yeah, I'm the cop," Raphael repeated again. "And I'm here to talk to you."

He saw the man smirk, knew he was sizing him up. He didn't care. He was here now. He followed behind Angela's brother and the guard to the meeting area and Raphael willed himself not to remember, not to think. He sat down at the table, forcing the muscles in his face to become hard. He couldn't allow himself to feel a damn thing in this place. He couldn't let the slightest weakness show.

Raphael knew about this place; he'd been in a dozen prisons in his earlier years, forced by his parents to visit uncles and cousins. Raphael's eyes closed and he swallowed. That had been a long time ago. He snapped his eyes open and looked around, surprised that for even a nanosecond he'd let his guard down enough to let them close.

"You tried to have me killed," he said without hesitation.

"You don't look dead," Adrian answered.

"I said you tried."

"Do I look like I'm in a position to do anything?"

Adrian laughed softly and looked around the room. Before he even opened his mouth Raphael knew he was going to come out with a smart-ass comment.

"Look around you." Adrian pointed with his index finger toward Raphael's chest then jerked it back. "This is a prison. I don't get day passes."

Raphael looked at a group of rough-looking Black men that were eyeing them sharply, making it obvious, not caring that Raphael saw them. "Those thugs, they work for you?" he asked.

"I don't have a payroll."

"You're a real smart-ass, aren't you?"

"Look, you came in here to see me. I guess that means you have all the answers."

"Did you know they wanted to kill your sister?" Raphael watched for some sign of emotion.

None.

"Whatever, man. I don't know what you're talking about."

Raphael was tired of playing games. "The men that you sent to shoot me wanted to waste your sister. Did you know that?"

"Hey, I just saw my sister a few days ago. She looked fine to me, no bullet holes. But if someone wants to shoot at the two of you, why are you bringing it to me? You're the big cop, why don't you take care of it?"

Adrian Reed's attitude was annoying the hell out of Raphael. He couldn't wait until he was done with the man and was on his way home. He bit his lip for a moment, glaring at the man seated in front of him before deciding on a different tactic.

"You told your sister I beat you. You don't even know me."

"I don't have to know you. I can tell you this much: She's been my sister for a lot longer than you've been screwing her."

Raphael jumped from the table so violently that a guard came over. Half the room turned in their direction. The guard whispered to him and he sat back down.

"Man, did you think that was going to impress me?" Adrian asked with a smirk.

"How can you talk about your sister that way?"

"What do you mean? Tell the truth, you are screwing her."

"You say that again and I'll going to smash you in your face," Raphael growled low in his throat.

"Good, then you'll be in here with me," Adrian laughed, "and you'll still get to screw, only this time it won't be my sister."

Just like that the veil was pulled away and all the memories he'd shoved away came rushing in. Raphael could feel the fear he'd felt then. His nerve endings were trembling and when he looked at his hands, he saw the outward flutter there also.

"What's wrong?" Adrian asked.

Angela's brother was deliberately going for the jugular. Raphael was aware of that. He was also aware that he couldn't let Adrian's words get to him.

"Is that really what you want? Do you like boys?" Adrian laughed and continued until the sound itself was deafening. "Wait until I tell my sister. That should end any idea she has of being in love with a cop."

Raphael thought of all the prison visits he'd been forced to make. He thought of his uncle's hands on his body, between his legs, feeling him, rubbing him, giving him dimes for the candy machine not to tell, to keep the secrets, telling him that it was the fault of the cops, that if it wasn't for them he wouldn't be there. It was all the fault of the cops.

Raphael's first orgasm had happened when his uncle had fondled him in the prison, not letting him go when he'd cried out, giving him money after. And he'd spent it. The shame of that day had been buried deep within his soul.

Raphael had wanted to right a wrong when he became a cop, a wrong done to him and probably a million other children who were forced to go visit relatives in prison.

His jaw was like granite as he glared at Angela's brother. He wanted badly to slug the man. He wanted to wipe the knowing look from his face. Raphael could feel his heart pounding rapidly in his chest. *He doesn't know*, he repeated silently to himself. No one knew, not even his father, not about his secret fears.

"You're willing to hurt your sister for a lie?" Raphael asked when he felt he could speak without strangling the man.

"I want out of here."

"You're guilty," Raphael said with assurance.

"How do you know that?"

"I've been checking around. I know that it was no accident that you were in the neighborhood. And I know that you were dating one of the local girls, Teresa Cortez."

Raphael saw a quick change come over Adrian and knew he was on the right track.

"What is it that you've asked your sister to do for you?"

No answer.

"She thinks she's there to bring down dirty cops, to find someone who can prove you're innocent." Raphael smiled. "She won't find anyone, will she? There is no possible way for her to find someone to say that you're innocent. Why? Because you're not." Raphael stared hard at Adrian. "I'm going to tell her."

"She won't believe you."

"You could be right."

"If you believe that, then why are you here?"

"I don't want you to take her down with you." Raphael spoke slowly and deliberately, trying to keep the pleading from his voice.

"Why do you care?"

"I love her."

"Are you sure it's her that you love and not the drawers?"

Raphael's hand was across the table so quickly that he surprised Adrian and himself. He applied pressure at the base of the man's elbow and saw his eyes smart from the pain. "If you ever speak disrespectfully about your sister again you won't have to worry about what will happen to you. I'm telling you, I'm going to kick your ass. Do we have this straight?" He applied a bit more pressure for good measure before releasing his grip.

Raphael watched as the group of men that had been eyeing them moved forward. Adrian held up a finger and the men stayed where they were, though their glares turned more vicious. Raphael didn't give a damn. He was not going to stand for anyone disrespecting his angel. Not even her brother.

"Your sister and I are not seeing each other any longer," Raphael explained through clenched teeth. "She is loyal to you, no matter what you think. The idea that I might have done something to hurt you is something that she can't live with or forgive. You don't have to worry about that."

"You think I'm going to tell her to be with you or give her my blessings, keep dreaming." Adrian laughed with a brittle coldness.

"I know that you're not going to do anything that might bring your sister or anyone else any happiness, because you're selfish. I also know you're not telling her the truth, and she needs to know that. If you want her to keep helping, she probably will, but at least tell her the truth. How do you think she's going to feel when she finds out that you betrayed her, you, her big brother, the one she gave up love for?"

"So this is about the two of you?"

"Like I said, it's about her. Tell her the truth. If you don't want to lose her respect, tell her the truth. For God's sake, give her a choice as to whether to keep helping you. Don't lie to her."

"I think I see what happened. You lied to her and got caught." Adrian laughed loudly. "Now you want me to help fix your blunder. Forget it. I told her not to go out with you in the first place. She should have listened. I don't think either of you hear very well. Maybe I should *habla Espanol?*"

Raphael didn't know how much longer he could stand being in the prison. Already his head was pounding and Adrian was bugging the hell out of him.

"Were you even beaten?"

"I had bruises."

"So did a lot of cops." *God, what a smart ass,* he thought. "Look, were you beaten by the cops?"

"What difference does it make? I'm in here."

"It makes a difference if your sister is doing this and nothing ever happened to you, at least not at the hands of the police. Do you know she hates the entire department because of you?"

"The entire department?" Adrian said with a sneer.

"She doesn't trust the police, and a lot of that distrust came from what you told her."

"You mean that she doesn't trust you."

"This isn't about me. I just don't think it's fair that she distrusts the entire department because of a lie that you told her," Raphael said, not daring to admit how much that knowledge hurt him. He was a policeman, so she didn't trust him.

Raphael heard the sound of a child screaming and rose immediately. He scanned the room and only noticed kids at play. Yet he continued to glance around for a child being hurt.

"You're a bit skittish, aren't you?"

Raphael felt the cords of his neck muscles straining and he forced himself to sit back down. "This is no place for kids," he said in distaste as he looked around again and saw the room filled with children of all ages.

No wonder he didn't get any respect from the little kids. They were more than likely being fed the same malarkey that he'd been feed when he was a kid. Cops were the bad guys.

"This is no place for anyone," Adrian answered softly.

Raphael looked at the man seated across from him. Something was different, a softer version of the hardened gang banger, which was precisely what he believed Angela's brother was.

"I agree," he said, "this isn't a place for anyone." Then more softly he added, "I would be afraid for my sister to come here so often."

"She's not coming as much as she used to, not in the last few months. Not since she became involved with you."

"She loves you. You're her big brother."

Adrian was now glaring at him, making Raphael believe that the one glimpse of something good in him had been merely a mirage. The man had returned to the coldness; his eyes reminded Adrian of the iced topaz of his angel's eyes.

"You don't have to tell me about my sister. She was family long before she ever met you, and she will be long after she's forgotten about you. Who do you think you are, coming in here telling me about my family? I know my sister loves me. I didn't need you to tell me that, fool."

"Too bad you don't love her the same way." Raphael stood and looked down at the man before shaking his head. "You did the crime. Be a man and do the time."

"You don't know a damn thing about doing time," Adrian said, rising from his seat.

"There are a lot of ways a man can do time," Raphael answered. "Being locked away in here is the easiest." He laughed softly, knowing that the man he was talking to didn't understand.

When your very soul is a prisoner, that's doing time the hard way. I'd take this any day, he thought, knowing that he meant it, knowing that he couldn't change the world.

He took another look around the immense room before he walked out. He saw several children dropping coins into the vending machines and his gut twisted. He looked around for the guards. At least they seemed more vigilant. Raphael walked back the way he'd come, barely noticing the guard escorting him out.

He was now assailed by memories as he walked out the doors of the prison and got into his car. As he drove away the memories continued. His parents taking him to visit his uncle, his favorite uncle, how each visit his uncle would slip away with him for a minute or two. The first time nothing had happened; he'd simply given him money for the vending machine and had introduced him to some of the other men.

Raphael couldn't remember when the visits had changed or when his uncle had begun touching him, making him feel dirty. He hadn't known how to tell his father. He'd simply begged not to go and had been told it was his family obligation to visit his relatives in prison.

His mother had even quoted the passage from the bible, the instance when Jesus asked how many had visited him in prison. "Of course you must go, you want to be a good boy," his mother had said. "You were given the name of an angel, an archangel with the power to heal. You must go."

And he'd gone and the day had come when his uncle had gone farther than he'd ever gone before and he'd fondled Raphael and held him tight when he'd squirmed to get away. In some way he'd enjoyed the feeling, yet deep inside he'd known it was sick and twisted and he hated himself for liking it. And he hated his uncle for doing it.

His uncle had laughed at him and told him that on his next visit he would teach him more. Then he'd shoved more coins in his hand and told him to go to the candy machine and buy something and he had. Raphael could remember stuffing the candy bars into his mouth one after the other until he puked and his mother scolded him and finally took him out of the prison. His uncle's laughter had rung in his ears all the way home.

It was that laughter that Raphael heard now. And it was his father's tears that he saw in his mind as he remembered the next visiting day.

Raphael had threaten to kill himself if he was forced to go. His mother had gone alone and his father had stayed at home with him, taking a strap to his behind for being disobedient and disrespectful. Somehow in the middle of the beating the words had come out. Raphael had told his father what had happened.

He'd cried, wondering if that meant he was a fag. His father told him no. He'd told his father everything except the fact that he'd enjoyed it. He even told him that his uncle had given him money and that was what he'd used to buy the candy bars.

His father had wanted to go to the prison and kill his brother. Only Raphael's begging him to keep his secret had stopped him. Within a week his father had moved them clear across the country, from California to Chicago, and he'd never told his mother what had happened. And when word came to his father that his brother had died in prison, his father had spit on the letter and burned it. He'd told Raphael that it was over. He'd said that Raphael had nothing to worry about anymore; God had taken care of his uncle.

Raphael sighed and for some reason thought of Nellie's question to him months before when she'd read his fortune and told him that he was going to meet a woman that he would love with his whole heart. She'd told him that he needed to reclaim his soul and he'd wondered if he even had a soul.

TWO SIDES TO EVERY STORY

He'd kept the memories buried so long that with them he'd also buried a part of himself, afraid of what he might find. Nellie had advised him to bring his soul into the light. He wished now he'd listened more carefully to her words. He would have run like hell to get away from it all.

CHAPTER 24

The call went out and Raphael responded. Chaos and pandemonium reigned. He saw the crowd advancing on several officers, shouting at them. Raphael ran toward the crowd and began talking rapidly, hoping that speaking Spanish would curtail what he felt in his bones was going to happen anyway. It wasn't a language barrier problem. It was a cop against crime problem.

"Rafe, look out," a shout rang out.

Without thinking Raphael dropped to the ground and rolled, pulling his gun from his holster as he did so. Tony, his partner, was in the line of fire and about to take a bullet that was meant for him.

Raphael hesitated a fraction of a second, remembering a similar night two years in the past, remembering Angela thinking he was a dirty cop. Then he pulled the trigger. His aim had been low, as he'd intended, wounding the leg of the man who'd tried to kill both him and his partner. The shot had been enough to cause the man to scream out in pain, dropping his gun as he reached for his leg. Within seconds several officers were on the man, taking him into custody.

And no, they were not gentle. Why should they be? The man had had a gun; he'd tried to kill them. Raphael spit. He was angry with himself for having doubted his motives. He'd done nothing wrong tonight. And he'd done nothing wrong when the gang fight had occurred with Angela's brother. He was what he'd always been.

A cop.

And a damn good one at that.

Raphael finished up and headed back to the station. There was paperwork that needed to be done and as always he had to talk to the commander. He'd shot someone; it would be investigated.

He turned in his weapon and received another. He didn't worry about the investigation; he'd done what he had to do. He'd saved his partner's life tonight, something he wouldn't have had to do if he'd not put him in the line of fire by not being alert in the first place. That wasn't going to happen again; he wouldn't let it.

The moment Raphael was off duty he headed for Angela's home. He intentionally kept his uniform on. That would stop things, should he become tempted to touch her. The ice in her eyes whenever she looked at the uniform would be enough to keep them a safe distance apart.

He'd made up his mind that he was going to give her what she needed to leave the neighborhood. If she needed to see Teresa Cortez, then he'd take her as close as he could get, but he wouldn't leave her thinking that her brother's side was the only side. When this day was over she would know it all.

Raphael rapped on Angela's door and waited impatiently for her to answer. He ignored her look of surprise when he entered, ignored the way his flesh jumped in his pants. He ignored the pounding of his heart and the memories of her moaning his name when they made love. He would also ignore how much he loved her and wanted to take her in his arms.

Keeping her safe was more important than loving her. He had checked the story the woman had told him and he was worried. He was determined to do everything he could to make Angela leave the neighborhood. He was determined to keep her safe or die trying. When the thought came to him, he knew it was true.

"What's wrong?" Angela asked. "You look so angry." She stepped away, eyed him up and down, knowing that he'd come deliberately from work to prove a point to her.

But the vicious look on his face scared her. He'd never glared at her in that fashion before. It was as though he hated her. Her heart seized in her chest and she licked her lips. She didn't want Rafe to hate her. Even if they couldn't be together, she didn't want that.

Why was she forever making the wrong moves, waiting too late to do the things that she should? She'd agonized over being shunned by her family and being thought a traitor, over right and wrong. Now she knew she was wrong and so was her family.

She'd decided that she had to tell Rafe as much as she could about what was happening. She should have called him before he showed up at her door in such a foul mood. Maybe then she could have convinced him how much she truly loved him.

"I can't take this anymore," Raphael began. "You've been messing with my head for months now. I wish the day I met you I had just ignored the fact that you were driving like a bat out of hell. I wish I had left it up to another officer to stop you."

"Rafe, I'm sorry about everything that happened but I think if you listen to me we can fix it. Just give me a chance to explain." She walked up to him and attempted to put her arms around his neck but he pushed her hands away.

"No, Angel, not this time. *Yo soy un hombre, no une nino.*" He glared at her, knowing he'd spoken too fast. She couldn't possibly know what he'd said. "*Yo soy un hombre, Angel, no une nino,*" he repeated more slowly. When he saw that she still didn't understand, he repeated it for a third time. "I'm a man, Angel, not a boy."

"I know you're a man," Angela whispered.

"You don't act like it. But it's my fault for letting you get away with it. I love you." He glared at her. "But I'm not going to let you beat up on me for everything that you think is wrong in your little world. I want you out of my life."

"Rafe, I don't want to be out of your life. I've been miserable. Just hear me out."

"You're not calling the shots any longer. I am."

"Let me explain," Angela tried again.

"No, Angel. No explanations. We broke up, remember?" he frowned. "But then like you said, I don't even know if we were ever together. We were sleeping partners. Isn't that what you said?"

"Rafe, no, it's not what you think."

She took in a deep breath. "You think I left you because I didn't love you. You're wrong. I couldn't stand looking at you and your family, knowing what I knew. It's my fault that you were shot. We both know it. You saved me."

"Do you think I would rather it had been you than me? If that's what you think, then you don't know me at all."

"No, that wasn't what I meant. If we'd never been together this wouldn't have happened. If I hadn't picked a fight with you in the restaurant . . ." She stopped short of telling him about her brother's threat, wishing that she could, but not knowing how.

"You didn't pull the trigger."

"But I'm the cause. We've talked about this before. I heard what those men said. You heard them," she said softly.

"We don't need to rehash it," he said, interrupting her, still trying to protect her, he realized. Sure, he knew her brother was involved. He hadn't come here to put her in the position of choosing between them. And he didn't want her to love him because she felt guilty for her brother's actions.

"I came here for one reason only," Raphael continued. "I'm going to help you with your damn investigation. We're going to put an end to this nonsense. I'm going to take you to get the information that you need. After that you leave Pilsen."

He moved even farther away from her, turning in order to say the next words, the things he really didn't mean but the things that he thought necessary.

"I don't ever want to see you again. I never asked for a woman in my life. I never wanted one. You've screwed me up so that I'll doubt my every move now, wondering how you'd look at my actions. It's bad enough that I've almost gotten myself killed twice. Now I'm endangering the lives of other officers because I'm too busy thinking about you."

"Did something happen to you? Were you shot again?" she asked, her eyes growing as large as tea cups. Fear gripped her and she shook but tried to hide her reaction from Rafe.

He stared at her, not missing the quavering in her limbs. He knew she was worried about him and it tore at him. He'd come to end her worries, not increase them.

He took a good look at her, noticing something that he'd missed before. There was more going on than her worrying about what he'd just told her. There was a fear in her eyes that had been there before he'd even opened his mouth. He'd just been too angry when he'd come in the room to take much notice of it.

Raphael wanted badly to hold her, find out what was wrong. Instead, he backed away before answering her. "Yeah, something happened, Angel. I almost got my partner killed. First, I wasn't focused; then I hesitated before I took the shot."

"You had to shoot someone?"

"Yes, does that make me a dirty cop?"

"Stop, Rafe."

"Stop," he laughed. "You want me to stop? Angel, you don't have the right to request anything of me."

"I don't know what happened with your partner, Rafe, but you have no right to blame me. I didn't do anything. I don't even know what you're talking about."

"I'm talking about us, about your not telling me what the hell is going on. My life is on the line every day that I go to work. I can't afford to worry about your not trusting me. I'm no good for myself and I'm no good for the officers I work with, not like this. So we're going to end it for good today."

He stopped and looked at her feet. "Put some shoes on. I'm going to take you to get your answers."

Angela was angry. Rafe wasn't making any sense. He didn't blame her for the things she felt responsible for, for his getting shot, but he blamed her for a shooting which she didn't even know about. He was angry, she acknowledged that much. Still, he was behaving irrationally.

When she'd heard his voice so ragged and filled with pain, she'd thought of telling him then and there that she still loved him. But he was being so damn stubborn. He was so determined not to be hurt. She wanted to tell him that she didn't care about finding information, that all she wanted was him. But all of that would have been a lie and he would have known it.

Curiosity got the better of her and she went for her shoes. She couldn't afford to let any information that could help her find a way to protect Rafe and his family be tossed away simply because he was being too stubborn to let her in. And this time the information she sought was to keep Rafe safe, not to get Adrian out of prison. It would do no good to tell him that, he wouldn't believe her. If she were honest, she couldn't blame him. She'd shut him out also.

Angela glanced at him as she slipped the shoes on her feet. She caught the quick look of desire that darted across his face. Then his look changed to something more. Love mixed with fear. She realized suddenly that the fear was for her. Rafe loved her still or he wouldn't be there. She'd tell him later that she loved him, when he was in a mood to listen to her.

"Where are we going?" Angela asked after they'd been driving for over fifteen minutes. They were on the Eisenhower Expressway and regardless of Rafe's hesitance to talk with her, she wanted to know where he was taking her.

"Rafe, answer me. I know you're a cop but I am not under arrest." She smiled to herself as he rolled his eyes and gritted his teeth.

"You wanted answers," he said finally. "Like I said, I'm taking you to get them."

"But where? I have a right to know."

Raphael settled himself into the seat more firmly, glanced out his window, then glared at Angela. "I'm going to show you what you've been risking your life for."

When they exited Angela wasn't sure where they were. She thought it was Oak Park, but couldn't be positive. She attempted to look for markers but Rafe turned off the main road before she could spot what she was looking for.

"Get out," he ordered, not coming around to open the door.

"*Sagana,*" she hissed loudly and got out of the car.

Raphael walked up to the door, ignoring Angela calling him a jackass, and knocked. A young woman came out. He spoke to her for a few seconds while Angela stood behind him, waiting for him to tell her what he'd said.

He didn't.

Another woman came to the door and again Raphael purposefully talked to her in Spanish, leaving Angela out of the conversation.

"I thought you said you would tell me what the conversation was about if you couldn't speak in English?"

He turned quickly, glaring at her. "That was before. I thought you weren't going to call me names anymore. Looks like we both lied."

Raphael took a step away from her. If he didn't he would be tempted to give in to the dictates of his heart. When the door opened again a man and woman came out together. "Jose Gomez, this is a friend of mine," he said, pointing at Angela, not giving her name, needing still to protect her, just in case. "She's a freelance reporter and she's writing a story of corruption. She wants to bring down the Chicago Police Department."

"You're kidding."

"No, I'm not kidding," Raphael answered, "and talk in English. I promised her there would be no secrets."

An air of hostility buzzed around them. Angela knew it was because of Rafe telling them that she was there to bring down the cops. Evidently they were friends of his and wondered why, being a cop, he was helping her. She could tell they didn't think it made any sense. Neither did she. If he thought this was helping she would hate to see his idea of hindering.

"Go ahead, miss, ask your questions," Jose said.

"Do you know where Teresa Cortez is?"

"Yes, she's my cousin." He stopped talking, glanced at her empty hands, then at Raphael. "Where is your notebook?"

"She's good," Raphael butted in. "She has excellent memory. Besides that, she has a recorder in her purse."

Angela almost stuttered. "Where is she . . . Teresa, I mean?"

"She went to Mexico."

"Are you sure? How do you know it's not a lie? Do you have proof?"

"My mother just came here one week ago and she saw her there. My mother has no need to lie," Jose said angrily. "Why do you want Teresa? Is the money she's spending yours?"

Bingo, Angela thought, and made a determined effort not to gloat. "Why did she go to Mexico?"

"She was dating this guy. Her brother and this guy had this deal going and the guy screwed him."

"What sort of deal?"

"Fakes, knock-offs. The dude went to New York a few times. Somehow he managed to convince Manuel to come in with him for the money he needed. I don't know how he managed to convince him to work with him but he did." Jose laughed. "How they managed to work together at all without someone getting killed is a real mystery."

"What happened?" Angela asked.

"They all pooled their money, bought this shit and sold it, passed it off as the real deal. The guy got cute. He was pissed that Teresa's brother didn't want him screwing his sister. So he doubled-crossed Manuel and gave the money to Teresa, who was supposed to bring it back when he told her to."

"Why did she go to Mexico?"

"She got pissed at her boyfriend, found out he was screwing around with someone else, so she took the money and ran, figured he deserved to get his ass kicked by her brother."

"But the big gang fight, what happened with that? I thought it was about drugs."

"There were some drugs involved, nothing major, a bag or two of weeds, a few pills, some lollypops, no big deal."

Angela grimaced but didn't say anything. To her any drug use was a big deal, but she wasn't there to pass judgment; she was there to get the truth.

"Then what landed them all in prison?"

"They shot a cop! Someone got crazy, must have been licking his own candy and hallucinated. When the cops rolled up in there it got wild. No one knew what the hell was happening. Everybody started swinging, cops, bangers. Hell, a few people that just happened to be in the area got popped a couple of times. The city is lucky nothing more happened."

"Did the cops beat up on the bangers?"

"That's pretty hard to say. Everyone was hitting everyone."

Angela stopped questioning Jose and looked at Rafe. She stared at him until he turned his green gaze on her and stared back, unflinching.

"Go ahead, we both know what you're thinking. Ask your next question."

"How do you know?" Angela turned back to Jose. "How do you know any of this?"

She watched as the man touched his shirt. "I was there. I work in the market right where everything went down. You came in once, remember? Raphael came in and took you out."

Angela stared at the man. She had not recognized him. Her eyes swung to Rafe's face. It was impassive as he stared back at her with green fire. "If you were inside the store working, you could have gotten things wrong," she said, looking back at Jose.

She watched as he rolled his eyes and clenched his teeth in possible annoyance. Then he lifted his shirt and pointed to the keloid scar on his belly.

"I know because I was right there in the thick of the action when it all went down. I should have kept my ass in the store instead of going outside to see what all the commotion was about."

"Who shot you, the cops?" she asked, looking pointedly at Rafe, angered that he was treating her so coldly.

"I don't know, could be, and could have also been a banger. I didn't ask. I was just glad to be breathing when it was all over."

"Do you know Adrian Reed?"

"Reed? Yeah, he was the Black guy Teresa was doing, why?"

"Do you have any idea why he's looking so desperately for her? I mean, if what you say is true and they broke up, why would he be looking for her?"

The man laughed. "Are you the one Teresa caught him cheating with? This interview sounds a little personal to me. I don't see how you can use anything I've told you to bring down the police department. You only seem to be interested in Teresa." Jose smiled. "At least that's what everyone in Pilsen says. Quite a few people know you've been looking for her. Like I said, she's my cousin. Do you have a grudge against her? Was some of that money supposed to go to you?"

Raphael touched Jose's arm. "Calm down. She's not out to hurt Teresa. She just really needs this information. You would be doing me a big favor if you told her everything that you know."

For an uncomfortable span of ten seconds they all glared at each other before Jose nodded at Angela to continue with her questions.

"Do you know why Adrian wants to find her so badly? He has to know she's been spending the money."

Jose didn't say anything for a moment but he relaxed and smiled at Angela. "Yeah, I know why he wants to find her. Teresa's brother is going to kick the crap out of him. Up till now Adrian's had some of the control in Statesville. Word is Manuel is going to be joining him there soon. Adrian doesn't want to become someone's bitch in there, and that's what Manuel has threatened to make him, someone's bitch.

"The brothers aren't offering him much protection because they figured he shouldn't have been playing it like that. He was doing it to both gangs. His own gang wants to kick his ass because he screwed them out of their cut. Matter of fact, he's already got his ass kicked in there a few times, but he's been promising both sides he's going to get money. He's been paying some guys to watch out for him. From what I hear his money is getting tight and he's running scared."

"How do you know all of this?"

"I have my ways."

"If all of this is true, why doesn't he just tell Teresa's brother that she has the money?"

The others laughed then and Angela felt stupid for a moment. "Of course Adrian couldn't tell Manuel that Teresa had the money. He'd take it all and Adrian would still be in trouble with his own gang."

"Bingo," Jose said.

All of this, she thought silently, feeling the sadness invading her body. Angela shook her head. She thought of Rafe being shot, her brother's threats against him and his family. All of this because of money, because he was trying to save himself.

"Is Teresa coming back?" she couldn't help asking.

"Probably when Adrian gets out of prison. She has a little boy. My mother said she heard her tell the boy that his *poppi* was away and she was going to take him to see him when he came home. So my mom asked her when he would be home and she said another two years. That's prison, man; everybody knows that. She just didn't want to tell the kid."

Angela felt as if the air had been knocked out of her. Adrian had a son. She wondered if he knew. Rafe poked her gently with his finger and there was compassion in his eyes when she looked at him. "Are you done with Jose?" he asked.

"If you know all of this about Manuel's sister, why doesn't he? How come you know that Teresa has the money and he doesn't?"

Jose grinned. "Like I said, I have my ways. Teresa has friends, loyal friends who've been helping her. She's been moving around. If her brother had really wanted to find her he would have. He thinks Adrian's sister has the money."

"Who told him that?" Rafe interrupted and Angela could sense the tension in his voice.

"Adrian told him, told him his sister ran off with the money. He told him his family hired a private investigator to look for her."

Now she just felt sick. What had Adrian gotten her into? He'd woven such a web of lies that Angela wondered if it would ever get straightened out.

"How much money are we talking about?"

"I think it's pretty close to three hundred and fifty thousand dollars."

Angela blinked. "Is that how much he owes or is that what he needs to satisfy both gangs?"

"I'm not sure. That's the figure I got for what Teresa took, so maybe it's both." Jose hunched his shoulders up as if to say, "I don't care."

"The word is that Adrian is expecting a big payday soon. Both gangs have backed off. They're giving him a couple more months to come up with the money."

Our parents' home, she thought. Their parents' home was going to be used to pay off Adrian's debt. She cringed, thinking of all her parents' money being used to chase dead ends when all the time Adrian had known they weren't going to find anything.

He must have gotten desperate when he sent her to live in the Pilsen neighborhood. What had he thought she was going to do if she found the woman? It sounded pretty much like she'd been using the money to remain on the run, that and to take care of her son. *Adrian's son*, Angela thought and trembled. "Thank you," she mumbled to Jose and stuck her hand out.

As Jose took it he said, "Hey, that night in the store we weren't going to hurt you. We had a few beers and we were just being silly. Raphael told us to knock it off. He came in the next day and got pretty angry about it. We knew there was something going on with the two of you. We've been watching out for you, making sure you stayed safe, just like he told us to do."

"Thank you," Angela mumbled, surprised that she hadn't known. At least this explained those funny feelings she'd gotten at times that she was being watched.

"Jose, is Manuel looking for Adrian's sister?"

"He was for the first year he was locked up. But since they transferred him to Menard he's had his own problems trying to not become somebody's bitch."

"When does he get out?"

"He got the same time as Adrian, only he got another year added for misbehaving." Jose laughed. "Adrian won't have to worry until

Manuel gets shipped back to Statesville. If he coughs up the money maybe it will square it. Maybe, you never can tell."

"You don't think there's any chance that Teresa will come back and just bring back the money she has left?"

"Naw, she's still pissed at Adrian. From what I understand he has this pretty woman that's been coming to see him two three times a week since he's been there. I think that's why Teresa hasn't come back. She heard about his new girlfriend, someone called Cassie Williams."

Angela closed her eyes in horror. She didn't doubt anything that Jose had said. No one, not even Simone, knew she'd being using the name Cassie Williams to get into the prison for the last two years to see her brother. He'd told her that he didn't want the convicts being able to find her, that he was trying to protect her. She had to leave before she started to cry.

"Are you really trying to bring down Raphael and the police department?" Jose called after her.

Angela looked at Rafe. "No, I'm not trying to hurt Raphael." She followed him to the car and waited. When he didn't open the door she did it herself, and got in.

"Rafe, I'm sorry, she said.

"Save it, we're not done yet. Everyone who's not a cop thinks it's such an easy job. I want to show you all of it. There is more to being a cop than just putting on a badge and bullying people."

There was nothing for Angela to do but sit there beside the stone-faced Rafe and wait.

—m—

"Latanya, how's it going?" Raphael said and kissed the woman's cheeks. "This is Angela, a friend of mine. She's a freelance reporter writing a story about the department. Would you mind talking with her for a few minutes?"

Angela watched as the pretty Black woman sized her up, trying to decipher if she was there to rip into the department. Angela decided to put the woman at ease. She was tired of people looking at her as if she were the enemy. She cringed inwardly as she caught Rafe's glare. She'd done the exact same thing to him and she knew he was thinking of it.

This was a different world, Rafe's world, where the citizens were the ones on trial and not the police department. For over two years she'd assumed everyone felt as she did. Now she was finding out that they didn't.

"I just want to put a human face on the police department, find out how the average person feels about them," Angela began.

"I'm not the average person," Latanya answered. "My husband was killed three years ago. Just a routine traffic stop and someone pulled a gun and shot my husband in the head. I was six months pregnant at the time. My daughter will never know her father. So if average is what you want, then Officer Remeris brought you to the wrong place."

Angela talked with the woman for over an hour, looked at her pictures and heard how the police department had helped her since her husband's death. She shook hands with the woman and told her how sorry she was for her loss, then headed back to the car with Rafe.

"There's no need for any more of this, Rafe. I get the picture; I know what you're trying to say."

"I want you to know it all," he answered. "I want you to know why I can't be thinking about you when I'm working. I want you to know why it's important to me to have you out of my life."

He was aware of her, more aware of her than he'd ever been. He knew it had to do with the fact that he wasn't planning on ever seeing her again, that after he made sure she was safe and out of the neighborhood, she would be out of his life. Regardless of his reasons, it hurt like hell to have her that close to him and not be able to touch her. He watched as the tears fell on her soft satin cheeks and he watched as she wiped them away, but he refused to acknowledge them.

"Rafe, we need to talk," Angela said between sobs. She could feel him moving away from her, closing his heart, shutting her out. She didn't want that. She loved him. It was killing her that he wouldn't even look at her unless he glared at her.

Sure, she'd been wrong in the way she'd treated him, but she'd planned for over a week to rectify her mistakes. She just hadn't gotten the chance.

"You haven't given me a chance to say what I want. You're making this so damn hard. Can't you just look at me?" she asked quietly.

"I'm driving. I have to keep my eyes on the road."

"I was wrong not to listen to you. I should have told you what was going on. I didn't know about Adrian dating Teresa, I didn't know about the money. Now I do. I was wrong, Rafe."

"It took you until today to come to that conclusion? I think that's wonderful. You listen to the words that a couple of strangers have to say and you trust them but not me. Is that your definition of love?" The muscle in his jaw twitched. "Leave me alone, Angel."

In less than a minute he stopped the car, got out without a word to her, went into a bakery and got back in. She eyed him but he still refused to look at her.

After another few minutes of silence, he stopped again in front of a nice brick ranch and got out, taking the pastries. "You coming?" He peered in at her, glaring, daring her with his look to call him *sagana* again.

She took the dare. "*Sagana,*" she whispered. And got out of the car and walked away from it.

Raphael knew he was being a jerk and a jackass. He didn't blame his angel for calling him on it. He was the all-time biggest jerk in the world. He was being mean and petty but he had to push Angela away from his heart. She had too much control over him and he couldn't afford to allow her back in.

He'd almost lost it when they were at Jose's. She'd looked so sad that all he'd wanted to do was take her in his arms and hold her, comfort her, tell her that he loved her. And he'd nearly gone crazy with fear when he'd heard what her dumb-ass brother had done. He'd thought he was being so smart but he had no idea the kind of danger he'd put his sister in.

Raphael was keenly aware that Angela thought he hadn't noticed her reaction when Jose had talked of Adrian's girlfriend Cassie. Raphael was no fool; he'd known immediately that the girlfriend was Angela. Another scheme Adrian had concocted.

He wanted to go back to the prison and strangle the man for putting his sister in harm's way. The pain in his chest had left only when he learned that she wasn't in immediate danger. Still, he wanted to hold her, comfort her.

So yes, he was being a jerk, not opening the door for her, afraid of touching her, afraid of the heat between them. He had to let her go and he had to begin by being a jerk, by making her not want him, not tell him what he already knew. She wanted to say that she loved him still. And Raphael needed it to be over.

But God, he didn't want it to. He loved her.

He waited for Angela to catch up with him before he walked to the door and rang the bell.

"Rafe, how are you, man? It's been awhile."

"I'm good." Raphael answered. "Shaun, this is a friend of mine, Angela. She's doing a paper on the department. I thought she needed to know what we're up against."

"Sure." Shaun rolled his wheelchair back and motioned for them both to enter his home. "Hi, I'm Shaun Donnelly." He stuck his hand out to Angela, then patted the arm of his wheelchair. "I got this courtesy of the department."

Angela didn't say a word. The charade of being a reporter had gone far enough.

"Don't you want to know how it happened?" Raphael asked, staring at her before he turned to Shaun. "Angela thinks I'm a dirty cop. She heard that I beat a guy in that gang war a couple of years back. I think she's still trying to find enough information to make it stick."

Angela stared in disbelief at Rafe, then at Shaun, who despite Rafe's words hadn't stopped smiling at her. Instead, he was looking at Rafe with a curious expression on his face.

"Is this the woman I heard about, the one who wrote you up a dozen times?"

"It's her."

Shaun shook his head and looked at her.

"So, Angela, do you want me to tell you how this happened?"

He didn't have to. She knew how it had happened. The same gang fight. She bit her lips and said softly, "It isn't necessary."

Shaun smiled again, looking from her to Rafe and back again. "I got a feeling it is. That night things were crazy. Rafe and I were both trying hard to calm the situation down, to not use violence. I hesitated for," he blew his breath on his fingers, "not even that long, and I got shot in the back. Rafe pulled me away, fighting as he did so. He never did pull his gun. I asked him why later and he told me he couldn't shoot and carry me at the same time." He smiled at Rafe. "I think he just forgot."

For a minute the men looked at each other. Then Shaun turned to Angela. "We went through the academy together. We both wanted to do a good job for our communities. We knew how dangerous it was going in." He patted the arm of his chair again. "This unfortunately sometimes comes with the territory."

She took a good look at the man seated in the chair. He couldn't be more than thirty-two and he was paralyzed. She trembled and looked at Rafe.

He'd told her he had hesitated, that he was thinking about her and had almost gotten killed. That could be him sitting in the chair. She licked her lips as her eyes filled with tears and a lump entered her throat. Rafe refused to look at her but Shaun did.

"I don't think you need me to say anything about the kind of man Rafe is, but just in case you don't already know, he's a hell of a guy. He's one of the good guys."

"That's not why I brought her here," Raphael interrupted. "I'm not trying to sell myself. I wanted her to see the other side to being a cop."

Shaun laughed, "Yeah, right." Then he looked at the two of them. "I'm glad to see you're not fighting anymore." Then he laughed aloud. Neither Raphael or Angela found the situation amusing. They stood as still as statues, not moving, not speaking.

They stayed for a few more minutes as the two men spoke together. Angel caught Shaun's, "So it happened to you too, huh? I thought you said you would never fall in love."

"I did, but it was a mistake. It's over," she heard Rafe answer and knew that he meant it. He didn't want anything more to do with her.

For some strange reason Angela didn't want to leave Shaun Donnelly's home. She knew Rafe was taking her home and that after that he never planned to see her again. She knew what he needed from her. Her trust.

She hugged Shaun and wished him well as she followed Rafe back out to the car. Adrian was guilty and he'd used her entire family. She dared a brief glance in Rafe's direction. She couldn't let him go. He was everything to her. Her heart ached with the knowledge that she really did know right from wrong.

CHAPTER 25

Raphael drove slower than normal, his determination firmly in place. He would take Angela home and that would be that. He would never see her again. He was a man, as he'd told her, not a boy. He'd get over not having her in his life. Still, he drove slowly to prolong the time.

When he couldn't prolong it any longer he turned into her street and drove to her door. "Get out," he ordered without looking at her. "You have what you need, now go."

"No, I can't," she answered.

"Get out," he repeated, reaching across her to open the door.

"No." she said again.

Why the hell is she making it so damn hard? he thought as he got out and angrily opened the passenger door. "Get out, Angel."

"I can't."

"You can."

"We need to talk," she whispered through her tears.

"We have nothing to talk about."

Raphael was getting angry with himself for wanting to hear her tell him that she loved him, and angry with her for not just getting out of the damn car and letting him go.

"Angel, don't make this any harder," he pleaded.

"I'm not trying to do that. You have to listen to me. It can't end like this, Rafe. It can't."

Her look was killing him more assuredly than any gun or knife. Hell, he'd rather be shot a million times than look into her eyes and see tears, than know he'd live the rest of his life without her. He saw her body tremble and reached for her before halting and cursing himself for allowing her to have that kind of effect on him.

"Get out, Angel," he barked hoarsely. "Get out now before it's too late."

"It is too late, Rafe. You said so yourself. It's too late for us."

He glared at her, saw her eyes glistening with tears and gave it one more shot. "Fine," he muttered. "Stay in the car, I don't give a damn. I'll leave," he said and walked away.

"Rafe, don't leave."

His back was to her. He took a couple of deep breaths, each costing him, each taking him away from her and out of her life. Damn, if she'd only listen to him, just let it be over, let him leave.

It had been hard enough riding in the car with her, smelling her scent, not reaching out to touch her. They both needed it to be over. They didn't need to draw it out.

"You've got what you need, Angel. Angela," he amended.

"No, I don't have what I need. What I need has his back to me and is about to walk out of my life. Don't leave, Raphael, please."

"Give me a reason to stay," he moaned, knowing he was about to cave. God, how he wanted her.

"I love you."

The world went quiet and Raphael stilled. Even his breathing ceased and he knew what was coming. His heart seemed to stop beating.

"Raphael, I love you. Raphael, *te amo*."

Her love will stop your heart but it will restart it again. And she will love you with the same fire as the ice with which she hates you.

"Don't leave me, Raphael. I would be lost without you. I love you." His heart slowly regained a normal rhythm. He turned to face her.

"I can't live in shadows anymore. I don't want to be just your bed partner. I'm not ashamed of being a police officer and I'm not going to quit the force."

"I didn't ask you to quit."

"Are you going to continue looking at me with disgust every time I put the uniform on?" He saw her eyes widen. "What, you didn't think I noticed that? What kind of a cop do you think I am? I noticed, *mi amor*."

Angela walked toward him, holding his gaze with her own. "Being with you has changed me also."

"How?" Raphael asked, holding his breath.

"I find it hard to hate the people who may have to save your life . . . or mine. I've tried but it's not working for me any more." She was now standing in front of him. "I respect what you do and I respect the other officers who put their own lives in danger. You can't blame me for wanting to help my brother. I couldn't see any other position. I didn't want to," she admitted. "But I know there are two sides to every story. I've always known that. I just chose to forget it for the past two years." He sighed as he looked at her, not taking her in his arms as he wanted to do. He wanted so much from her, not just her love, but her respect. Above all, he wanted her trust. There were still things she didn't trust him with. He could see it in her eyes.

"I want you to trust me, Angel," he said, walking up the stairs to her apartment. The conversation they were having was not one to have in the open.

"I do trust you," she replied, following him up the stairs, handing over the keys to her apartment.

"Then tell me, was your brother involved in my getting shot?"

"Rafe, don't do this to me, please. Isn't it enough that I love you and I respect the job that you do? And believe me, I trust you. I trust you with my life. There are just certain things that I have no control over telling you. Please tell me it's enough."

It wasn't enough, not for them to make a life together. He desperately needed her to trust him with everything.

"Are you going to make me beg?" she asked.

Raphael thought about it. She'd made him beg and still it hadn't mattered. He smiled. No, he wouldn't make her beg, not for his love, never for his love. "Angel, I love you." He turned back to face her as he whispered the words. He took the few steps necessary to return to her and wrapped her in his arms for a long moment before bringing her back to face him. "*Te amo*, Angel," he said as his lips claimed hers. He loved her, she knew it with every breath she took. She thought of

Adrian and his threats against Rafe and his family. She shouldn't be in his arms if she wanted to keep them safe but she couldn't send him away again. She had to find a way to protect him and keep him in her arms at the same time.

"Rafe, you were right all along," she began. "My brother was responsible for your getting shot and he's not innocent. He wouldn't tell me what happened but I figured it out from some things I heard. I had already figured out that he was dating this Teresa woman and that she ran off with the money she was holding."

Rafe held Angela tighter. "I know, baby. Manuel and your brother went in on this deal together; your brother got greedy and stole all the money and he gave it to Teresa to hide. Jose doesn't have all the facts.

"Adrian thought Manuel wouldn't suspect his sister, but with your coming here asking questions about her, the word got back to Manuel and he now knows that she was involved. Jose doesn't know that."

"About that, you didn't tell Jose my name. Why? Don't you trust him?"

"I trust him with my life." Raphael kissed her gently on the forehead, then her nose and finally he stared at her lips and touched them lightly. "But not with yours." For a long moment they gazed into each other eyes.

"How long have you known this?" Angela asked.

"For awhile."

"And you didn't do anything about it. Why, Rafe?"

"Because I needed you to tell me, Angel. I needed you to trust me. I would never do anything that would bring you pain. And giving this information to the authorities would bring you pain."

"Rafe, he threatened your family. He said if I didn't break up with you something might happen to them."

The words were out and she didn't want to recall them. She wanted him to know. She felt his muscles bunch.

"Is that why you were pushing me away? You were trying to protect me and my family?"

Angela closed her eyes, biting on her lips to keep back the tears. "*Te amo*, Raphael. I couldn't let anything happen to you."

"And I can't let anything happen to you. You're moving away from here tonight. I don't want either your brother's goons or Manuel coming after you."

"No, Rafe, if I leave, Adrian will know. He has his friends watching me. They're going to tell him that we're back together," she whispered and shivered in his arms.

"I can take care of myself and my family, Angel."

"I'm not leaving you. I'm staying right here where you are. If there's going to be trouble, I'm sticking around."

"You're too stubborn, you know that?"

"I'm not being stubborn. I just can't leave you here with this mess."

"None of this is your fault, Angel. You don't have to worry about that."

"I'm not blaming myself."

He smiled at her and she smiled back. "Okay, just a little," she admitted, "but I don't want to be away from you. I want to be near you. I'll think of something to do. I promise."

"We'll think of something." He kissed her. "Together, baby, we'll keep my family safe and I won't betray your trust."

"Your family's going to hate this as much as Adrian, aren't they? What are we going to do about that?"

"We'll manage. Now will you shut up and kiss me? I want to make love to you. I need to make love to you and I need to do it now."

Angela's body quivered in his embrace. Her head fell back as he kissed the column of her neck. She heard his moan deep in his chest; the primitive sound was filled with need and she moaned in response.

Together they sank to the floor. She barely noticed Rafe's hand moving to grab the pillows from the sofa; she just felt the softness as he laid her down. She shivered in anticipation as he pulled the top from her shoulder and began kissing her skin, caressing her with his lips.

She pulled his head down to her breast and moaned again as he suckled her. Her fingers moved frantically over his body. His hard, corded muscles seemed to beg to be touched.

"You are mine, Angel, and I am yours," Raphael whispered into her ear.

"Yes, I am yours and you are mine," she answered and lost herself in his love.

CHAPTER 26

Raphael pulled into the lot of the prison and killed the engine. He had no desire to go back inside, no desire to see Adrian Reed because he didn't know if he'd be able to restrain himself from hitting the man. He was sweating and used the back of his hand to wipe it away.

"Are you okay?" Angela asked.

He turned toward her. "I'm okay."

"I guess I should have thought about how hard it would be for a policeman to walk into a prison. I suppose a lot of people hate you in here. You don't have to go in, Rafe, I can do this alone."

"Going in together was our plan. We discussed it and decided it was the best way."

"Our plan, Rafe? I'd say you badgered me until I gave in," Angela said with a smile. "It really doesn't take both of us to accomplish this, so you can wait for me here in the car."

"No more doing things alone, Angel. We're doing this together."

"But you don't have to, really it's alright. I understand."

He smiled. "What do you understand?"

"I read. I know how it is."

"Sorry to disappoint you, Angel, that's not how it is in my case."

"Then what is it?"

"Memories."

"Memories? You haven't ever been arrested, have you?"

"No, but I have been to visit relatives in prison. I know the kinds of things that go on. I know that after awhile the men don't care about themselves or anyone else."

He smiled at her. "As much as I hate it, I can understand why your brother has gone to so much trouble to remain a man. It's no joke," he said.

"Were you molested visiting someone in prison?" she asked.

He looked into her eyes, looked for the disgust, the pity. He didn't want either from her. But he wanted her to know the truth. He held her gaze. "When I was eight." He paused, waiting for her to digest that information.

She remained silent.

"My uncle. I was visiting him in prison, and he touched me," Rafe said softly, still watching her. "After awhile I guess he did a bit more than touch me. He gave me money afterward and I kept quiet."

"Did he rape you?"

"Not my body."

"It's a pity what kids have to go through to reach adulthood," Angela said. "With me it was one of my parents' friends. I was about ten. He gave me five dollars to let him put his hands in my pants. I never told anyone," she said.

There was neither pity nor disgust in her eyes. What Raphael saw was understanding.

"I felt like a whore," he whispered.

"So did I," Angela answered.

"I wondered if I were a man." He shrugged his shoulders. "I doubted myself for years."

"You are a man." She smiled at him. "Take my word for that." She traced his face with the tip of her finger. "You're the man of my dreams, the one I thought didn't exist except in fantasy." She traced his lips, felt the tingle of electricity, and kissed him. "I thought all men, with the exception of my brother and my father, were dogs."

"And now?"

"I was never looking for love, Rafe. I didn't really think it existed. You've proven me wrong time and again. You saved my life, you saved your partner, and you've lived by a set of values that should make you proud. You're very much a man."

Her eyes closed, and she felt his lips pressing against hers. His tongue pushed at her, and she opened her mouth to receive him, sucking on his tongue, leaning in closer.

He ended the kiss. "We'd better go in before we get arrested."

He got out, came and opened her door.

"I meant it, Rafe, you don't have to go inside."

"Like you said, I'm a man and I'm not sending my woman in there alone." He reached for her hand, closed his fingers around hers and tugged her along toward the door of the prison. The feeling of tightness that always prevailed when he thought of his past was gone.

Rafe couldn't believe how easy it had been. Something that had plagued him his entire life had been taken care of in less than a minute—no pity, no disgust, no questions, just understanding and anger that they'd both had to endure the same pain. Nellie had been right all along. Raphael had found his soul mate and he'd found his soul. He gave his angel's hand a little squeeze.

No, he still didn't want to go inside the prison. He would probably never want to go in, but he would walk through hell for the woman who now held his soul. He would do whatever it took to bring her to heaven, and keep her there.

Rafe pulled out his driver's license and gave his name and waited as Angela pulled out her ID and gave the name Cassie Williams.

He smiled to himself; he'd known it. At least her brother had had the sense to keep his sister safe by preparing for her visits.

Adrian Reed came to the room and looked at his sister before his gaze barely flicked over Rafe. He frowned at the two of them, turned and walked away, and they followed.

"I don't believe this shit," Adrian said in a voice loud enough to carry to his sister and Rafe.

"What don't you believe?" Raphael asked. "Did you think you were going to get away with terrorizing your sister? I told you if you hurt her I would kick your ass."

Adrian turned suddenly. "And if you're here to do that, bring it on."

Before either man could make a move, Angela was between them, pulling Rafe's hand, moving him away from her brother. "We didn't come in here for this," she said sternly to Rafe. "I'm not leaving this place without you at my side, so cool it." She faced her brother. "Besides, I can handle this."

She looked at Adrian, hoping her disappointment showed on her face. "I know the whole story," she said softly, sitting down and motioning for Rafe to do the same. "Matter of fact, I know more about it than you."

"What do you know?" Adrian asked, curious.

"I know that your not wanting me to date Rafe is personal. You know how Spanish men feel about Black men dating their women because you were dating Teresa. You're a hypocrite." She bit out the words coldly.

"So what?"

"So there is a difference. I'm in love with Rafe and he's in love with me. Teresa was not important to you. You only wanted me to find her to get your money back."

Something flickered and glowed in her brother's eyes and Angela blinked. Some of her anger retreated. She saw something in her brother she'd not seen in over a year, a caring.

"She is important to you, isn't she? You love her."

Adrian didn't answer.

"Why did you cheat on her if you loved her?"

Again Adrian didn't answer. He glanced at Rafe, then back at his sister.

"Adrian, talk to me. Why all the lies? Why are you letting Mom and Dad sell the house?" She closed her eyes for a second; it hurt to breathe. "Why did you hurt Rafe?"

"That wasn't supposed to happen. No one was supposed to get hurt. I just wanted you to stop seeing him."

"Because he's Spanish?"

"Because he's a cop," Adrian growled. "Did you really think I wanted a cop messing around in my business? Look what happened. You've brought him here with you. What does that tell you? I was right not to want you with him."

He bit down on his lip and opened and closed his hands before making them both into fists. "I had people looking out for you. I'm not a monster. I made sure you were safe. I knew you were fighting with the cop before you told me. My friends thought it was funny."

"I never saw anyone."

"You weren't supposed to. But they told me that you almost spotted them one night and ran into a store. When you came out you were with the cop." He turned and glared at Rafe. "He stayed the night. The fighting between the two of you was no longer funny. Then he took it upon himself to have his friends watch out for you. By doing that he made it harder for my people to keep an eye on you without anyone knowing they were doing it."

"So you told them to shoot him?" Angela couldn't believe it. How could so many people have been watching her without her knowing it?

"You can't prove anything." He glared at Rafe.

"I'm not here to prove it," Rafe growled. "Do you think I would be here with your sister if that were the case? You're not going to get her killed over money. I'm not going to let you. You've got gang bangers looking for her."

"They don't know who she is."

"For now." Rafe was not appeased. "Okay, that was good that you thought to make her into someone else, but people aren't stupid. A fake license is easy to come by. Sooner or later they're going to find out who she is. I know you don't care about your sister but I do. And I plan on keeping her safe."

Angela moaned without meaning to. She looked across the huge common room at all the other families. None of this was supposed to happen. Adrian had no business being in prison. He was smart. He could have done anything with his life but get involved with gangs.

She felt someone touching her hand, holding it, and at first thought it was Rafe but the electrical tingle wasn't there. She turned and stared at her brother.

"I was scared," Adrian began. "I did it because I was scared." He held her hand tighter. "You have no idea how it is in here." He gripped her hand. "I hardly sleep. Sleeping can get you killed or worse. I'd rather die than . . ."

"Why didn't you just tell me that? I would have understood. You could have told me the truth."

"How? You always thought I was so perfect, that I couldn't do anything wrong. I couldn't disappoint you."

"I never thought you were perfect, Adrian. You were my brother and I loved you, so I supported you. It never meant that I was a fool."

Angela held her brother's gaze, then squeezed his hand in return. "I just need you to be honest with me about all of this. That whole fight that night, what happened?" she asked.

"I don't know. It had nothing to do with me and that's for real. I was there doing business. I had teamed up with the Latin Lords, just a few of them. We were trying to diversify, go legit."

"Legit is not selling knock-offs," Rafe interjected.

Adrian ignored him and continued talking to his sister. "We were trying to end the war between us, Blacks against Latinos, at least in the beginning. We were trying to do something together, then Manuel found out I was dating his sister and he got pissed. And I got pissed that he didn't like it.

"I wanted to show him I didn't need his sister. I thought I didn't need her." He paused. "I was with someone else. I wanted Manuel to see me, but I never intended for Teresa to see me.

"She did. She got pissed. She split," Adrian finished.

"But the fight," Angela insisted. "Tell me about that."

"What happened after that, I don't know, except everyone thought they'd been double-crossed and before you knew it, the cops were there and it was crazy. Now I'm here." He looked around. "It wasn't supposed to go down like this, I shouldn't be here."

"And you're really going to let our parents lose everything because you shouldn't be here? Maybe initially you didn't belong here but for all the things you've done since, you do belong here, Adrian." Angela shook her head sadly. "You brought all of this on yourself."

Her brother cringed and looked away and the sting of tears burned the back of her eyes like crushed stones.

"I understand your reasons, but you went about it in the wrong way," Raphael offered.

Angela glanced at him. She'd not expected sympathy from him for her brother's actions. He'd been hurt the most by her brother and with the threat hanging over his family she wondered how Rafe could even speak civilly to Adrian.

"That's not the only reason I want to get out of here." For the first time since they'd entered the room Adrian was addressing Rafe.

"There are other more important things I have to do. I have to get out of here."

"You want to find Teresa?"

"Yes."

"For the money?" Angela asked. "So you can give it to her brother?"

Adrian's eyes closed and he shook his head. "That's not the reason I need to find her."

Angela stared at Rafe and found him staring back at her. "You knew she was pregnant, didn't you?" she asked. She saw a genuine look of surprise on her brother's face. "Yes, we know," she said. "She has a son." She watched as tears filled her brother's eyes. "You have a son. I have a nephew."

"She said she was going to get rid of it." Adrian sighed, closing his eyes and shutting Angela and Raphael out. "She didn't do it."

"Apparently not. But now that you're a father you've got to think about the legacy you want to leave your son. Your sister didn't do the crime with you, Adrian, but she's been doing the time. It's time she was paroled."

"What are you planning on doing? I wasn't selling drugs, I didn't shoot a cop and I didn't tell those fools to shoot you."

"I know you didn't have a weapon. I checked your records. That's why you're not doing more time. You're lucky. And I also know you weren't found with drugs on you. That's why you got off easy. Still, you weren't clean. I know that also," Raphael answered Adrian.

"As for what I plan to do, the answer to that question is nothing. I can't, this is between you and your sister."

"Angie, looks like it's falling to you. What are you going to do?" Adrian asked, worry and hope coloring his voice.

"If I could convince Daddy not to sell the house I would. But they think I'm a traitor. They want you out regardless of what you've done, so it doesn't matter," she answered.

"So why did the two of you really come here together today?"

Rafe spoke first. "Because we're together. We want you to know that your threats are not going to stop us. But to tell you the truth, if something happens to my family you're going to wish for the days that you were only afraid of Manuel. Those will seem like the good old days."

"What about my sister?"

Rafe looked at Angela. "Do either of us want her to make a choice?"

"Seems like she's already made her choice," Adrian answered.

"You have to pay for what you've done, Adrian," Raphael said softly.

"You have to do the right thing," Angela said softly to her brother, then stood to leave.

When they were inside the car Rafe turned to Angela. "Hand it over," he said. He held his palm open and waited for Angela to fish the fake license from her wallet. She dropped it into his palm and smiled. "To serve and protect, baby," he grinned. "And to stop crime."

For two weeks Angela had walked two worlds, one of fear, one of supreme joy. Whenever she was in public with Rafe her stomach knotted and she waited for the sound of a gun. It was only at night in bed when she was lying in his arms that she could give in to the joy that flooded her heart; it was only then when she felt safe, when she held him to her and knew that he was alive for yet another day. She'd left Pilsen and moved back to Naperville but the fear for Rafe's safety hadn't left her.

"You've got to stop worrying so much about me, Angel," Rafe said to her one morning as they lay on the couch together watching some show on television.

"I can't help it."

"Are you worrying about your brother?"

"No, I'm worrying about anyone out there that hates cops."

"Like you?"

"I would have never shot you."

"But you hated me."

"I don't anymore."

"I'm glad." He smiled at her. "Very glad."

His green gaze was as hypnotic as ever. It caught her and she saw the lust competing with the love and she smiled. "I know what's on your mind."

"Of course you do, you. You're always on my mind," he said, reaching for her, kissing her, caressing her soft skin. "Let's go back to bed," he suggested.

But before she had a chance to answer, a knock sounded on the door and they exchanged glances. No one had rung the bell. Rafe's mood immediately changed as he pushed her behind him. He raced to the bedroom to get his gun before answering the door.

"Angela."

Angela looked in shock toward the door, then motioned for Rafe to put his gun away. "It's my mother," she whispered as she rushed to answer the door. Within seconds Rafe had returned and was facing her parents.

The two couples stood uncomfortably for a few seconds until Angela regained her senses. "This is Raphael Remeris," she announced and waited. Her father stuck his hand out and the tension eased.

"We just wanted you to know that we're not selling the house. We're taking out a loan instead."

"Why?" Angela asked.

"Your brother, he told us not to." Her father looked away. "He told us everything."

"So why are you taking out a loan?"

"We're going to pay the money that he owes. He's still our son and we want him safe. If paying money will keep him safe, we don't care, we're going to do it. We would have done it two years ago. All he had to do was tell us."

Rafe came closer to Angela and slid his arms around her. "I love your daughter," he said, looking at the two of them. "Do you have any objections to our being together?"

"And if we did, would it stop you?" her father asked.

"Not a chance."

"We didn't think so," her father said and slapped him on the back. "We were wrong about so many things, maybe having a cop in the family won't be the end of the world."

"One more thing," her mother said. "Adrian said he has a son. He said you know where he is. We'd like to see him. Will you tell us?"

"I don't know exactly where he's at but I'll try to find out. I want to see him also," Angela answered her mother.

"I'll help her find him," Rafe offered.

For the next several hours Angela and her parents did what they could to repair the rift. Having a new baby was going to go a long way toward that. She wondered if that had been the catalyst for her brother's change of heart as well. She didn't know, but she sure hoped so.

When her parents were gone at last, Rafe looked at her, the desire still glowing brightly in his eyes. "Want to pick up where we left off?" he asked.

"What if I say no?"

"I might be forced to convince you," he said, licking the side of her neck and sliding his hand beneath her short skirt, burning her with his touch.

"We've gotten just one set of parents out of the way," Angela teased. "Are you sure you don't want to wait for a Hispanic woman to fall in love with? It would make your mother happy."

"I want the woman that I've already fallen in love with, the only one with the power to stop my heart," he smiled at her, "and to restart it again. What about you, Angel? What is it that you want?"

"I want you, the man who makes my skin burn when he touches me, who risked his own life to save mine. I want the man whose love forced me to remember something that I tried to forget, that there are two sides to every story. I want you, *Poppi*. *Te amo*, Raphael Remeris."

She ran her tongue over his lips, feeling his passion, feeling her own. "You never did tell me the meaning of your name. I know Raphael is the name of an archangel—anything else? I remember what your *madrina* said, and the way she looked at you. What does Raphael mean?" she asked as her hand brushed against the bulge in his crotch.

"Yes, there's more," Raphael answered as he ran his tongue across her lips. "Raphael is the angel of healing."

It figured, Angela thought as Raphael slid the panties from her hips, and inserted his fingers deep inside her while his tongue, inside her mouth, was doing all sorts of magical things to her. Raphael was the perfect name for the man who'd brought so much healing to her heart and her life.

The End

ABOUT THE AUTHOR

Award winning author Dyanne Davis lives in a Chicago suburb with her husband Bill, and their son Bill Jr. She retired from nursing several years ago to pursue her lifelong dream of becoming a published author.

An avid reader, Dyanne began reading at the age of four. Her love of the written word turned into a desire to write. Her first novel, *The Color of Trouble*, was released July of 2003. The novel was received with high praise and several awards. Dyanne won an Emma for Favorite New Author of the year.

Her second novel, *The Wedding Gown* was released in February 2004 and has also received much praise. The book was chosen by Blackexpressions, a subsidiary of Doubleday Book Club, as a monthly club pick. The book was an Emma finalist in March 2005 for Steamiest Romance, and for Book Of The Year. *The Wedding Gown* was also a finalist for Affaire de Coeur Reader's poll.

Dyanne's *Misty Blue* is a sequel to *The Wedding Gown*. It received a four star rating from Romantic Times. In December of 06 *Let's Get It On* also received a four star rating from Romantic Times. Dyanne has been a presenter of numerous workshops. She has a local cable show in her hometown to give writing tips to aspiring writers. She has guests from all genres to provide information and entertainment to the audience.

When not writing, you can find Dyanne with a book in her hands, her greatest passion next to spending time with her husband Bill and son Bill Jr. Whenever possible she loves getting together with friends and family.

TWO SIDES TO EVERY STORY

A member of Romance Writers of America, Dyanne now serves as Chapter President for Windy City. Dyanne loves to hear feedback from her readers. You can reach her at her website. *www.dyannedavis.com* She also has an on-line blog where readers can post questions and photos. *Http://dyannedavis.blogspot.com* She's also started a romance reader and writers on line book club with more than a dozen authors, and would love to have you join them. *http://bookmarked.Target.com.* The group is called, Romancing The Book. Any problems getting in, send Dyanne an email and she will send you a personal invitation.

2007 Publication Schedule

January

Corporate Seduction
A.C. Arthur
ISBN-13: 978-1-58571-238-0
ISBN-10: 1-58571-238-8
$9.95

A Taste of Temptation
Reneé Alexis
ISBN-13: 978-1-58571-207-6
ISBN-10: 1-58571-207-8
$9.95

February

The Perfect Frame
Beverly Clark
ISBN-13: 978-1-58571-240-3
ISBN-10: 1-58571-240-X
$9.95

Ebony Angel
Deatri King-Bey
ISBN-13: 978-1-58571-239-7
ISBN-10: 1-58571-239-6
$9.95

March

Sweet Sensations
Gwendolyn Bolton
ISBN-13: 978-1-58571-206-9
ISBN-10: 1-58571-206-X
$9.95

Crush
Crystal Hubbard
ISBN-13: 978-1-58571-243-4
ISBN-10: 1-58571-243-4
$9.95

April

Secret Thunder
Annetta P. Lee
ISBN-13: 978-1-58571-204-5
ISBN-10: 1-58571-204-3
$9.95

Blood Seduction
J.M. Jeffries
ISBN-13: 978-1-58571-237-3
ISBN-10: 1-58571-237-X
$9.95

May

Lies Too Long
Pamela Ridley
ISBN-13: 978-1-58571-246-5
ISBN-10: 1-58571-246-9
$13.95

Two Sides to Every Story
Dyanne Davis
ISBN-13: 978-1-58571-248-9
ISBN-10: 1-58571-248-5
$9.95

June

One of These Days
Michele Sudler
ISBN-13: 978-1-58571-249-6
ISBN-10: 1-58571-249-3
$9.95

Who's That Lady
Andrea Jackson
ISBN-13: 978-1-58571-190-1
ISBN-10: 1-58571-190-X
$9.95

TWO SIDES TO EVERY STORY

2007 Publication Schedule (continued)

July

Heart of the Phoenix
A.C. Arthur
ISBN-13: 978-1-58571-242-7
ISBN-10: 1-58571-242-6
$9.95

Do Over
Jaci Kenney
ISBN-13: 978-1-58571-241-0
ISBN-10: 1-58571-241-8
$9.95

It's Not Over Yet
J.J. Michael
ISBN-13: 978-1-58571-245-8
ISBN-10: 1-58571-245-0
$9.95

August

The Fires Within
Beverly Clark
ISBN-13: 978-1-58571-244-1
ISBN-10: 1-58571-244-2
$9.95

Stolen Kisses
Dominiqua Douglas
ISBN-13: 978-1-58571-247-2
ISBN-10: 1-58571-247-7
$9.95

September

Small Whispers
Annetta P. Lee
ISBN-13: 978-158571-251-9
ISBN-10: 1-58571-251-5
$6.99

Always You
Crystal Hubbard
ISBN-13: 978-158571-252-6
ISBN-10: 1-58571-252-3
$6.99

October

Not His Type
Chamein Canton
ISBN-13: 978-158571-253-3
ISBN-10: 1-58571-253-1
$6.99

Many Shades of Gray
Dyanne Davis
ISBN-13: 978-158571-254-0
ISBN-10: 1-58571-254-X
$6.99

November

When I'm With You
LaConnie Taylor-Jones
ISBN-13: 978-158571-250-2
ISBN-10: 1-58571-250-7
$6.99

The Mission
Pamela Leigh Starr
ISBN-13: 978-158571-255-7
ISBN-10: 1-58571-255-8
$6.99

December

One in A Million
Barbara Keaton
ISBN-13: 978-158571-257-1
ISBN-10: 1-58571-257-4
$6.99

The Foursome
Celya Bowers
ISBN-13: 978-158571-256-4
ISBN-10: 1-58571-256-6
$6.99

Other Genesis Press, Inc. Titles

A Dangerous Deception	J.M. Jeffries	$8.95
A Dangerous Love	J.M. Jeffries	$8.95
A Dangerous Obsession	J.M. Jeffries	$8.95
A Dangerous Woman	J.M. Jeffries	$9.95
A Dead Man Speaks	Lisa Jones Johnson	$12.95
A Drummer's Beat to Mend	Kei Swanson	$9.95
A Happy Life	Charlotte Harris	$9.95
A Heart's Awakening	Veronica Parker	$9.95
A Lark on the Wing	Phyliss Hamilton	$9.95
A Love of Her Own	Cheris F. Hodges	$9.95
A Love to Cherish	Beverly Clark	$8.95
A Lover's Legacy	Veronica Parker	$9.95
A Pefect Place to Pray	I.L. Goodwin	$12.95
A Risk of Rain	Dar Tomlinson	$8.95
A Twist of Fate	Beverly Clark	$8.95
A Will to Love	Angie Daniels	$9.95
Acquisitions	Kimberley White	$8.95
Across	Carol Payne	$12.95
After the Vows	Leslie Esdaile	$10.95
(Summer Anthology)	T.T. Henderson	
	Jacqueline Thomas	
Again My Love	Kayla Perrin	$10.95
Against the Wind	Gwynne Forster	$8.95
All I Ask	Barbara Keaton	$8.95
Ambrosia	T.T. Henderson	$8.95
An Unfinished Love Affair	Barbara Keaton	$8.95
And Then Came You	Dorothy Elizabeth Love	$8.95
Angel's Paradise	Janice Angelique	$9.95
At Last	Lisa G. Riley	$8.95
Best of Friends	Natalie Dunbar	$8.95
Between Tears	Pamela Ridley	$12.95
Beyond the Rapture	Beverly Clark	$9.95
Blaze	Barbara Keaton	$9.95

Other Genesis Press, Inc. Titles (continued)

Other Genesis Press, Inc. Titles (continued)

Echoes of Yesterday	Beverly Clark	$9.95
Eden's Garden	Elizabeth Rose	$8.95
Enchanted Desire	Wanda Y. Thomas	$9.95
Everlastin' Love	Gay G. Gunn	$8.95
Everlasting Moments	Dorothy Elizabeth Love	$8.95
Everything and More	Sinclair Lebeau	$8.95
Everything but Love	Natalie Dunbar	$8.95
Eve's Prescription	Edwina Martin Arnold	$8.95
Falling	Natalie Dunbar	$9.95
Fate	Pamela Leigh Starr	$8.95
Finding Isabella	A.J. Garrotto	$8.95
Forbidden Quest	Dar Tomlinson	$10.95
Forever Love	Wanda Thomas	$8.95
From the Ashes	Kathleen Suzanne	$8.95
	Jeanne Sumerix	
Gentle Yearning	Rochelle Alers	$10.95
Glory of Love	Sinclair LeBeau	$10.95
Go Gentle into that Good Night	Malcom Boyd	$12.95
Goldengroove	Mary Beth Craft	$16.95
Groove, Bang, and Jive	Steve Cannon	$8.99
Hand in Glove	Andrea Jackson	$9.95
Hard to Love	Kimberley White	$9.95
Hart & Soul	Angie Daniels	$8.95
Havana Sunrise	Kymberly Hunt	$9.95
Heartbeat	Stephanie Bedwell-Grime	$8.95
Hearts Remember	M. Loui Quezada	$8.95
Hidden Memories	Robin Allen	$10.95
Higher Ground	Leah Latimer	$19.95
Hitler, the War, and the Pope	Ronald Rychlak	$26.95
How to Write a Romance	Kathryn Falk	$18.95
I Married a Reclining Chair	Lisa M. Fuhs	$8.95
I'm Gonna Make You Love Me	Gwyneth Bolton	$9.95
Indigo After Dark Vol. I	Nia Dixon/Angelique	$10.95

Other Genesis Press, Inc. Titles (continued)

Indigo After Dark Vol. II	Dolores Bundy/Cole Riley	$10.95
Indigo After Dark Vol. III	Montana Blue/Coco Morena	$10.95
Indigo After Dark Vol. IV	Cassandra Colt/	$14.95
	Diana Richeaux	
Indigo After Dark Vol. V	Delilah Dawson	$14.95
Icie	Pamela Leigh Starr	$8.95
I'll Be Your Shelter	Giselle Carmichael	$8.95
I'll Paint a Sun	A.J. Garrotto	$9.95
Illusions	Pamela Leigh Starr	$8.95
Indiscretions	Donna Hill	$8.95
Intentional Mistakes	Michele Sudler	$9.95
Interlude	Donna Hill	$8.95
Intimate Intentions	Angie Daniels	$8.95
Ironic	Pamela Leigh Starr	$9.95
Jolie's Surrender	Edwina Martin-Arnold	$8.95
Kiss or Keep	Debra Phillips	$8.95
Lace	Giselle Carmichael	$9.95
Last Train to Memphis	Elsa Cook	$12.95
Lasting Valor	Ken Olsen	$24.95
Let's Get It On	Dyanne Davis	$9.95
Let Us Prey	Hunter Lundy	$25.95
Life Is Never As It Seems	J.J. Michael	$12.95
Lighter Shade of Brown	Vicki Andrews	$8.95
Love Always	Mildred E. Riley	$10.95
Love Doesn't Come Easy	Charlyne Dickerson	$8.95
Love in High Gear	Charlotte Roy	$9.95
Love Lasts Forever	Dominiqua Douglas	$9.95
Love Me Carefully	A.C. Arthur	$9.95
Love Unveiled	Gloria Greene	$10.95
Love's Deception	Charlene Berry	$10.95
Love's Destiny	M. Loui Quezada	$8.95
Mae's Promise	Melody Walcott	$8.95
Magnolia Sunset	Giselle Carmichael	$8.95

Other Genesis Press, Inc. Titles (continued)

Matters of Life and Death	Lesego Malepe, Ph.D.	$15.95
Meant to Be	Jeanne Sumerix	$8.95
Midnight Clear	Leslie Esdaile	$10.95
(Anthology)	Gwynne Forster	
	Carmen Green	
	Monica Jackson	
Midnight Magic	Gwynne Forster	$8.95
Midnight Peril	Vicki Andrews	$10.95
Misconceptions	Pamela Leigh Starr	$9.95
Misty Blue	Dyanne Davis	$9.95
Montgomery's Children	Richard Perry	$14.95
My Buffalo Soldier	Barbara B. K. Reeves	$8.95
Naked Soul	Gwynne Forster	$8.95
Next to Last Chance	Louisa Dixon	$24.95
Nights Over Egypt	Barbara Keaton	$9.95
No Apologies	Seressia Glass	$8.95
No Commitment Required	Seressia Glass	$8.95
No Ordinary Love	Angela Weaver	$9.95
No Regrets	Mildred E. Riley	$8.95
Notes When Summer Ends	Beverly Lauderdale	$12.95
Nowhere to Run	Gay G. Gunn	$10.95
O Bed! O Breakfast!	Rob Kuehnle	$14.95
Object of His Desire	A. C. Arthur	$8.95
Office Policy	A. C. Arthur	$9.95
Once in a Blue Moon	Dorianne Cole	$9.95
One Day at a Time	Bella McFarland	$8.95
Only You	Crystal Hubbard	$9.95
Outside Chance	Louisa Dixon	$24.95
Passion	T.T. Henderson	$10.95
Passion's Blood	Cherif Fortin	$22.95
Passion's Journey	Wanda Thomas	$8.95
Past Promises	Jahmel West	$8.95
Path of Fire	T.T. Henderson	$8.95

Other Genesis Press, Inc. Titles (continued)

Path of Thorns	Annetta P. Lee	$9.95
Peace Be Still	Colette Haywood	$12.95
Picture Perfect	Reon Carter	$8.95
Playing for Keeps	Stephanie Salinas	$8.95
Pride & Joi	Gay G. Gunn	$8.95
Promises to Keep	Alicia Wiggins	$8.95
Quiet Storm	Donna Hill	$10.95
Reckless Surrender	Rochelle Alers	$6.95
Red Polka Dot in a World of Plaid	Varian Johnson	$12.95
Rehoboth Road	Anita Ballard-Jones	$12.95
Reluctant Captive	Joyce Jackson	$8.95
Rendezvous with Fate	Jeanne Sumerix	$8.95
Revelations	Cheris F. Hodges	$8.95
Rise of the Phoenix	Kenneth Whetstone	$12.95
Rivers of the Soul	Leslie Esdaile	$8.95
Rock Star	Rosyln Hardy Holcomb	$9.95
Rocky Mountain Romance	Kathleen Suzanne	$8.95
Rooms of the Heart	Donna Hill	$8.95
Rough on Rats and Tough on Cats	Chris Parker	$12.95
Scent of Rain	Annetta P. Lee	$9.95
Second Chances at Love	Cheris Hodges	$9.95
Secret Library Vol. 1	Nina Sheridan	$18.95
Secret Library Vol. 2	Cassandra Colt	$8.95
Shades of Brown	Denise Becker	$8.95
Shades of Desire	Monica White	$8.95
Shadows in the Moonlight	Jeanne Sumerix	$8.95
Sin	Crystal Rhodes	$8.95
Sin and Surrender	J.M. Jeffries	$9.95
Sinful Intentions	Crystal Rhodes	$12.95
So Amazing	Sinclair LeBeau	$8.95
Somebody's Someone	Sinclair LeBeau	$8.95

Other Genesis Press, Inc. Titles (continued)

Someone to Love	Alicia Wiggins	$8.95
Song in the Park	Martin Brant	$15.95
Soul Eyes	Wayne L. Wilson	$12.95
Soul to Soul	Donna Hill	$8.95
Southern Comfort	J.M. Jeffries	$8.95
Still the Storm	Sharon Robinson	$8.95
Still Waters Run Deep	Leslie Esdaile	$8.95
Stories to Excite You	Anna Forrest/Divine	$14.95
Subtle Secrets	Wanda Y. Thomas	$8.95
Suddenly You	Crystal Hubbard	$9.95
Sweet Repercussions	Kimberley White	$9.95
Sweet Tomorrows	Kimberly White	$8.95
Taken by You	Dorothy Elizabeth Love	$9.95
Tattooed Tears	T. T. Henderson	$8.95
The Color Line	Lizzette Grayson Carter	$9.95
The Color of Trouble	Dyanne Davis	$8.95
The Disappearance of Allison Jones	Kayla Perrin	$5.95
The Honey Dipper's Legacy	Pannell-Allen	$14.95
The Joker's Love Tune	Sidney Rickman	$15.95
The Little Pretender	Barbara Cartland	$10.95
The Love We Had	Natalie Dunbar	$8.95
The Man Who Could Fly	Bob & Milana Beamon	$18.95
The Missing Link	Charlyne Dickerson	$8.95
The Price of Love	Sinclair LeBeau	$8.95
The Smoking Life	Ilene Barth	$29.95
The Words of the Pitcher	Kei Swanson	$8.95
Three Wishes	Seressia Glass	$8.95
Through the Fire	Seressia Glass	$9.95
Ties That Bind	Kathleen Suzanne	$8.95
Tiger Woods	Libby Hughes	$5.95
Time is of the Essence	Angie Daniels	$9.95
Timeless Devotion	Bella McFarland	$9.95
Tomorrow's Promise	Leslie Esdaile	$8.95

Other Genesis Press, Inc. Titles (continued)

Truly Inseparable	Wanda Y. Thomas	$8.95
Unbreak My Heart	Dar Tomlinson	$8.95
Uncommon Prayer	Kenneth Swanson	$9.95
Unconditional	A.C. Arthur	$9.95
Unconditional Love	Alicia Wiggins	$8.95
Under the Cherry Moon	Christal Jordan-Mims	$12.95
Unearthing Passions	Elaine Sims	$9.95
Until Death Do Us Part	Susan Paul	$8.95
Vows of Passion	Bella McFarland	$9.95
Wedding Gown	Dyanne Davis	$8.95
What's Under Benjamin's Bed	Sandra Schaffer	$8.95
When Dreams Float	Dorothy Elizabeth Love	$8.95
Whispers in the Night	Dorothy Elizabeth Love	$8.95
Whispers in the Sand	LaFlorya Gauthier	$10.95
Wild Ravens	Altonya Washington	$9.95
Yesterday Is Gone	Beverly Clark	$10.95
Yesterday's Dreams, Tomorrow's Promises	Reon Laudat	$8.95
Your Precious Love	Sinclair LeBeau	$8.95

Order Form

Mail to: Genesis Press, Inc.
P.O. Box 101
Columbus, MS 39703

Name _____

Address _____

City/State _____ Zip _____

Telephone _____

Ship to (if different from above)

Name _____

Address _____

City/State _____ Zip _____

Telephone _____

Credit Card Information

Credit Card # _____ ☐ Visa ☐ Mastercard

Expiration Date (mm/yy) _____ ☐ AmEx ☐ Discover

Qty.	Author	Title	Price	Total

Use this order

form, or call

1-888-INDIGO-1

Total for books _____

Shipping and handling:
  $5 first two books,
  $1 each additional book _____

Total S & H _____

Total amount enclosed _____

Mississippi residents add 7% sales tax